"Even if you never watched the TV show, read these mysteries! Sly humor, endearing characters, tricky plots—Lee Goldberg's smart writing is what makes these terrific *Diagnosis Murder* books something to tell all your friends about."
—Jerrilyn Farmer, bestselling author of the Madeline Bean mysteries

"Lee Goldberg takes the utterly familiar Dr. Mark Sloan and surprises us with heartbreaking glimpses of the past that allow the good doctor to step off the television screen and into a flesh-and-blood reality. Well plotted and beautifully rendered."
—Margaret Maron, Edgar®, Agatha, and Macavity Award–winning author of the Deborah Knott mysteries

"Just what the doctor ordered, a sure cure after a rash of blah mysteries. *Diagnosis Murder: The Past Tense* has more plot twists than a strand of DNA."
—Elaine Viets, author of *Murder With Reservations*

"Lee Goldberg's *Diagnosis Murder* books are fast-paced, tightly constructed mysteries that are even better than the TV show. You'll read them in great big gulps."
—Gregg Hurwitz, author of *The Program*

"Lee Goldberg takes you on a streamlined ride through forty years of LA history with a busload of suspicious characters. *The Past Tense* will quicken the pulses of longtime *Diagnosis Murder* fans and newcomers alike while Dr. Mark Sloan's quest for justice is sure to warm hearts."
—Denise Hamilton, author of the Eve Diamond crime novels

"A clever, twisting tale. *The Past Tense* leaves you guessing right up until the heart-stopping ending. This was my first time reading a *Diagnosis Murder* novel, but it won't be my last."
—Lisa Gardner, author of *Gone*

continued . . .

DIAGNOSIS MURDER

THE
LAST WORD

Lee Goldberg

BASED ON THE TELEVISION SERIES CREATED BY
Joyce Burditt

A SIGNET BOOK

SIGNET
Published by New American Library, a division of
Penguin Group (USA) Inc., 375 Hudson Street,
New York, New York 10014, USA
Penguin Group (Canada), 90 Eglinton Avenue East, Suite 700, Toronto,
Ontario M4P 2Y3, Canada (a division of Pearson Penguin Canada Inc.)
Penguin Books Ltd., 80 Strand, London WC2R 0RL, England
Penguin Ireland, 25 St. Stephen's Green, Dublin 2,
Ireland (a division of Penguin Books Ltd.)
Penguin Group (Australia), 250 Camberwell Road, Camberwell, Victoria 3124,
Australia (a division of Pearson Australia Group Pty. Ltd.)
Penguin Books India Pvt. Ltd., 11 Community Centre, Panchsheel Park,
New Delhi - 110 017, India
Penguin Group (NZ), 67 Apollo Drive, Mairangi Bay,
Auckland 1311, New Zealand (a division of Pearson New Zealand Ltd.)
Penguin Books (South Africa) (Pty.) Ltd., 24 Sturdee Avenue,
Rosebank, Johannesburg 2196, South Africa

Penguin Books Ltd., Registered Offices:
80 Strand, London WC2R 0RL, England

First published by Signet, an imprint of New American Library,
a division of Penguin Group (USA) Inc.

First Printing, May 2007
10 9 8 7 6 5 4 3 2 1

To Dick Van Dyke,
the one and only Dr. Mark Sloan

ACKNOWLEDGMENTS

I would like to thank my wife, Valerie, and my daughter, Madison, for their love and support during the long days and nights it took me to write this book. I thought I'd never finish it and I know that they did, too. I'm also grateful to Dr. D. P. Lyle, Diane Stavroulakis, Robin Burcell, Paul Bishop, Karen Dinino, Joel Goldman, Colleen Casey, and Peter Keane for their advice and wise counsel. Whatever medical or legal errors I've made or creative liberties that I've taken are entirely my own.

The story you are about to read picks up characters and events from my previous books in this series as well as the *Diagnosis Murder* episodes "Retribution," "Obsession," and "Resurrection," which I cowrote with William Rabkin, with whom I produced the TV series.

Fair warning: If you haven't read the previous *Diagnosis Murder* books, you might want to set this one down until you have, because I spoil some of the surprise endings in this novel.

I've been associated with *Diagnosis Murder*, on-screen and in print, for well over a decade and it has been one of the highlights of my career as both a TV writer and a novelist. I've enjoyed every minute that I've spent with Dr. Mark Sloan, and I hope that you have, too. Let me know at www.diagnosis-murder.com.

CHAPTER ONE

Carter Sweeney was a pale, slight man with a receding hairline and a meticulously groomed goatee. He wore a loose-fitting bright orange jumpsuit and sat in a stiff-backed stainless-steel chair. His wrists and ankles were in irons, which were looped around his waist and strung through an eyebolt in the concrete floor.

Despite these restrictions, Sweeney seemed completely relaxed, as if he were lounging on a beach instead of sitting in the chilly, sterile visitation room at Sunrise Valley State Prison, home to extremely violent offenders. That's because the visitation room was a luxury suite compared to solitary confinement in his twelve-by-seven-foot cell, where his bed, writing shelf, and stool were all made of poured concrete.

During his first year at Sunrise Valley, he was allowed outdoors for only one hour each day, by himself, in a concrete cavern known as the Dog Run. After three years of incarceration, he was allowed three hours per day in the Dog Run with two other prisoners. With continued good behavior, that was the most sunlight and social interaction he could expect to enjoy until his execution.

So the opportunity to spend time in the visitation room with someone from the outside world was truly an experience to be savored for as long as possible. Unfortunately for Sweeney, his reluctant guest didn't share his eagerness to prolong the visit.

"You don't call. You don't write. I was beginning to wonder if you still cared about me," Sweeney said in the smooth, calming voice that had made him a Los Angeles talk radio star at one time.

Dr. Mark Sloan sat across from Sweeney in a stainless steel chair that felt like it had been carved from a block of solid ice. He was shivering from the cold, but he couldn't let Sweeney see it.

Sweeney would interpret the shaking as fear and use it as a psychological weapon against him.

Mark knew it would be foolhardy to underestimate Sweeney simply because he was chained and imprisoned. Sweeney was the most dangerous man Mark had encountered in his forty years as a homicide consultant to the LAPD.

It wasn't that Sweeney was a violent man, at least not physically. As far as Mark knew, Sweeney had never hurt anyone with his bare hands. His preferred method of killing was an explosive encased in an ornately crafted, hand-carved wooden box. Sweeney and his younger sister, Caitlin, had learned their bomb-making and wood-carving skills from their father, Regan, a furniture maker who set off bombs all over Los Angeles after his store was condemned by the city to build a new freeway.

But Carter Sweeney's true weapon was his mind, which Mark was sure the years of near-solitary confinement hadn't broken. He was a brilliant analytical thinker, with the frightening ability to manipulate others into doing exactly what he wanted, often without them ever being aware of it.

"I didn't come here to play games with you," Mark said, despite knowing full well that he was deluding himself. Simply by showing up, he was already playing whatever game Sweeney had begun.

"Of course not," Sweeney said. "We both know how much you dislike games—unless there's a corpse involved."

"You kill people," Mark said. "I don't."

"So that must have been a different Dr. Mark Sloan I read about a few months ago," Sweeney said. "*That* Mark Sloan gunned down a woman in his own home."

"It was self-defense," Mark said. "Not premeditated murder."

For an instant, that horrible moment played out in front of Mark's eyes again. He was in bed, helpless, recovering from a head injury. She was going to smother him with a pillow. He had to shoot. But the first shot didn't stop her. *She just kept coming—*

He blinked hard, willing the image away, but he knew it was a temporary reprieve. The memory of that blood-soaked night would haunt him for the rest of his life.

"But you knew she would show up," Sweeney said. "If you didn't intend to kill her, why were you waiting for her with a loaded gun?"

"I tried to reason with her," Mark said. "I didn't want her to die."

"Sure you didn't." Sweeney winked at him.

So was *that* what this visit was about? Mark wondered. Did Sweeney want to revel in Mark's deadly misfortune? If that was it, Mark wasn't going to play along.

"You're in no position to judge me or anybody else," Mark said. "You're a mass murderer. You blew up a hospital, maiming and killing dozens of innocent people."

"Come now, Mark. You know I didn't do that. My poor, disturbed sister, Caitlin, planted those bombs. You saw her there yourself, right before the hospital fell on top of you."

"She was acting on your orders," Mark said. "You wanted revenge against me for sending your father here."

"You killed him."

"I *caught* him," Mark said. "The State of California executed him."

Within days of Regan Sweeney's execution, Carter Sweeney embarked on a copycat bombing campaign to make it appear that Mark had framed an innocent man. Sweeney also used his popular radio program to expertly turn public opinion against Mark, the LAPD, and the district attorney's office. But Carter ultimately failed, undone by his own arrogance, which Mark used to trick him into incriminating himself in the bombings.

But Mark didn't know that Carter's sister was also involved in the plot. She remained free and blew up Community General Hospital, trapping Mark, his son, and many of his closest friends in the flaming rubble.

That was just the beginning of the nightmare for Mark Sloan.

Caitlin joined the Revolutionary Order for Armed Rebellion, or ROAR, a white supremacist group, using them to hijack the bus that was taking her brother to prison. Together, Carter and Caitlin kidnapped Mark and forced him to help them steal a hundred million dollars from the Federal Reserve.

But Mark outsmarted them once again. Now the Sweeneys were finally imprisoned, and Carter was sentenced to death by lethal injection. Like father, like son.

"As much as I enjoy reliving your downfall," Mark said, "I'm sure you didn't invite me here to rehash your history of violence."

"I'm an innocent man," Sweeney said.

"Oh spare me," Mark said.

"I couldn't possibly do that," Sweeney said with a gleam in his eye. "I wanted you to hear the good news directly from me. I'll be out of here in a few weeks."

"The only way you're leaving prison is in a coffin," Mark said. "All your appeals have been denied."

"Not all," Sweeney said. "The court has granted my writ of habeas corpus. There's going to be a hearing soon. I have a feeling it's going to go very well. I might even be freed in time to cast my vote for mayor. But it's such a difficult choice. Do I vote for John Masters, the police chief whose department unjustly arrested me? Or Neal Burnside, the district attorney who railroaded me into this hellhole?"

"The evidence against you is overwhelming and irrefutable. No court will ever overturn your conviction," Mark said. "But go ahead—enjoy your fantasy. I'm sure it makes the hours pass more swiftly in your cell."

"I won't be the second innocent Sweeney wrongly put to death because of you."

"You're wasting your act on me," Mark said. "We both know the truth."

Sweeney broke into a broad grin. "Haven't you heard? Clinton never had sex with that woman and Iraq has weapons of mass destruction. The truth doesn't matter anymore. Truth is so last century. The new currency in our culture is perception. And everyone's perception of me is about to change."

"Not mine," Mark said.

"I'm counting on that," Sweeney said. "So tell me, Mark, how's your health these days? I heard you took a nasty fall."

"I'll live."

"That's good, because I want you to enjoy a very long life."

"It's too short to waste any more of it here with you," Mark said. "Make your point."

"I already have. Weren't you listening? Let's have lunch when I get out. How do you feel about Chinese food?"

"This is the last time we'll be seeing each other." Mark rose from his seat. "At least until your execution."

"Now *that's* more like the Mark Sloan I know," Sweeney said. "You never miss an opportunity to see someone die, do you?"

Mark went to the door and pounded on it a little too urgently.

"Guard, I'm ready to go."

"What's your hurry? There are so many of your friends in here. You should really say hello to them before you leave. I know they'd love to see you."

"I'll pass," Mark said.

The serial killer known as the Silent Partner was here. So was former councilman Matt Watson, psychiatrist Gavin Reed, Detective Harley Brule, Mob accountant Malcolm Trainor, and many others Mark had helped capture. He didn't need to see how the years of incarceration had taken their toll on the minds and bodies of all those murderers.

He took no pleasure in their suffering, even though they deserved it. His investigations weren't about vengeance. They were about seeing that justice was served, but he'd come to accept the fact that that wasn't his primary motivation. It was the chase. It was the intellectual challenge of the hunt, the methodical piecing together of the clues that led to the killer. *That* was what drove him.

Mark never wanted to see the faces of the killers he'd caught again, not in the flesh or in his memory. And yet here he was, in a room with Carter Sweeney, the worst of them all.

What was he thinking, coming here?

Why was it taking so long for the damn door to open?

"Think of all the vacancies they'd have in here if not for your diligence, Mark. They should really have named this prison in your honor," Sweeney said. "Maybe they're just waiting until you die."

Finally, Mark heard the electronic hiss of the locks opening automatically inside the thick steel door. A guard stepped in, eyed Sweeney warily, and escorted Mark out. The big door closed behind them, the locks sliding into place with a heavy, satisfying *thunk*.

Carter Sweeney was chained in place behind a steel door. He couldn't do Mark, or anybody else, any harm ever again. Even so, it took every ounce of self-control Mark possessed not to run all the way out of the prison.

CHAPTER TWO

Mark was almost at the door of his car, which he had parked at the far end of the prison lot, when he was overwhelmed with nausea. He dashed to the nearest garbage can and vomited, heaving until his stomach was empty and his throat was raw, trying to purge the past hour from his life.

He staggered to his Lexus SC 430, opened the door, and slumped into the driver's seat, too light-headed at the moment to drive, too dazed to care about the burning sting of the sunbaked leather upholstery against his back.

There was a bottle of water in the cup holder. He took a sip of hot water, swished it around in his mouth, and spit it out on the cracked asphalt. He watched the water evaporate almost instantly in the dry July heat and wished he'd never come here.

When Sweeney's lawyer had called yesterday to relay his client's invitation, Mark had flatly refused to see the killer.

That should have been the end of it.

But it wasn't.

Mark couldn't stop thinking about the call. What was Sweeney up to? Why did he want to talk to Mark?

His curiosity about Sweeney was too strong to ignore, just as Sweeney had known it would be. Mark knew he was being manipulated, which only made it harder for him to decide whether or not to go.

Which reaction was the one that Sweeney was expecting? Which one would play into his scheme, whatever it was?

He found himself second-guessing every decision he had made and wondering if that, too, was part of Sweeney's plan. He hadn't even spoken with Sweeney again and already the killer was playing with his head.

Mark thought about getting his son Steve's advice, but he

knew what it would be: Don't go. Don't give Sweeney the pleasure of toying with you again.

Steve was the homicide detective who'd arrested Sweeney. He believed that once murderers were imprisoned, their existence was no longer worth acknowledging. They deserved no one's care or attention. So he certainly wouldn't have approved of Mark paying a visit to Sweeney.

Mark considered getting an opinion from Dr. Amanda Bentley, the adjunct county medical examiner and Community General's pathologist, but she'd nearly died in the hospital blast, and she wouldn't approve of Mark's consenting to any request from the man who'd almost killed her.

The only one of Mark's friends who might have told him to visit Sweeney was Dr. Jesse Travis, the young ER resident whose enthusiasm and curiosity often trumped his common sense and better judgment. In fact, Jesse would probably have insisted on tagging along with Mark.

So, after a day of indecision, Mark decided it would be easier just to face his adversary and get it over with than to continue obsessing over what Sweeney might be up to.

And now that the visit was over, Mark sat baking in his car outside the prison, a concrete island amidst a sea of cotton fields two hundred miles north of Los Angeles. He went over their conversation again, word for word. The exercise didn't provoke any fresh insights, only another wave of nausea, which thankfully passed quickly.

Mark was no closer to understanding Sweeney's reasons for wanting to see him than he had been before the visit. But he was sure Sweeney hadn't summoned him merely to announce his latest legal maneuvering.

So what message was Sweeney actually trying to convey?

And why now?

He told himself to let it go; the answers didn't matter anyway. Unlike Carter Sweeney, Mark still had a life to live.

CHAPTER THREE

Corinne Adams did everything she could to ensure that she would have a long, healthy life. The blond-haired twenty-four-year-old didn't smoke, drink, or do drugs. She was even reluctant to take Advil for a headache, preferring massage, meditation, or a bracing cup of herbal tea as a way of relieving her pain.

She ran for thirty minutes each day on her treadmill, which was strategically placed in front of the TV in her one-bedroom apartment. She watched *House Hunters* while she exercised, dreaming of what she would buy when she finally sold one of her screenplays and gave up secretarial work forever.

She was a vegetarian and brushed her teeth after every low-cal, low-fat, organic meal. She was the thinnest, healthiest member of her obese family, none of whom had ever stood on a scale and seen the needle point to anything below two hundred pounds.

One night four years ago, when Corinne still lived at home in Woodland Hills, the whole family went out to dinner at Home Sweet Home Buffet. It was seafood night. Her mother, Noreen, was going back for thirds when she dropped dead of a massive heart attack. The other diners paused, confused, in their lemming-like march to the fried shrimp, until management stepped in and ushered everyone to the opposite side of the restaurant.

The tragedy at Home Sweet Home Buffet had a profound effect on Corinne. She moved out of the house, went on a strict diet, began exercising regularly, and earnestly pursued her dream of becoming a screenwriter. All of her scripts, regardless of their plots, were titled "Home Sweet Home Buffet," which made it difficult, even for her, to tell her screenplays apart without reading the first few pages.

The scripts, which were either family dramas or romantic comedies, had nothing to do with her mother's death. Corinne just thought "Home Sweet Home Buffet" sounded clever, and she liked all the meanings that could be read into the title.

She'd written all of her screenplays with Reese Witherspoon, Julia Roberts, or Sandra Bullock in mind, because they played characters who were just like her: spunky, adorable, independent, and desirable.

A big part of her desirability came from her new breasts. She'd had to work three jobs for two years to save up enough to get them. It wasn't an issue of vanity, but rather a matter of basic survival. In LA, having a nice rack meant she would get better jobs, better pay, better health benefits, and better men.

But so far the only men she seemed to date were her miserable screenwriting instructors at UCLA's extension school. They were hack writers who never got the money or recognition they knew they deserved, so now, for a measly $1,500 a quarter and a healthy serving of irony, they taught other people how to compete against them. Corinne couldn't help wondering if her instructors were taking her money and intentionally sabotaging her scripts with bad advice.

Even so, that didn't stop her from sleeping with her instructors, who, in the absence of recent screen credits, measured their self-worth by how many students they could seduce.

She didn't mind that. The part she didn't like was sitting in the classroom with nineteen other wannabes, their desperation to break into the Industry as palpable as body odor. Ben Bovian, the instructor on this particular night, was no less desperate, though his aspirations were focused on breaking into Corinne's pants.

That wasn't going to happen, partly because Corinne was bored with his fumbling foreplay, which consisted of sticking his tongue in her ear while they watched his unforgettable episodes of *Sue Thomas F.B.Eye*, and his postcoital whining six minutes later about all the less talented, but more successful, screenwriters who were getting all the work.

But mostly Ben wouldn't be going to bed with her tonight because Corinne would never sleep with anyone again, though she didn't know that at the time.

The first hour of class was spent giving notes to Jeremy Glatz, a thirty-four-year-old travel agent, on his 257-page, handwritten, epic screenplay about a thirty-four-year-old travel agent who was irresistible to women.

Ben went through the atrocious script page by page, commenting in detail on lame lines of description and inept dialogue. It was an excruciating and pointless exercise, Corinne thought. The most constructive advice Ben could give Jeremy would be to chuck the whole screenplay into the trash and give up the idea of ever becoming a writer.

By the time the ten-minute break came around, Corinne was so eager to escape Jeremy's horrendous writing and Ben's hungry glances that she bolted out of the third-floor classroom and rushed down the stairs, taking them two at a time.

That was a mistake.

She missed a step on the second flight and went tumbling down the stairs with a shriek, banging off the steps, the walls, and the handrails until she finally landed headfirst on the linoleum floor of the lobby with a sickening, bone-cracking *smack*.

But she didn't hear it.

She didn't feel it either.

She was past hearing or feeling anything ever again.

CHAPTER FOUR

It was a slow night in the emergency room at Community General Hospital. Dr. Jesse Travis sat in the waiting room, his feet on a coffee table, watching an episode of *Grey's Anatomy* and eating a bag of Cheetos. His wife, Susan, an ER nurse, sat next to him, her head on his shoulder.

Jesse liked the weight of her, the pressure of her, the warmth of her against him. He couldn't imagine how he could ever survive without it. And he didn't think he was just romanticizing his need for her. He'd read about studies done on monkeys that died, despite terrific diets and comfortable environments, because they were deprived of the "contact comfort" of other monkeys.

A full bag of Cheetos and a big-screen TV weren't enough for him anymore. He needed Susan, too.

He'd become one of those monkeys.

He was a love monkey.

Jesse was about to tell Susan what he was thinking, but then he thought better of it. He had a feeling that telling Susan that he realized they were just like monkeys wouldn't strike her as the most romantic thing he'd ever said.

He and Susan were newlyweds and spent most of their waking hours at the hospital. Home was just the place where they slept, showered, and changed clothes. So the ER waiting room had become their family room, one they reluctantly shared with the general public and, on occasion, a few homeless people seeking shelter from the elements.

Jesse gestured to the TV. "This is a show about the worst doctors in America."

"But that Dr. McDreamy guy is cute," Susan said.

"Every one of those oversexed doctors is guilty of malpractice, unethical behavior, and unbelievable stupidity."

"But they're cute," Susan said.

"So nothing else matters."

"It's television, Jesse."

"Tens of millions of people watch this show," Jesse said. "They think that's how doctors are supposed to behave. No real doctor could make the mistakes that they do on a consistent basis and still be allowed to practice medicine."

"Real doctors aren't nearly as entertaining," she said. "Or cute."

"What about me?"

"I married you, didn't I?" she said.

"That's not an answer," Jesse said.

She kissed him on the cheek. "You'll just have to live with it."

"The patients would be better off operating on themselves with garden tools," Jesse said. "That hospital is a death trap."

"Full of cuties," she added.

"I had no idea you were so superficial," Jesse said.

"I thought that's what attracted you to me," Susan said.

"No, it was your body," Jesse said.

"At least you're not superficial," Susan said.

"I've got so much depth that people have been known to fall to their deaths just looking into my eyes."

"I can vouch for that," Susan said.

An ambulance pulled up outside. Jesse and Susan got up, put on surgical gloves, and met the paramedics as they came in, wheeling their bloody patient on a gurney.

The paramedics were two stocky men who looked like they needed to catch up on sleep. One of them was pumping an Ambu bag to keep the patient breathing. The other paramedic gave Jesse the rundown on their patient, who had a cervical collar around her neck, a cardboard splint around her left wrist, and an IV line in her right arm.

"The victim's name is Corinne Adams, age twenty-four. She took a header down a staircase," the paramedic said. "And I mean a header. Cracked her skull open like an egg. She's also got a broken wrist. She's not breathing on her own. Her blood pressure is one hundred over fifty, pulse one-twenty-five, her sats are ninety-five percent on four liters. We started an IV of D-five with lactated ringers."

Jesse lifted her eyelids and shined a light in both of her eyes. Her pupils were wide open, big and black. It was like staring into the eyes of a Barbie doll.

It wasn't a good sign.

"Let's get her into trauma one," Jesse said, leading the way. "Anyone contact her family?"

"The police are on it," the paramedic said.

They wheeled her into the trauma room. Jesse, Susan, and the paramedics lifted Corinne onto the table and transferred her IV bag to a stand. Several more nurses spilled into the room. They started getting the things that they knew from experience Jesse was going to ask for. Susan took over pumping the Ambu bag to keep Corinne Adams breathing.

Jesse listened to Corinne's heart and lungs, which she'd worked so hard to keep healthy and strong. They hadn't failed her now. She had good heart and breath sounds. The organs were working.

He palpitated her belly, the one she'd kept flat and firm with diet and exercise, checking for internal injuries and unusual masses. It was clear.

"I need blood gases, CBC, SMA-seven, and type and cross for four units of blood in case we have to do some surgery." Jesse rattled off the orders to the nurses while he tapped Corinne's right elbow and knees with a tiny rubber hammer, checking her reflexes. She didn't have any. "Get me a skull X-ray, cross-table lateral C-spine, and a CT of the head. Make it fast."

One of the nurses hurried out. Susan looked across Corinne's body to Jesse, who was preparing to intubate the patient and put her on a ventilator that would take over her breathing.

"What do you think?" Susan asked.

"Check her driver's license," Jesse said. "We need to find out if she's an organ donor."

CHAPTER FIVE

The parked cars along the south side of the 2300 block of Messmer Avenue in Canoga Park were riddled with bullet holes. Shattered glass sprinkled the sidewalks and glittered in the light cast by the streetlamps, headlights, and the multicolored light bars atop the police cruisers. There was something magical about the glimmer of the glass shards that made Lieutenant Steve Sloan think of Christmas trees, the Las Vegas Strip, and pirate treasure.

He stepped carefully over the sidewalk to the manicured lawn in front of one of the nearly identical ranch-style homes that lined the San Fernando Valley street.

There were three bullet holes in the living room window of the house. One of the bullets had hit the big-screen TV that dominated the room. Another bullet had traveled clear through the house, out the kitchen window, and into the back fence, where several crime scene techs were digging out the slug and taking pictures. The remaining bullet had passed through the neck of Wilbur C. Gant and become entangled in the springs and stuffing of the recliner he was sitting in.

Wilbur C. Gant was a thirty-seven-year-old accountant who lived in his childhood home, which he had bought from his mother so she could fulfill her dream of retiring to a mobile home in Twentynine Palms. He was single, wore suspenders because he liked the look of them, and bled to death watching a rerun of *CSI*.

Steve peered in the window but didn't bother going inside the house. He could see Dr. Amanda Bentley, chief pathologist at Community General, leaning over the body in her blue MEDICAL EXAMINER Windbreaker. Her path lab did double duty as an extension of the county morgue, and so did she—as an adjunct county medical examiner. She was African American and a few years younger than Steve, whom she treated like her older brother.

He already knew that Gant wasn't the intended target of the bullets. That honor belonged to LaShonda Wilkes, who was sitting on the curb across the street with her two children, three-year-old LaTisha and five-year-old Chase. The hairstylist and unwed mother had been driving home from work with her children when her estranged boyfriend, Teeg Cantrell, pulled up alongside her in his pickup truck. When she turned to look at him, he pointed an automatic weapon at her. LaShonda slammed on her brakes at the same moment he started firing.

Teeg missed her and the children but managed to spray half the block and Wilbur C. Gant's living room with bullets before speeding off, sideswiping a car in the intersection on his way.

Fearing that Teeg would come back to finish what he'd started, LaShonda shifted her car into reverse and floored it without looking back, immediately colliding with the minivan right behind her and injuring the driver, a gardener named Julio Martinez.

Julio, who didn't speak much English, was less concerned about the damage to his van and the nasty cut on his forehead than he was about being arrested for driving without a license, insurance, or U.S. citizenship.

All in all, the situation had the makings of a long, miserable night for Steve.

He called out to Amanda. "Any surprises?"

"Yeah, there's a big one." She looked up at him with a perplexed expression on her face. "This man was already dead when the bullet hit him."

Steve felt a stab of anxiety in his chest. "What do you mean, he was already dead?"

"As in no longer living," she said. "That kind of dead."

"Then how did he die?"

"He was killed by a rattlesnake bite," she said.

"Oh hell," Steve said. "Are you sure?"

"I think I know a rattlesnake bite when I see one," she said. "You may want to bring Mark in on this."

"I'm perfectly capable of figuring out what happened here myself," Steve said.

"He's really good at this stuff," she said.

"So am I," Steve said. "I'm sure there's a simple explanation for everything."

"Really? What do you figure the odds are of a guy getting bitten by a rattlesnake and then getting hit by a stray bullet in a drive-by shooting?" Amanda asked. "Doesn't that sound a little unbelievable to you?"

It did.

And his father had a special ability to make sense of unbelievable situations like this.

He groaned and reluctantly fished around in his jacket pocket for his cell phone. There was no doubt that Mark would end up insinuating himself into the investigation anyway, so Steve figured he might as well bring his father into it now. It meant Steve would get a lot of grief from his superiors, who felt that every time Mark was brought in on a case it made the LAPD look incompetent.

He was about to speed-dial his father's number when Amanda burst out laughing. So did her two assistants, who were standing off to one side waiting with a gurney and a body bag.

Steve glared at her. "You were kidding."

"I told you it was unbelievable and you *still* bought it," she said, a big smile on her face. "I really have to play poker with you again. I could use the money."

Steve shoved his cell phone back into his pocket. "You took advantage of my trust."

"I took advantage of your gullibility," she said. "It's a wonder to me that you catch any bad guys at all."

"It was the context of the conversation. You're at a crime scene, engaging in your official duties," Steve said. "I naturally assumed you were behaving in a professional manner. Obviously, I was wrong."

"Oh, Steve, don't get all grouchy on me. A girl is allowed to have a little fun. Besides, you didn't need me to tell you how this man died. Isn't it obvious? He was shot in the neck."

Steve turned his back on Amanda, furious with himself for letting her fool him again. She loved to tease him, which he wouldn't mind if she wasn't always doing it in front of other people. He'd told her that. But she didn't think there was much fun in teasing him if there wasn't some potential for embarrassing him, too.

At least only her assistants and a couple of crime scene techs had heard her. He never would have lived it down if any other cops had witnessed it.

He strode over to question LaShonda Wilkes, but she held up her hand to stop him as he approached. She was busy yelling at someone on her cell phone, using some inventive combinations of profanity that Steve hadn't heard before, and she didn't want to be interrupted.

Steve nodded, said a few words to a uniformed cop, and was jotting down some of LaShonda's more colorful phrases for future reference when an unmarked LAPD Crown Vic drove up and a Hispanic woman got out, a badge and a gun clipped to her belt.

She strode over to him. He liked the way she strode. She was in her thirties, had black hair, dark skin, and even darker eyes. She introduced herself as Detective Olivia Morales, West Valley Homicide. They shook hands. She had a handshake firm enough to crack walnuts.

"Do you speak Spanish?" Steve asked.

"You think just because my name is Morales that I speak fluent Spanish."

"Yeah," Steve said, "I do."

"That's racial stereotyping, Lieutenant."

"No, it's not," he said.

"Just because you're Nordic, I don't immediately assume you speak Norwegian."

"You think I'm Nordic?" Steve asked.

"You're tall, blond, and look like you'd be comfortable wearing a Viking helmet." She shrugged. "That's Nordic to me."

"Do Nordics speak Norwegian?"

She shrugged again. "How the hell would I know what Nordics speak? I was trying to make a point. So, why do you want to know if I speak Spanish?"

Steve gestured to Julio Martinez. "Could you tell him that he's free to go after he gives us his statement and that we aren't going to arrest him or turn him over to immigration?"

She nodded. "I'll get around to it when I'm finished here. I'm surprised you didn't ask me to take care of those two kids, seeing as how I have a uterus and you're Nordic and all."

"That was going to be my next request," Steve said.

"Aren't you curious why I'm here?"

"I thought it was to talk to the gardener and keep an eye on those kids," Steve said, smiling. "Was there something else?"

Olivia gestured to LaShonda. "Her boyfriend, Teeg Cantrell, is a wanted fugitive."

"What is he wanted for?"

"He went into a 7-Eleven in West Hills last Friday night. He bought a six-pack of beer, three Milky Way bars, and a box of donuts. The cashier rang him up, but Teeg was two dollars short. When the cashier wouldn't give him the stuff anyway, Teeg shot him twice and walked out."

"The cashier still alive?"

"Would the hottest Latina homicide detective in the San Fernando Valley be standing here if he was?"

"Teeg sounds like a terrific guy," Steve said. "I wonder why LaShonda let him go."

"We could ask her," Olivia said.

"She's talking on the phone and doesn't want to be interrupted."

"And you're waiting?"

"Actually, judging by her use of language, I'm guessing she's talking to her ex-boyfriend right now."

"What kind of language?"

Steve showed her his notes. One of Olivia's thin, etched eyebrows arched. He liked the way it arched.

"Yeah," she said. "She's talking to her boyfriend. Are we tracing the call?"

"We are," Steve said. "But it's only going to give us the general area."

"If he's on the move," Olivia said, "maybe we can get a chopper up and spot his car."

"That's the idea," Steve said.

LaShonda abruptly snapped her phone shut and stomped over to the two detectives.

"How much longer do I have to stick around here?" LaShonda said irritably, her hands on her wide hips. "We haven't had dinner yet."

"We'll get you and the kids some burgers in a few minutes," Steve said, then introduced himself and Olivia to her.

"I know who she is," LaShonda said, glaring at Olivia. "I told you before I don't know where Teeg is. Ask one of his sluts."

"I've been talking to his sluts," Olivia said. "They send their regards. You want to tell us what happened here?"

"What's it look like to you?" LaShonda asked. "Teeg tried to smoke me."

"Why did he want to do that?" Steve asked.

"Because I threw his sorry ass out of the house for partying with sluts," LaShonda said. "And then I told him he couldn't see his kids until he started paying me some support."

"Was that your boyfriend you were just talking to?" Steve motioned to her phone.

"Teeg isn't my man no more and never will be again,"

LaShonda said. "Nobody shoots at me and gets back into my bed."

"I have the same policy," Steve said. "Did he call you or did you call him?"

"He called me. He said he was gonna come after me again and he wasn't going to miss this time. I laughed at him. I told him he can't even hit the toilet when he aims his—"

Steve interrupted her before she could finish that lovely thought, but he got the image anyway. "Could I see your phone, please?"

She gave it to him. Steve flipped it open and scrolled through the menu to see if he could find the number of the last call received. He could.

He turned the phone towards Olivia so she could see the number on the screen.

"We call this police work," he said.

"Impressive," Olivia said. "You've been watching *Law and Order*, haven't you?"

"I have to do something while I'm shining my Viking helmet."

CHAPTER SIX

Mark got back to Community General shortly after eleven p.m. No one was expecting to see him there, least of all Jesse, who was reviewing Corinne's X-rays and CT scans with Ramin Akhavan, the radiologist.

"What are you doing here?" Jesse asked Mark.

"I couldn't sleep," Mark said.

It wasn't exactly a lie. On the drive down from Sunrise Valley, alone in the car, all he could think about was Carter Sweeney. Mark knew that if he went back to his empty beach house in Malibu and tried to go to bed, he'd be up all night, churning over the events of the day and the nightmares of the past. So he chose distraction. And the absence of a homicide to solve left the hospital as his only salvation from his thoughts.

"So you get up, get dressed, and drive to work," Ramin said. "Haven't you heard of the Internet? Television? A good book?"

"I'm a people person," Mark said.

"That's what chat rooms are for," Ramin said. "You don't even have to get dressed."

The idea of sitting naked at a computer talking to strangers didn't strike Mark as very appealing under any circumstances.

"How is it going tonight?" Mark asked Jesse.

"It was slow until this patient came in," Jesse said, referring to the X-rays. "Her name is Corinne Adams. She fell down a flight of stairs at UCLA."

One glance at the X-rays and CT scans showed Mark what Jesse was dealing with, but he didn't say anything. He'd let Ramin go through the formality of explaining the results. He knew how much experts enjoyed the opportunity to show their expertise.

"What's the prognosis?" Mark asked Ramin.

"Not good. As you can see, she has a skull fracture here."

Ramin pointed to a long crack on the left side of the head. "And massive bleeding."

"I don't see a subdural hematoma," Jesse said.

"All the bleeding is inside the brain," Ramin said.

"What's her EEG look like?" Mark asked.

"What you'd expect with these test results," Jesse replied. "There are no sparks at all. Her pupils are blown, her reflexes are shot. We've got her on a ventilator in the ICU."

Mark nodded. There was nothing more that could be done for her. She was brain-dead, with no hope of recovery.

"Is she a good candidate for organ donation?"

"One of the best I've ever seen. Young, fit. She didn't smoke or drink. She's even got a donor card," Jesse said. "It's like her whole life was leading up to this."

"Maybe it was," Ramin said. "Maybe she was put on this earth for the sole purpose of saving the lives of a dozen other people."

The actual number of sick and injured people who could receive organs or other parts of her body, like corneas, tendons, and bones, was far higher than a dozen. Both Mark and Jesse knew there could easily be three times that many people whose lives could be saved or made markedly better by recycling Corinne Adams.

"I believe in fate," Ramin said.

"Does she have a family?" Mark asked Jesse.

"She was single, no husband or kids, if that's what you mean," Jesse said. "Not even a boyfriend."

"Fate," Ramin repeated to himself.

"Her sister Lurline is downstairs," Jesse said. "I spoke briefly with her. I didn't have much to say at the time."

He still didn't. The situation was pretty simple, just painful to share with a loved one.

She had a donor card, so at least that spared him the uncomfortable task of convincing her grief-stricken sister to let him harvest her organs. Corinne had already given her consent.

Over the next twenty-four hours, Jesse would have a lot of work to do. First, he'd have to find out who was next in line for each organ and work with the pathology lab to oversee the battery of tests to determine their compatibility with the donor. At the same time, he'd have to schedule the operating rooms and recruit surgical teams, as well as keep the brain-dead patient's body alive and healthy until the operation.

"Would you like me to talk to the sister?" Mark asked Jesse.

Grateful and relieved, Jesse nodded. "That would free me up to start making calls."

Mark could have offered to take over all the other work, too, so Jesse could return to the ER. But he knew how much Jesse wanted to coordinate the complex organ transplantations.

It wasn't Jesse's first time. In fact, he'd harvested kidneys and a liver from a donor only a week earlier. But each new experience further honed his skills, both administratively and surgically. Even so, Mark would keep his eye on the process, helping out where he could and smoothing over any wrinkles that emerged.

The first wrinkle was the grieving family. Although they didn't need the sister's permission to proceed, Lurline could make things a lot harder than they had to be if she disapproved of the procedure.

Mark found Lurline in the cafeteria, eating a piece of banana cream pie. Eating was clearly how Lurline dealt with stress and, judging by her obesity, there was a lot of it in her life. He introduced himself and sat down across from her. She was silent for a moment, shoveling more pie into her mouth. Her cheeks were big, round, and red.

"It's bad, isn't it?" she asked him.

Mark nodded. "She cracked her skull and there's bleeding in her brain."

"Can't you stop the bleeding and put a plate in her head or something?"

"I'm afraid not. If the bleeding had been around her brain, we could have relieved the pressure by drilling a hole in her skull."

Which is exactly what Jesse did to Mark only a few months ago. Mark rubbed the spot on his head where a piece of bone from the cadaver of an organ donor had been used to plug the hole.

It was pure luck Mark hadn't ended up like Corinne and that his bones weren't being reused today to fill gaps in other people's bones. He was a registered organ donor, too.

"But with the bleeding and bruising throughout her brain tissue, there is nothing we can do," he continued somberly. "Her brain is no longer functioning."

"You're saying she's dead," Lurline said.

"Her brain is dead," Mark said. "Her body is still alive."

"Because you've got her hooked to machines," she said.

"She's on a ventilator to keep her breathing," Mark said. "And we have her on an IV to keep her hydrated and nourished."

Lurline sighed, gathering her thoughts before speaking, stabbing at her piece of pie with her fork.

"We've got this three-foot-tall Santa Claus in the garage. We bring him into the living room every Christmas, dust off his red suit, and plug him in. This candle in his hand lights up and he looks around and says 'Ho ho ho' every couple of minutes. He used to play 'Jingle Bells,' too, but that part broke years ago." Lurline finished her pie and licked the whipped cream off her lips. "Corinne never liked that Santa Claus much. I think she'd like being him even less. Unplug her."

"Are you aware that Corinne agreed to become an organ donor in the event of a situation like this?"

"She didn't think this would ever happen. She was just doing the politically correct thing."

"But she did it," Mark said.

"Why can't you take her off the machines?"

"We need to keep her alive until we are ready to remove her organs."

Lurline grimaced and ran her finger along the rim of her pie plate, wiping up the cream that remained. She licked her finger clean.

"So you're going to gut her like a fish," Lurline said. "Remove her organs while she's still alive."

Basically, Lurline was right. But Mark wasn't going to say that. He put it as delicately as he could.

"Her organs are healthy and we need to keep them that way until the last possible moment," Mark said. "That means keeping her as physiologically functional as possible until surgery."

"You've turned her into a cocoon."

"Corinne is gone. Wherever it is we go in our afterlife, she's already there. Now the body she has left behind can be used to save lives."

"But not her own," Lurline said.

"I'm sorry," Mark said.

"She went on a diet, kept herself in shape, even got herself some new boobies," Lurline said. "And for what?"

Mark thought about what Ramin Akhavan, the radiologist, had said about fate.

"Maybe for this," Mark said.

"Screw *this*." Lurline got up, went back to the cafeteria counter, and snagged another piece of pie.

CHAPTER SEVEN

Steve Sloan often spent his weekends wearing short-sleeved shirts and shorts, and he thought he looked pretty good in them. His body was muscular and tan from years of weightlifting, jogging, and surfing. He was built for casual attire.

So it must have been some flaw in the design of the mud brown short-sleeve shirt and matching shorts of the United Parcel Service uniform he was wearing that made him look so awkward and pudgy. The uniform made him feel like an adult who still lived at home with his parents, which, of course, he was.

But Steve wasn't living with his dad because he was some socially inept loser afraid of leaving the nest. He had lived on his own for years. The only reason he'd moved back home, so to speak, was because his dad bought an incredible two-story beach house and invited Steve to share it. Steve loved the beach. He loved surfing. And there was no way he could ever afford to live on the beach in Malibu on a cop's salary. It was too good an opportunity to pass up. That was all there was to it. Not that anyone in the department really believed that story.

He was afraid that other cops saw him the way he felt when he put on the UPS uniform, which, for some bizarre reason, matched the color of the company delivery truck he was now driving through a neighborhood of tract homes in Simi Valley. Judging by the idiotic smirks on the faces of the six heavily armed SWAT guys and the one Latina detective in the back of the truck, Steve was right.

"Nice knees," Olivia said.

"Thanks," Steve muttered.

"They really pop with the brown socks and loafers," she said. "It's a shame you aren't wearing the UPS cap, too."

"I thought women love a man in uniform," he said.

"If the uniform makes him look like a man," she said, her implication painfully clear to Steve.

He turned the corner and headed into a cul-de-sac. It was nine a.m.

"We're moving into position," he said.

"Ten-four," the SWAT commander radioed back.

Teeg had called LaShonda from a landline. The police traced the phone to one of the cookie-cutter homes in this recently built neighborhood, which was inhabited almost exclusively by young middle-class families. There were SUVs, bicycles, and basketball hoops in the driveways. The lawns were all freshly laid mosaics of sod.

It seemed like a strange place for Teeg to hide out, especially if he wanted to go unnoticed. Steve was surprised the cops weren't called by every neighbor in the cul-de-sac the moment Teeg stepped out of his truck.

It was probably a good thing they hadn't called. If a black-and-white had driven up, Teeg was trigger-happy enough that he would've started firing the instant the cops got out of the car. And the guy's aim wasn't very good.

With that in mind, the LAPD was approaching the apprehension of this particular felon with care. They couldn't risk provoking a shoot-out in this cul-de-sac. The possibility of civilians getting hit by Teeg's stray bullets was way too high. And the police didn't think they could evacuate the neighbors or move large numbers of officers into offensive positions without tipping off the suspect and sparking a firefight.

So they had to get clever.

It was the SWAT commander who came up with the idea of dressing Steve as a UPS deliveryman and having him drive a van full of cops right into the suspect's driveway. Then Steve was supposed to walk up to the front door and deliver a package.

The front door of the house was set back far enough from the driveway that Teeg's view of the truck would be obscured, especially with Steve standing in front of him. The plan was that team would scramble out of the front passenger side of the van, surround the house, and wait for the signal to strike.

Steve's job was to see whatever he could through the open door and report back if there were other people in the house. That was assuming that Teeg opened the door wide enough or that he even answered. The box Steve was delivering contained a tear-gas bomb that would explode in Teeg's face when he opened it.

That was the primary signal.

If Teeg didn't open the box, then the SWAT team would burst in on Steve's command. One way or another, they were going in.

Steve could see Teeg's pickup parked in front of a single-story house with a red tile roof and a large, three-car garage at the front.

He parked in the driveway on the side farthest from the front door. Teeg would be able to see the rear of the van, but not the front.

So far, so good.

Steve picked up the package, strode to the door, and leaned on the bell. He could hear it ring inside the house. It was a hollow sound, like the ring was bouncing around empty rooms. After a moment, he heard footsteps padding up to the door and saw a flicker behind the peephole. Someone was looking at him and seeing a harmless geek in goofy brown shorts.

"What is it?" Teeg demanded.

"UPS," Steve said. "I have a delivery for you."

"Is it something good?"

"I don't open the boxes," Steve said. "I just deliver them."

The door opened. Teeg was shirtless and barefoot, wearing only a pair of white Jockey shorts. He was a bald, light-skinned, African-American Hispanic with prison yard muscles. There was a tattoo on his hairless chest that the artist had probably intended to be a vicious cobra, but it looked to Steve like a tapeworm with bad teeth. Behind Teeg, Steve could see that the entry hall and the living room were vacant of furniture, artwork, and other people.

So Steve handed Teeg the box and punched him in the face.

Teeg staggered back, stunned by the blow.

Steve stepped into the house and punched him again to keep him hospitable.

"LAPD. You're under arrest."

Steve took the box back from Teeg so he wouldn't set off the tear gas bomb when he hit the floor.

Teeg dropped.

Steve watched Teeg crumple and heard the SWAT team members crashing into the house simultaneously through various doors and windows. The SWAT guys each shouted "clear" as they swept the rooms for occupants and found no one.

The cops all converged in the entry hall around Teeg, who, when he was able to focus his eyes again, looked up into eight gun barrels pointed at his face.

Steve rolled Teeg over on his stomach, yanked his arms behind his back, and handcuffed him while informing him of his rights. Outside, several black-and-whites drove into the cul-de-sac, and neighbors started coming out of their houses to see what was going on.

He lifted Teeg to his feet and handed him off to the first officer who came through the door.

Olivia came into the entry hall, holstering her gun. "I don't think one of the signals we agreed on was smacking the guy in the face."

"The opportunity presented itself," Steve said.

"I feel sorry for the next UPS guy Teeg meets," Olivia said.

"I don't think they deliver to death row," Steve said.

CHAPTER EIGHT

Mark got home from the hospital at about two a.m. and went straight to bed. When he awoke shortly after nine a.m., Steve was already gone. The only sign that Mark and Steve had been in the same house that night were his son's coffee cup in the sink and a butter knife left by the toaster.

He made himself some coffee, poured a bowl of Wheat Chex, and sat down at the kitchen table, facing the beach.

The *Los Angeles Times* was on the table, the front page dominated by a story analyzing the hotly contested mayoral race between Police Chief Masters and District Attorney Burnside. Mark couldn't bring himself to read it. He didn't care who won. The city would survive either one of them and so would he.

There was also a story about the safeguards being implemented at area hospitals in the wake of the arrests of two nurses who'd been killing patients for years. Mark didn't bother reading it. He'd lived it. It was his investigation that exposed them.

And there was a story about sentences being handed down against the corrupt cops exposed by private eye Nick Stryker's surveillance and subsequent blackmailing scheme.

It seemed that Mark had a connection to every story on the front page except the labor unrest in France, the efforts in Southern California to eradicate mosquitoes that carry West Nile virus, and a human-interest feature on a man who wallpapered his apartment with cocktail napkins.

Mark pushed the *Times* aside and glanced outside while he ate. Looking at his million-dollar view was a much less stressful way to start the day.

It was a typically gray morning, the fog hanging thick over the beach, keeping it a good ten to twenty degrees cooler than the rest of Los Angeles and the San Fernando Valley. By noon, most of the fog would burn off and the beach would be covered with people seeking relief from the three-digit temperatures by frolicking in the salt water and sewage of Santa Monica Bay.

The waves were pretty to look at, but the days when Mark would stroll in the surf in anything but a HazMat suit and rubber boots were long gone. There were times when the stench of rotting seaweed, soaked in the raw affluent that poured into the bay, made Mark contemplate a life in the mountains instead.

It wasn't just the contaminated water that prompted him to think about making some changes in his life. It wasn't that he was unhappy, but ever since the three days he'd spent in a coma, he'd been restless and uneasy. His encounter yesterday with Carter Sweeney had only made things worse.

He felt like he was a prisoner of his past, like a TV series character experiencing variations of the same story, over and over again for hundreds of episodes, season after season, without anything really changing. It was only an illusion that his life was moving forward; in fact, he was simply running in place.

While Mark was comatose, he'd dreamed his life from a different perspective. He was living in the same world, only everyone had changed in significant ways. He'd even married again.

The strange thing was, once he regained consciousness, that restlessness and uneasiness he'd been feeling were much stronger. He found himself missing his imaginary life with Emily, his new wife.

It was silly. He knew that. Emily wasn't a real person. She merely symbolized an aspect of the murder he was trying to solve at the time. But he couldn't help wondering if Emily was more than that, if she was his subconscious expressing his dissatisfaction with his life.

Mark was in his mid-sixties. He could retire and still have a long life ahead of him. But then what would he do? How would he occupy his time? How would he keep his mind sharp? Could he walk away from a life devoted to medicine and homicide investigation? And even if he could, was that what he wanted?

That was the real problem. He didn't know what he wanted.

Maybe he was just lonely.

Wasn't that really why he'd bought this house after his wife, Katherine, died, all those years ago, as a way to keep Steve from leaving him alone?

No, he couldn't possibly be that selfish or manipulative. It wasn't in his character. It wasn't who he was. Or who he thought he was anyway.

Maybe the only change he needed in his life was to find a new woman to love. He hadn't made much of an effort in that regard in the decades since Katherine died. Sure, he'd had some relationships, but the women all ended up moving on. They grew tired of competing with the hospital and the LAPD for his attention and losing.

He couldn't blame them for leaving him. He'd refused to change. Perhaps he always would.

Mark glanced at his watch. It was time to go to the hospital—it always was when his thoughts started taking him down roads he'd rather not travel.

CHAPTER NINE

Jesse was on his way to the ICU to check on Corinne Adams when Mark caught up with him in the hallway. The young surgeon looked terrible.

"Have you slept at all since I last saw you?" Mark asked.

"Susan and I managed to sneak into one of the new maternity suites for a couple of hours," Jesse said and then winced with regret. "I probably shouldn't have told you that."

The maternity suites were part of a new initiative by Hollyworld International, the owners of the hospital, to lure upscale couples to Community General for their maternity needs.

Hollyworld owned several amusement parks and resorts and brought that design expertise to the lushly appointed maternity suites, which looked like upscale hotel rooms and offered well-heeled couples the opportunity to, as the advertisements put it, "enjoy the birth of your child in a relaxing environment of unsurpassed comfort, luxury, and style for mother, father, and newborn."

The theory was that couples would check in to the maternity ward as if it were a Ritz-Carlton, staying a few days before and after the birth of their child for a "maternity vacation that you will enjoy so much, you'll start thinking of having another child before you leave."

But few couples could afford the daily rates, which looked more like monthly mortgage payments. It was a poorly kept secret that the only couples taking advantage of the plush new suites were doctors and nurses sneaking away for a few intimate moments in the middle of their long, grueling shifts.

"You need your sleep," Mark said. "As long as you don't nod off while you're behind the wheel of a car or operating on a patient, why should I care where you get your rest?"

"Because you're an administrator here and we're supposed to sleep alone on the hard, narrow cots in the doctors' lounge," Jesse said, lowering his voice to a conspiratorial whisper. "Not with our wives in the comfy king-sized beds with the four-hundred-thread-count sheets and heavy comforters that they've got up in the maternity suites. Those rooms are a lot nicer than our apartment. It's almost pointless to go home."

"Did you change the sheets?" Mark asked.

"Of course we did."

Mark shrugged.

"What matters to me is that you're at the top of your game and providing the best possible care to our patients. You need to be rested and undistracted by problems in your personal life to do that. If sleeping with your wife in an empty maternity suite is what it takes to maintain that level of quality care, then so be it. No one is getting hurt. If anything, the patients and the hospital are benefiting."

"I like your enlightened attitude," Jesse said.

"The hospital doesn't."

"So what else is new? Speaking of which, Clarke Trotter has been looking for you."

Mark made it a habit to avoid Trotter, the hospital's legal counsel and hatchet man.

Trotter did whatever he could to limit the hospital's legal exposure in any given situation. But that was Trotter's job, and Mark could respect that. What Mark couldn't abide was Trotter's unwillingness to factor the medical and human consequences of his actions into his decisions.

"I'll stay on the lookout for him," Mark said. "Where do things stand with Corinne Adams?"

Jesse stopped outside the doors to the ICU and turned towards Mark.

"She's stable. I've sent out her lab work to all the hospitals that have patients at the top of the various waiting lists for organs. They're getting back to me with their tissue samples and lab results to match with the donor. I'd like to see the donor on the table by the end of the week."

Mark noticed that Jesse was referring to Corinne not by name but as "the donor." It was a subtle shift, but he knew it was a necessary one for someone in Jesse's position. It was an act of emotional self-preservation.

Jesse had to stop thinking of her as a person. Otherwise the complex task of arranging for and performing her organ removal would be too emotionally difficult, even for someone who'd intellectually accepted that she was already dead.

"Any takers yet?" Mark asked, knowing that it could be days before the right candidates with the same compatibility antigens as Corinne, were found.

And the longer the wait, the greater the chances that her physical condition could change for the worse, putting her organs at risk.

"Just one. We've got a thirty-five-year-old patient right here with Eisenmenger's syndrome. His name is Ken Hoffman. He's at the top of the list for a heart-lung transplant and happens to be compatible with the donor."

That was a lucky break, Mark thought.

The heart and lungs would stay viable for only two to four hours after harvesting, so the best possible situation was to perform the extremely delicate organ removal and transplanting at the same hospital, preferably in adjoining operating rooms.

Corinne's heart and lungs would be the last organs removed from her body in order to keep the other organs viable for as long as possible. The kidneys and liver could last for up to twenty-four hours with proper packing and care after removal, which meant they could be sent just about anywhere in the United States.

"Have you lined up the heart surgeons?"

"David Carren is on deck for the removal and Larry Carroll is coming over from Cedars-Sinai for the implant."

They were both excellent surgeons, though Carroll was known as a risk junkie. When he wasn't in the operating room he liked to climb mountains, jump out of airplanes, and swim with sharks. Mark worried that anyone who enjoyed gambling with his life might be more likely to gamble with someone else's. Then again, it often took a personality like that to excel at the kind of delicate surgeries Carroll took on.

"Are the other organs going to local patients?"

"I'm still working on that, but it looks like at least one kidney is headed to Houston. We'll probably be dividing up the liver among three or four people, though I'm not sure who or where yet."

Mark wasn't surprised. A healthy liver was often divided among several patients, and there were undoubtedly many, many desperate people vying for a piece of this one.

"It sounds like you've got everything under control," Mark said.

"It's a big relief to hear you say that, Mark. Because if I've got you fooled, there's a chance everyone else will be, too."

They entered the ICU. The practice of medicine had become so high-tech that the unit looked less like a hospital ward than a Best Buy that happened to have a few people on gurneys plugged into the computers, cameras, TVs, and PlayStations on sale. The bright colors on the walls and the blue scrubs worn by the staff only added to the effect.

There was a nurse at Corinne's bedside, reviewing her chart, when Mark and Jesse entered. She had a scowl of dissatisfaction on her face. Her name was Mercy Reynolds and she was one of the hordes of utilization nurses that descended on Community General not long after Hollyworld International took over. The utilization nurses had free run of the hospital, roaming every floor and department, ostensibly to review the treatment of patients to ensure that they were receiving appropriate care.

In truth, the utilization nurses were tasked with finding ways to save the hospital money and maximize resources, which meant second-guessing doctors and suggesting cutbacks in care whenever possible.

"What is she still doing here?" Mercy asked.

"Does she look like she's ready to be released to you?" Jesse replied.

"She looks dead to me," Mercy said.

She was in her early thirties, about the same age as Jesse, but she didn't have one-tenth of his medical experience or knowledge. She was an accountant with a stethoscope, in Mark's opinion.

Mark wondered if she was truly as arrogant and confident as she acted or if it was all a cover for her insecurity and incompetence. It didn't matter. Hollyworld had given her the authority to challenge doctors far more qualified than she was, under the guise of being an objective advocate for the patients. She reported to the chief of staff, a Hollyworld bureaucrat who usually sided with the utilization nurses over the frequent objections of the doctors.

"She's an organ donor," Mark said. "We're in the process of arranging for the transplant surgery."

"How long will that take?" she asked.

Mark glanced at Jesse, who shrugged.

"Another day or two," Jesse said.

"Is that the best you can do?" Mercy demanded, impatience oozing from every word. "Every day this patient is in the ICU means there is one less bed available for someone else."

"You mean someone who can pay," Mark said. "I'm guessing that Corinne Adams isn't adequately covered by her insurance for catastrophic injury."

"She isn't covered at all," Mercy said. "She's uninsured, which means she's costing us money we'll never recover, money that could go towards bettering patient care throughout the hospital."

"What about the money the hospital is going to make off the transplant surgery?" Jesse asked.

"At best, we'll break even," Mercy said. "We aren't allowed by law to profit financially from the organs themselves."

"What counts is that this surgery will save half a dozen lives," Mark said.

"Only one of those patients is at this hospital," Mercy said. "If the others were here, too, we might see some profit from this."

"We're in the business of saving lives," Mark said. "That's how we measure profit and loss."

"Last time I checked, Dr. Sloan, you were drawing a salary, and a sizable one at that," Mercy said. "Where do you think that money comes from?"

"Money is not my primary motivation for being a doctor," Mark said.

"And it's not mine for being a nurse either," Mercy said. "I'm not your enemy. I wish you'd stop treating me that way."

"You want to hustle this patient out of the ICU because she can't pay for the treatment she's getting," Jesse said. "How do you expect us to take that?"

"It's about more than the money to me and this hospital," Mercy said. "Look at her, Dr. Travis. Is this a dignified way to die? Do you think being kept alive as a brainless sack of flesh is what she had in mind when she agreed to donate her organs? Do you think her family wants to see her like this any longer than absolutely necessary? The sooner we get her out of here, the sooner we end her suffering and theirs."

"And ours," Mark said. "Financially speaking."

"Yes," Mercy said, studying Mark's face. "You seem shocked that I'd say that, Dr. Sloan. Does acknowledging the truth make me the bad guy or just the only honest person in the room?"

She walked away without waiting for either one of them to answer.

Jesse looked after her and shook his head in dismay. "What possessed her parents to name her Mercy?"

CHAPTER TEN

Technically, Steve's job was done.

He'd apprehended Teeg Cantrell, the shooter responsible for killing a bystander in a drive-by shooting and for gunning down the cashier during a robbery at a West Hills convenience store.

Forensic evidence irrefutably connected Teeg to the murder weapon. Ballistic experts matched the bullets recovered from the victims with the semi-automatic weapon found at the home where Teeg was apprehended. Teeg's fingerprints were all over the weapon, and his clothing tested positive for gunpowder residue.

On top of that evidence, Steve could place Teeg at the scene of both murders. The CSI unit matched Teeg's smashed truck to paint chips recovered from the car he collided with while speeding away from the scene. And Steve had surveillance camera footage of Teeg shooting the 7-Eleven cashier.

Case closed. Teeg was on his way to death row. It was time for Steve to move on to the next homicide investigation that came along.

But he couldn't. Not quite yet.

He was still wondering why Teeg was hiding out with the desperate housewives on Wisteria Lane. Teeg didn't exactly fit in with the soccer moms and dads.

The easy way to find out was to ask Teeg about it. But Steve doubted Teeg would be very forthcoming with the guy who'd punched him in the mouth. Twice.

So while Teeg was busy being booked and processed for his lifetime in the prison system, Steve sat at his computer researching the ownership of the Simi Valley house.

It took only a couple of minutes to get the information from the county tax assessor. The house was owned by Gold Mountain Investment Partners, who, based on their history of frequent property purchases and quick sales, were playing the housing market. They'd buy a home, make some minor cosmetic changes, then resell it a couple of months later, cashing in on the increased property value since their purchase, a practice known as flipping. When the housing market was soft, they'd hold on to the home as a rental property and then sell it the moment the market upticked again.

The headquarters of Gold Mountain Investment Partners was a post office box rented by a Gaylord and Bette Yokley at a Mailboxes America outlet two blocks from their home in Palmdale.

Steve ran a background check on the Yokleys and discovered that the couple, both of whom were in their forties, had criminal records.

Bette Yokley had been arrested several times over the years for marijuana possession, drunk driving, indecent exposure, and disorderly conduct. She liked to party. She currently worked as a dog groomer in a pet salon located in the same strip mall as their post office box.

Her husband, Gaylord, was an ex-marine and former gun dealer who spent five years in prison for selling illegal firearms and unlawful possession of explosives. His defense was that he was an "off the books" military operative for the CIA, supplying weapons on its behalf to groups attempting to overthrow anti-U.S. governments in South America and Africa. The jury didn't buy it. After his release from prison, Gaylord went into the used-car business.

On a hunch, Steve checked to see who'd sold Teeg his truck. Sure enough, it was Yokley Motors.

It didn't take a huge intellectual leap for Steve to figure out that Yokley was back in the firearms business and might have sold Teeg some weapons.

So why was Yokley being so generous to Teeg? What exactly was their relationship? It had to be more than a simple truck sale or a gun transaction. And whatever it was, it probably wasn't legal.

He had an inkling where this case might eventually lead. And it was big.

Steve took a moment to consider his options. He could take this bust and all the glory for himself. Or he could spread the wealth and bring Detective Olivia Morales into it, too. Not that anyone would blame him if he didn't. He had no professional or ethical obligation to her; he'd found this strand on his own and followed it where it led. It was unrelated to any legwork Olivia had done.

Even so, the last thing he needed was another enemy in the department, especially at a time when his enemies seemed to outnumber his friends by three to one.

The more he thought about it, the more he became convinced that this Yokley thing could turn out to be an opportunity to win some favor with a few people in the law enforcement community who'd put him on their shit lists. So what if he had to share the credit for the bust with half a dozen other people? In the long run, it might do him more good than hogging it all for himself.

He picked up the phone and made three calls. One was to Olivia Morales; the next was to assistant district attorney Karen Cross. And then he called down to the holding cells and asked an officer to bring Teeg up to one of the interrogation rooms.

Chapter Eleven

Teeg snarled and tried very hard to appear fearsome, but his swollen lip made the snarl too painful to maintain and he just didn't have Anthony Hopkins's gravitas. When Steve walked into the interrogation room, he took one look at Teeg and immediately pictured the guy in his undies, flexing that silly tapeworm tattoo on his chest. Even Teeg, clueless about most aspects of human nature, could read the amusement on Steve's face and saw himself as he must be seen. It was a pitiful moment of realization.

So Teeg dropped the snarl and slumped in his chair, humiliated and depressed before Steve had uttered even a single word.

"Lousy day, isn't it, Teeg?"

"Hell yes," Teeg mumbled.

"We've got you on two counts of murder, one count of armed robbery, and that's just for starters. The evidence against you is so strong, the DA is sending some kid, an intern straight out of law school, to try the case for some courtroom experience. I met the kid. He's seen cases on *Judge Judy* that are more complex. He thinks it might take him ten minutes to present his case, if he drags things out, and maybe five minutes for the jury to reach a verdict, and that's counting the time it takes them to get from the jury box to the jury room. All things considered, you could be on death row before lunch."

Teeg didn't know who Judge Judy was, but he'd seen parts of two or three *Law & Order* episodes, which just about covered his knowledge and understanding of the U.S. judicial system. The one thing he knew was that cops don't bother talking to you unless their case is shaky. Maybe his situation wasn't as bad as the cop was making it seem.

"So if I'm this badly screwed," Teeg said with all the cocky bravado he could muster, "why are you in here talking to me?"

"Because you're such a pathetic criminal, and your stupidity has made catching and prosecuting you so easy, I get absolutely no career bump at all for arresting you," Steve said. "I want something out of this."

"You think I give a crap about you?"

"No, but I think you care about yourself. You're going to prison for the rest of your life. That's a done deal. There's nothing either one of us can do about that. But it's up to you whether you get a lethal injection or serve a life sentence somewhere, and whether that time is spent in a hellhole or in a Ramada Inn with bars on the windows."

"I'm not confessing to nothing, if that's what you want."

Steve leaned on the table and got in Teeg's face. "You're not listening to me. I don't need you to confess. I've got you. But you could save your ass and enormously improve your future standard of living in prison by telling me about Gaylord Yokley's black-market arms business."

Teeg's eyes bugged out. "You *know* about that?"

Steve did now.

"You bought your guns from him. You bought your truck from him. You were hiding out in a house owned by him. Yeah, Teeg, we know about you and Yokley."

"Did he rat me out? Is that how you found me?"

That was some mighty faulty logic as far as Steve was concerned. He couldn't see what possible upside there would be for Yokley to let Teeg hide out in his house and then turn him in to the police. But Steve also didn't see any benefit to telling Teeg how inane his reasoning was. He decided to let Teeg think whatever he wanted to if it would get him to talk.

So Steve simply shrugged, which communicated volumes to Teeg.

"Damn," Teeg said. "After everything I done for him? He's made a lot of money off me and my homeys."

"What were you doing in his house?"

"I told him I smoked a *vato* and needed a place to go where nobody would look for me until things cooled off. Me and my homeys are his best customers. So he let me crash at his place in Simi."

"You thought you'd just blend right in."

"Why not?" Teeg asked without a trace of irony. He honestly didn't see how a tattooed gangbanger might stand out in a cul-de-sac full of middle-class families. And not just anywhere, but in

Simi Valley, the city that let the cops who nearly beat Rodney King to death walk with only a finger-wagging and a stern warning.

"My mistake," Steve said. "So tell me what you and your homeboys were buying from Yokley."

"Guns, man," Teeg said. "We go in like we're buying cars, and he delivers the *quetes* in the trunk with the spare tire."

"But you bought a pickup truck," Steve said. "What kind of weapons did you need a cargo bed for?"

"Rifles, shotguns, like that."

Like that.

Steve glanced at the mirror on the wall. On the other side of the glass, he knew, Detective Olivia Morales and ADA Karen Cross were watching, along with invited guests from LAPD's Gang Intervention Unit, the Federal Bureau of Investigation, and the Bureau of Alcohol, Tobacco, and Firearms, or ATF. They were all absorbing the news that Yokley was supplying LA street gangs with weapons and using his profits to buy and sell real estate.

Getting a search warrant and raiding Gaylord Yokley's home and business with a multi-agency task force would be a no-brainer now.

Steve turned back to Teeg and smiled. "Suddenly your future is looking a little less bleak."

"Like how?"

"I can guarantee that in return for your testimony against Gaylord Yokley, the State of California won't be strapping you to a table and injecting lethal drugs into your veins."

"Can I get a TV in my cell?"

"Sure," Steve said. "Under the rules of the Geneva Conventions, depriving you of *American Idol* would constitute cruel and inhuman punishment."

"Make it a wall-mounted flat screen," Teeg said. "I don't know what prisons are like in Geneva, but the cells here are cramped."

CHAPTER TWELVE

The executive dining room was another improvement Holly-world International made after it purchased Community General. The senior staff and upper-level administrators were served the same food on the same dishware as the people dining in the cafeteria, but somehow the dim lighting, tablecloths, and absence of bothersome patients, worried loved ones, and harried interns made it taste better.

Mark hadn't visited the executive dining room, even though his position at the hospital allowed him the privilege. He disapproved of the class structure that the existence of an executive dining room created among the hospital staff. To him, the dining room personified the insensitivity of Hollyworld towards its employees. The company seemed to be actively sowing bitterness and distrust between administration and the doctors, nurses, technicians, and orderlies who worked there.

So, naturally, the executive dining room was where Janet Dorcott, Community General's thirty-three-year-old chief administrator, summoned Mark for an urgent meeting.

She'd replaced Noah Dent after his mysterious, and quite unexpected, departure from the job a year or so earlier. Dent slashed budgets, laid off dozens of nurses, and tried to shut down the adjunct county medical examiner's office, which Mark had established. It was run by Dr. Amanda Bentley out of the hospital's morgue. But no sooner had Dent made those massive changes than he abruptly reinstated everything and left. That was one mystery Mark had never felt compelled to investigate.

Janet was recruited by Hollyworld from a big box retailer, where she'd been in charge of the company's aggressive efforts to build superstores on the outskirts of small towns. The retailer dramatically undercut local, family-owned businesses on price and selection and drove them into bankruptcy, leaving behind empty storefronts and deserted streets. When the local businesses died, so did the culture and character of the rural communities they'd served for generations.

She saw that as a successful outcome.

Of course, Janet would argue that she was bringing much-needed jobs and a wide range of affordably priced products to the poverty-stricken communities that needed them most and, in doing so, was revitalizing stagnant local economies. She didn't care that, at the same time, the superstores were stripping the communities of their character and history, assimilating them into a homogeneous landscape of bland box stores.

That was her idea of progress.

She brought that same attitude to medical care, treating hospitals as box stores and patients as customers. The only difference was the products weren't cut-rate; only the service was.

Janet liked to paint herself as a simple country girl and play up her Texas twang to disarm people. But Mark saw the performance for what it was—a show of contempt for her rural upbringing and anyone who was charmed by it.

Mark toyed with refusing to meet her in the executive dining room and instead making the woman come to him in the cafeteria. But then he'd be playing the same kind of power games that she did, and he didn't want to lower himself to her level. So he met her in the executive dining room as requested.

Janet smiled at him when he came in, her unnaturally whitened teeth gleaming in the pinpoint halogen light that illuminated her private booth. He figured that his presence reaffirmed her sense of superiority in the hospital hierarchy and his tacit acknowledgment that he was answerable to her.

She set aside her BlackBerry, her chef's salad, and her glass of ice water, which Mark assumed she kept cold by holding it against her bosom.

"Dr. Sloan, it is so good to see you," she said. "I was beginning to think you were avoiding me."

Mark shivered, struck by the eerie parallel between her greeting and the one Carter Sweeney had given him twenty-four hours earlier.

"I haven't been avoiding you," he said, sliding into the booth across from her. "I've been avoiding Clarke Trotter."

"It's the same thing," she said. "The legal counsel works for me. As a matter of fact, so do you."

"And here I am."

"That's exactly what I'd like to discuss with you," she said. "We'd like you to go."

"Already? I haven't even ordered lunch yet."

He was being facetious. He knew what she meant. She was hardly the first chief administrator who'd wanted to get rid of him. She was the fourth or fifth.

"I have no doubt that you were an excellent physician once, respected in your field, and that Community General was proud to have you on its staff," she said. "That time is long gone."

"You're questioning my competence as a doctor?"

"I wouldn't know. Since I took over this hospital, I haven't seen you practicing much medicine. Most of what I know about you I've learned from reading the *Los Angeles Times*, *The New York Times*, and *USA Today*."

She picked up a stack of newspapers from the seat beside her and dropped them on the center of the table. The papers had been collected over the last few months. The front pages were filled with stories relating to the killer nurses scandal that Mark had uncovered.

"That's your problem, Janet. Instead of learning about the hospital by walking the halls, meeting the staff, and getting to know people over lunch in the cafeteria, you sit in here reading newspapers and spreadsheets," Mark said. "You won't discover what I'm doing as a doctor by reading the *Los Angeles Times*."

"You're right. I won't. I'd much rather be reading about the wonderful accomplishments you're achieving as a doctor and the prestige it brings to Community General. Instead, what I'm reading about is your obsession with homicide investigation, which has brought nothing but calamity and shame to this hospital and to the entire medical profession. There isn't a hospital in Los Angeles, or anywhere else in the country, that would hire you today."

"Do you think that this hospital and our profession were better off when there were nurses killing patients for sport?"

"Of course not. But in the wake of exposing those killers, there have been weeks of negative media coverage calling into question the vetting and oversight of our nursing staff, the privacy and security of our medical records, and the health and safety of the patients in our hospitals."

"That is a good thing," Mark said.

"It's a disaster, Dr. Sloan. It undermines public confidence in our hospital. It costs us business. And that's not even counting the millions of dollars we stand to lose settling the lawsuits arising from all this. Or the long-term costs of any additional regulations that the government, provoked by this scandal, could impose on our hiring and supervision of medical personnel."

"In the long run, it will improve medical care and save lives," Mark said. "I don't feel guilty about that."

"What about the people who lost their lives when this hospital was bombed? The killer was after *you*. Do you feel guilty about that?"

"I do," Mark said quietly.

"But that hasn't stopped you from continuing with your dangerous hobby, has it? Since the bombing, there have been three attempts on your life at this hospital, all provoked by your investigations. It's pure luck that no one else has been injured or killed as a result. And yet you're still here, willfully endangering the lives of our patients, their loved ones, and our medical staff while you selfishly indulge your obsession with murderers."

There was some truth to that, more than Mark wanted to admit. He'd rationalized that he couldn't be held responsible for the actions of killers. But it was just that, a rationalization. Even so, Janet Dorcott's argument would have been more convincing to Mark if he'd thought she actually believed it herself. Her rationale for wanting to get rid of him wasn't nearly so altruistic.

"It's all about the bottom line for you," Mark said. "You aren't concerned about anyone's safety."

"And *you* are?" Janet asked incredulously. "If you were, you would have taken this generous severance package when it was first offered to you."

She slid a file across the table to him. Mark was familiar with the terms. Noah Dent had made him the same offer, preceded by an unpleasant meeting very much like the one he was having now. It seemed as though Mark had sat through this meeting repeatedly over the years, with one chief administrator after another. It always ended with Mark refusing to quit and vowing to fight any efforts to force him out.

Sitting there, looking at that file, Mark was struck again by the feeling that his life was on an endless loop, the same events replaying themselves over again.

He was tired of it. He didn't want to live a rerun. He didn't want to have this meeting every time a new chief administrator came to Community General.

Mark took the file.

"I'll think about it," he said.

CHAPTER THIRTEEN

Steve spent the afternoon in the SWAT tactical command center with agents from the FBI and the ATF, examining blueprints of Gaylord Yokley's home and car dealership in preparation for the simultaneous raids they were going to conduct, assuming all the warrants came through and the agencies could settle their turf issues.

Gaylord Yokley's house was in a flat expanse of open desert. The big problem was that he would see them coming. Steve was worried about him destroying any evidence, although handguns and rifles aren't easily flushed down the toilet. He was more concerned about the raid turning into another Waco, with Gaylord hunkering down with his wife and kids in an armed standoff with law enforcement.

So it was decided that they would wait to strike until after Bette left to drive the kids to school and as Gaylord was on his way out to work. At the worst, only Yokley would be left to make a stand.

Gaylord Yokley's used-car dealership was in an industrial area on the corner of two wide, busy streets. It catered to low-income customers. An alley ran behind the dealership, with warehouses on either side.

In addition to Gaylord, surveillance revealed that the dealership's employees included one salesman, one secretary, an accountant, two mechanics, and roughly four illegal Mexican immigrants whom the salesman or one of the mechanics picked up on the street each day to wash cars.

The location of the dealership made it easy to coordinate the raids; they would hit it at the same instant they struck the house. Steve and his law enforcement colleagues suspected the guns were kept at Yokley's home, or at a third location, and brought to the dealership for delivery. Keeping the weapons at the dealership made it too likely that they'd get robbed someday by one of their less than reputable customers. Plus Steve wasn't entirely sure that anyone at the dealership but Gaylord knew about the black-market weapons sales.

Once the logistical details of the raid were agreed upon, and the various responsibilities doled out among the agencies, all the agents retreated to their offices to brief their superiors. That left Steve alone with Olivia Morales and Karen Cross.

The ADA started making some calls. Olivia stepped close to Steve and lowered her voice so Karen couldn't overhear what she said.

"I've got a boyfriend."

"Good for you," Steve said. "Any particular reason I should know?"

"In case you were thinking of putting the moves on me."

"I'm not," Steve said, though he had been until that exact moment.

"Then why this?"

"Why what?"

"Why the sparkling repartee and the invite to share this bust?"

"Because I'm a witty and generous fellow."

"No," Olivia said. "Really."

"That's it. There's more pie here than I can eat, so I am sharing it."

She narrowed her eyes. "You must need friends."

"Desperately," he confessed.

"You've got one."

"But I can't sleep with you," he said.

"I thought you weren't interested," she said.

"I'm not."

"Just so we're clear," she said.

"We're clear," he said.

"So why aren't you interested? Is something wrong with me?"

She said that a little bit too loud, enough so Karen Cross, who'd just hung up the phone, raised an eyebrow, intrigued by the innuendo. Karen was half Caucasian, half Asian, and exceedingly thin, which gave her a deceptively frail look. She was anything but frail.

"You don't want to get involved with him," Karen said.

"You know this from experience?" Olivia asked.

"I'm relying on instinct and good taste," she said.

"Gee, thanks," Steve said. "It's so nice to be wanted."

"The warrants aren't going to be a problem," Karen said, ignoring Steve's show of false indignation. "I just hope Teeg isn't lying and all of this effort actually leads to a cache of illegal weapons."

"You say that like you have some doubts about this," Steve said.

"I always do when you or your father are involved," she said. "I've been burned before."

"You've also gambled and won," Steve said. "Prosecuting those killer nurses rehabilitated your career."

"It wouldn't have needed rehab if it wasn't for the Lacey McClure debacle."

Karen was referring to her prosecution of movie star Lacey McClure, who was accused of murdering her cheating husband and his lover. It was a scandalous case, tried on live television, and it nearly ruined Karen, Steve, and Mark before it was over.

She had also been part of the team that prosecuted corrupt cop Harley Brule and his Major Crime Unit cronies, another case that Mark and Steve handed the DA. The way Steve looked at it, his debt to Karen had been repaid twice over. After the Yokley bust, she was going to be owing him some favors.

"Assuming you're right about Yokley, and he has been selling guns to LA street gangs," Karen said, "this arrest could cause us some serious political problems."

"How?" Olivia asked. "It's a win for everybody."

"But which mayoral candidate gets to exploit it?" Karen asked. "DA Burnside or Chief Masters? If I'm smart, I'll tip off Burnside about this. And if you two are smart, you'll alert Masters."

"There's an easy way to cover all of our butts," Steve said. "We'll tip them both off to the raid at the same time. Let them duke it out for bragging rights."

"Works for me," Karen said just as her cell phone rang. She answered it, listened for a moment, then fixed her gaze on Steve before mumbling a "yes, sir" and ending the call.

"You can tell Burnside about the raid yourself," she said to Steve. "He wants to see you right now."

CHAPTER FOURTEEN

District Attorney Neal Burnside's office was huge, large enough for his massive desk and leather chair, two guest chairs, a couch, two armchairs, a coffee table, a round conference table with six more chairs, and a flat-screen TV the size of a sport utility vehicle.

Outside his door, the ADAs on his staff were crammed into windowless offices that were roughly the size of the prison cells they were struggling to fill with criminals. The prosecutors had to wriggle their way into their chairs, which were wedged into what little open space they could clear amidst the jammed file cabinets, the computer monitors, and stacks of bulging case files.

Steve doubted that any of the ADAs would vote for their boss. Burnside was lucky his peasants didn't rise up in armed rebellion and drag him off to the guillotine.

That happy thought kept Steve entertained as he stood patiently in front of Burnside's desk, waiting for his own head to be handed to him by the DA; for what offense, he didn't know. He doubted that Burnside had called him down to his office for praise, promotion, or a fervent appeal for his vote.

Burnside took his time reviewing some document on his desk before finally, reluctantly, acknowledging Steve's presence.

"Carter Sweeney's habeas corpus plea is being heard in court soon," he said. "Are you aware of that, Detective?"

"No, but I'm not going to lose any sleep over it," Steve said. "Are you?"

Burnside didn't appreciate having his question turned back in his direction, which was, of course, exactly why Steve did it.

"The hearing happens to fall within days of the election," Burnside said. "Interesting timing, don't you think?"

"I wouldn't expect anything less of Carter Sweeney," Steve replied. "Would you?"

The questions were being volleyed back and forth like a tennis ball. Burnside's face reddened. He wasn't going to be put on the spot in his own office.

"This isn't simply his last appeal for freedom. It's a strategic political move designed to influence the outcome of the mayoral race," Burnside said. "I want to know whose campaign Sweeney is hoping to derail with this stunt."

Steve admired the way Burnside couched his latest question as a statement.

"Ask Carter Sweeney," Steve said.

"I'd rather ask your father," Burnside said.

"Sweeney blew up Community General Hospital with Dad and me in it," Steve said. "Ever since that little tiff, they haven't really stayed in touch."

"Oh really?" Burnside pushed a photo across the desk to Steve. "Your father visited Carter Sweeney a few days ago."

The photo was lifted from a prison surveillance camera video, and it showed Mark sitting across from Sweeney in the visiting room.

Steve was shocked. If he hadn't seen the photo, he never would have believed it.

Why was his father meeting with Sweeney? Why did Mark keep it secret from him?

"What did they talk about?" Burnside demanded.

"I have no idea." Steve passed the photo back to Burnside. "This is the first I've heard about this."

"I don't believe you," Burnside said.

"I don't care," Steve said.

"If your father thinks he can use Carter Sweeney's pathetic bid for freedom to smear me or my campaign, he is sorely mistaken."

"My father put Carter Sweeney in prison. He has no interest in seeing him freed," Steve said. "Not that there's any chance of that happening. Is there?"

"Of course not," Burnside said, "The case against him is rock solid and has withstood every one of his insipid attempts to overturn his conviction."

"Then I don't see what you're so worried about."

"This," Burnside said, and slammed his fist down on the photograph. "So far, the press doesn't know anything about Sweeney's habeas corpus hearing. They will. But when it comes

out, and *how* it comes out, will determine whether it's a front-page story or a one-paragraph filler buried in the back pages."

"I don't know what they were talking about, but I'm sure it has nothing to do with this election. My father isn't interested in politics."

Steve resented Mark for putting him in this position. Had Mark really thought he could talk to Carter Sweeney without anyone finding out about it?

Burnside studied Steve for a long moment. "Is this some stunt that Chief Masters has cooked up? Is he using your father as his go-between? Because if he is, he's going to look pretty damn stupid getting in bed with a serial killer just to smear me."

Steve sighed. "My father doesn't like the chief any better than he likes you. When the chief finds out about this prison chat, I wouldn't be surprised if he accuses my father of working behind the scenes on *your* behalf."

"What possible reason would your father have for aligning himself with me?"

"That's a good question. But I'm sure the chief realizes that if it wasn't for the Stryker blackmail files that my dad handed to you, and all the high-profile prosecutions and publicity that came from that case, you wouldn't be a serious contender in the mayor's race."

"Oh, so that's the game." Burnside rose from his desk and pointed a finger at Steve. "I don't owe Mark Sloan a goddamn thing. He can't use Carter Sweeney to leverage any kind of influence with me. You tell him that."

Steve shook his head. "You're paranoid."

"I'm the next mayor of Los Angeles," he said. "Now get the hell out of my office. You might want to think about moving to another city while you're at it. This isn't going to be a very pleasant place for you and your father to live anymore."

CHAPTER FIFTEEN

Steve and Jesse were both forty-eight hours away from leading major operations in which the slightest miscalculation could cost lives. So, naturally, there was only one thing they could do to prepare: They gorged themselves on barbecue.

They met Mark and Susan for dinner at Barbeque Bob's, the restaurant that Steve and Jesse had bought several years back when the original owner retired. The two of them shared the responsibility of running the place, arranging their work schedules so that one of them was there most of the time. And when one of them couldn't be there, they could always count on Susan to take up the slack.

The restaurant was still the run-down, ramshackle dive it had always been when Steve and Jesse were its best customers. The Formica countertops were chipped, the vinyl on the stools was cracked, and the tables were covered with names and drawings crudely carved into the wood with knives and forks.

Despite the pressure on them, Steve and Jesse were in a festive mood, eating ribs and pie, running the grill in the kitchen, delivering orders, and cheerfully hobnobbing with the customers.

Susan stayed in the booth with Mark. She was trying not to be too obvious about her concern for him, but he saw the way she was sneaking looks at him.

"I'm fine," he said. "You can stop looking at me like that."

"Are you worried about the transplant surgery?"

"No," Mark said. "Jesse has done a great job arranging everything, and the surgeons he's got lined up are top-notch. It will go smoothly."

"Are you worried about the raid?"

"Steve has taken bigger risks with far less preparation and

backup before," Mark said. "He's in more danger just crossing the street."

"Then it must be the severance package that's on your mind."

"How did you know about that?"

"You dropped it off with some charts at the nurses' station," she said, reaching into her purse and passing the paper to Mark.

"I guess I was a little distracted today," he said, pocketing the offer. "It's a good thing you found it. Did you read it?"

She nodded guiltily. "You and Jesse have been a bad influence on me. It's a generous deal."

"So they keep telling me," he said ruefully.

"The fact that you even kept the document means you're actually considering their offer."

"There's no harm in that," he said.

"There was a time you would never even have looked at it. You would have just walked away from the table and left it behind."

"Times change."

"You've been at Community General for over forty years," she said. "It's part of you. Do you really think you can leave?"

"I've been feeling restless and uneasy for a while now," he said. "It's been worse since the accident."

"It wasn't an accident, Mark. Someone tried to kill you. That's enough to make any sane person restless and uneasy," she said. "Maybe what you should give up is homicide investigation. None of your patients has ever tried to whack you."

"Because I'm so lovable and avuncular."

"That hasn't stopped the killers from trying to murder you."

"That's because killing is what they do, whether or not you're lovable and avuncular."

"Does Steve know about this?"

Mark shook his head. "There's nothing to talk about until I get some idea of what I want to do."

"Who says you have to do anything? You can keep on going the way you are. Or you can take a long sabbatical to figure stuff out. Or you could simply retire and enjoy the good life."

"You make it seem like I have a world of possibilities."

"You do," she said. "More than most people have. Embrace it."

Mark looked at Jesse at the cash register, cheerfully ringing up an order for a satisfied BBQ-sauce-splattered customer. And then he glanced over at Steve, who was happily delivering a heaping platter of ribs to a table of eager diners.

"I could always work here," Mark said.

"Now you're talking," Susan said.

CHAPTER SIXTEEN

Steve didn't bring up his conversation with Neal Burnside to Mark until they were walking in the door of the beach house.

"How's our good friend Carter Sweeney enjoying his stay at Sunrise Valley?"

Mark looked at his son. "How long have you known about my visit?"

"Neal Burnside told me about it tonight before dinner."

Mark nodded and went into the kitchen to make them both some hot tea. He didn't really want tea, but it gave him something to do to avoid a direct confrontation with his son.

"When were you going to tell me about it?" Steve asked.

"I wasn't."

As Mark prepared their tea, he told Steve about the call from Sweeney's lawyer and the details of their conversation.

By the time Mark was done with his story, they were sitting outside on the deck sipping their tea and watching the waves crash, the frothy white surf glowing in the moonlight.

"Why weren't you going to tell me?" Steve asked.

"Because I was ashamed of how easily I let myself be manipulated by him. I'm a slave to my own curiosity."

"You're being too hard on yourself."

"I can't help but feel that I've done exactly what he wanted me to do and that Burnside's reaction was part of his plan, too."

"What's his plan?"

"I don't know," Mark said. "But whatever it is, I'm already playing my part."

"Then so am I," Steve said.

"What do you think he's up to?" Mark asked.

Steve finished his tea and watched the sea breeze fan the dune grass. It reminded him of a girlfriend he hadn't thought about in twenty years. She had long blond hair and she liked to let the wind blow through it. Her name was Natalie or Naomi or something like that. She'd said she loved him and he'd pretended that he hadn't heard her.

"He's powerless and forgotten in prison. So he's using this hearing, his final moment in the outside world, to do as much damage as he can," Steve said. "Burnside is right, Sweeney is going to throw a grenade into the mayor's race and hope as many of his enemies get fragged in the blast as possible. The thing is, I don't see what damage he can do."

"That's what scares me," Mark said. "I can't see it either."

CHAPTER SEVENTEEN

The harvesting of Corinne Adams's internal organs began at six a.m. in Operating Room #1. Dr. Jesse Travis led the surgical team that spent the next several hours removing her kidneys and liver. Mark watched it all from the observation room, along with a standing-room-only crowd of curious surgical residents.

It was an emotionally difficult operation for Jesse, who, like all doctors, had taken the Hippocratic oath, to "first do no harm." Gutting this patient of her vital organs was definitely doing her harm, brain-dead or not. And yet, even as Jesse was ensuring her doom, he had to keep her alive on the operating table long enough for her heart and lungs to be plundered.

Jesse knew Corinne was brain-dead, and that her organs would save lives, but he still felt as if he was doing something wrong as he sliced open her belly, tied off the veins and arteries leading to her kidneys, and removed the organs.

Susan and her team of nurses packed the organs in saline and ice and put them in ice chests, which were labeled with the names of their intended recipients. The ice chests were then handed to couriers, who hurried off to personally deliver the organs to desperate patients in San Francisco and Phoenix.

Meanwhile, Jesse extracted Corinne's liver and divided it into three parts, like cuts of beef. The three liver sections were then packaged and sent by couriers to hospitals in Seattle, Houston, and San Diego.

Jesse's work was done. He stepped aside and heart surgeon David Carren took over. Dr. Carren had the unenviable task of killing Corinne Adams by removing her heart and lungs.

Jesse had trouble rationalizing his actions with the vow to first do no harm, so he couldn't imagine the ethical and emotional conflict Dr. Carren had to be dealing with. Then again, perhaps Dr.

Carren had made his peace with such surgeries long ago. Jesse didn't know, and he certainly wasn't going to ask now.

Dr. Carren worked with precision, carefully timing his procedures so that the heart and lungs were kept "alive" until the last possible moment.

Once they had been removed, Jesse delivered the organs to an adjoining operating room, where thirty-five-year-old Ken Hoffman was waiting with his chest cracked wide open and heart surgeon Larry Carroll and his team were standing by.

Dr. Carroll would have to perform a delicate balancing act, removing one set of heart and lungs and implanting another without killing his patient in the process. And he had to do it all while watching the clock. The donor heart and lungs would remain viable for only a few hours.

He was methodical and coolheaded, and he insisted on doing the *New York Times* crossword puzzle aloud while he worked, giving answers to a nurse whose only responsibility was to query him with questions like "What's a seven-letter word for an element named after a mythical queen?" Mark had to resist the temptation to yell out "Niobium" from the observation room.

While Dr. Carroll raced against time to perform his medical miracle and complete the crossword, Susan wheeled Corinne's gutted corpse down to the pathology lab, where Dr. Amanda Bentley took over the final steps in the organ-donor process.

First, Amanda performed a brain autopsy, confirming Corinne's medical condition prior to her death on the operating table. There wasn't much else to base the autopsy on, considering that most of Corinne's vital organs were on their way to cities all over the West Coast. But Amanda took tissue and fluid samples and then began the grim, solitary task of dismantling Corinne Adams.

Unlike Jesse, Amanda had no ethical or moral qualms about her work. It was much like a full autopsy, but much more extreme and far less wasteful. These body parts weren't going to be buried or incinerated.

Amanda cut, pulled, and peeled away almost everything. Bones. Tendons. Vertebrae. Ligaments. Corneas. Fingernails. Skin. She took all that from Corinne and more, logging and packing everything for shipment to MediSolutions International, the Phoenix tissue-processing company that would dole out the body parts for a wide variety of uses, from orthopedic reconstruction and cosmetic surgeries to medical testing and training.

By the end of the day, there was very little left of Corinne for cremation. The rest of her, the bulk of her corporeal self, would live on in dozens of other people who didn't even know her.

If it was fate that determined Corinne Adams's demise, then fate also had a wicked sense of timing. The mortuary came to get Corinne's body at the exact same moment that Federal Express showed up to pick up the packages that contained her bones and tissues.

Mark strode smiling into the path lab just as the mortician wheeled the body bag out on a gurney and the FedEx guy hauled his packages away on a hand truck.

The three of them nearly collided in the doorway.

Mark politely sidestepped the mortician and the FedEx guy and let them pass. He was completely unaware that the men were carrying away all that remained of Corinne Adams.

But her role in Mark Sloan's life was only just beginning. Fate wasn't finished with either one of them yet.

"The heart-lung transplant was completed without a problem," Mark said. "And the patient is doing remarkably well."

"That was the easy part," Amanda said. "The big question is whether or not Dr. Carroll finished his crossword puzzle."

"I had to scrub in and give him an assist," Mark admitted.

"What stumped him?"

"A fifteen-letter phrase for 'frustration.' "

Amanda thought for a moment. " 'Tear one's hair out.' "

"You should have been a heart surgeon," Mark said.

CHAPTER EIGHTEEN

While the doctors at Community General were raiding Corinne Adams's body, a multi-agency law enforcement strike force was simultaneously raiding Gaylord Yokley's home and office.

Steve Sloan and Olivia Morales led the raid on Yokley's house because they assumed that was where his weapons were most likely stashed. The two detectives wanted to be where the real action was.

The raid went off exactly as planned, taking place after Bette Yokley left the house to drive her kids to school. Gaylord Yokley was nabbed without incident as he walked to his Escalade.

Gaylord seemed relaxed, almost resigned to what was happening, as if he'd imagined it already a thousand times before. He was Mirandized, handcuffed, and taken to a holding cell downtown while the search of his 4,800-square-foot house and two detached garages was conducted.

At first glance, Steve didn't see anything unusual about the home or its furnishings. It appeared to be the home of a typical family. Report cards and vacation photos were taped to the door of the refrigerator. PlayStation cartridges were scattered on the coffee table in the den. Car magazines and old issues of *Vanity Fair* were collected in a basket beside the toilet in the master bathroom.

Home sweet home.

In the initial sweep, a gun was found in a nightstand drawer in the master bedroom and another in a box on the top shelf of the kitchen pantry. Both weapons were legally registered to Bette Yokley.

But things got a lot more interesting once Steve and the other officers and agents began emptying the closets. They discovered false walls that hid automatic weapons, semi-automatic weapons, rifles, and handguns.

That was only in the closets.

Steve took a broom from the pantry, turned it upside down, and tapped the kitchen floor with the handle, listening for a hollow echo that would indicate a space under the tiles.

He motioned to an officer with a sledgehammer. All it took was two whacks of the sledgehammer to break away the travertine and reveal row after row of rifles, neatly laid out side by side.

Olivia looked at the cache of weapons at Steve's feet. "We're going to need another truck."

Steve picked up a sledgehammer and swung it at the nearest wall, smashing the plaster away until the studs were revealed, along with the handguns stuffed in the spaces between them.

"Better make that *two* trucks," Steve said.

"Who knew guns made such good insulation?" Olivia asked.

Steve wandered into the den and examined the bookcase. None of the books looked like they'd ever been opened. They were missing their dust jackets and seemed to have been picked by a decorator for their size and color. He tried to take a book off the shelf and discovered it was glued in place.

On a hunch, he grabbed the edge of the bookcase and pulled. The entire bookcase swung open like a vault door, revealing a deep, cinder-block-walled room with a target taped to the far end. The floor was covered with spent shells. It was a hidden shooting range.

"Unbelievable," Olivia muttered.

Steve looked over his shoulder at her. "You must live in an old house. Family rooms are history. Indoor shooting ranges are the newest thing."

"Nothing brings a family together like shooting AK-47s," Olivia said.

"Makes you wonder what Yokley's kids have in their school lockers," Steve said.

"I'm not going to wonder," Olivia said. "I'm going to get search warrants and find out."

The search of Yokley's home went on well into the late afternoon. By the time it was done, the multi-agency strike force had recovered 1,372 weapons, from AK-47s to Uzis, as well as a dozen hand grenades and ten pounds of C4 explosive. The weapons and explosives were hidden all over the house, under floors, behind walls, and in secret compartments in the furniture.

The tally didn't include the ammunition, scopes, silencers, and other assorted "accessories" that were also found in various hidden cubbyholes.

Yokley possessed enough weaponry to either overthrow a small country or arm a mid-sized rap music company. It took five large trucks to haul all the weapons downtown to be logged, traced, and examined by ballistics and forensics experts from the LAPD, the ATF, and the FBI.

At six p.m., Chief Masters and District Attorney Neal Burnside called dueling press conferences. Each man took full credit for the arrest of a "major black-market supplier of weapons" and for keeping scores of guns off the LA streets, thus preventing an untold number of robberies, shootings, and murders, perhaps even an all-out gang war.

The FBI and the ATF also held their own press conferences, trumpeting the interagency cooperation and the unprecedented number of weapons seized in the raid, which, they intimated, was a monumental victory in the war on terror.

No one in any of the press conferences, however, saw any reason to mention Steve Sloan. But he didn't mind. He was used to his work being overshadowed or ignored. What counted to him was that he'd accomplished what he'd set out to do.

His reward would come later. And when it did, it would not be at all what he expected.

CHAPTER NINETEEN

The next two weeks were uneventful compared to most weeks in Dr. Mark Sloan's life. He was inundated at the hospital with mind-numbingly boring administrative tasks, requiring him to shuffle from one meeting to another and leaving him little time to practice any actual medicine. If Janet Dorcott was planning to drive him out by making his job intolerably dull, she was succeeding.

But she wasn't putting any pressure on him to go—because, he assumed, the pressure was off of her. The killer nurses scandal had been pushed off the front page and the nightly newscasts by daily updates on the Gaylord Yokley investigation, heightened fears about the spread of the West Nile virus, the contentious mayoral race, and the discovery that a famous movie star had fathered a child out of wedlock.

The boring routine at the hospital wouldn't have been so hard to take if Mark had at least had an interesting homicide investigation to keep him occupied. The murder rate in Los Angeles had not suddenly plunged; rather, the current cases weren't difficult or puzzling enough to require Mark's deductive skills. And he hadn't stumbled on any mysteries to solve on his own, though he supposed he could always jet out to Scotland and see if he could prove the existence of the Loch Ness monster once and for all.

Steve had been kept busy on the Yokley case, uncovering the gun merchant's ties to ROAR, the homegrown but loosely organized antigovernment terrorist group. According to e-mails and documents found at Yokley's home and car dealership, ROAR was plotting to plunge the city into anarchy by supplying gangs with assault weapons and provoking a street war among them that would overwhelm the resources of the police force.

But the leaders of ROAR had never been known for their stunning intellect, and Steve didn't think Yokley was smart enough to have concocted the plot on his own.

Mark and Steve believed that Carter Sweeney was probably behind it, even though there was no evidence of any kind linking him to Yokley. Sweeney didn't really believe in any of ROAR's dogma, which was liberally cribbed from the KKK and Aryan Nations, but he would find the group easy to manipulate for his own purposes. Creating havoc in Los Angeles on the eve of the mayoral election was just the kind of thing that would keep Sweeney amused in captivity.

Even if Steve could find ties to Sweeney, there was nothing more the law could do to him. He was already sentenced to death. He could die only once. In a sense, Sweeney had a free pass to commit any crime he wanted, assuming he could pull it off from inside his cell.

If throwing Los Angeles into turmoil was Sweeney's master plan, then Mark could relax, knowing that it had been foiled—though if Teeg hadn't tried to shoot his estranged girlfriend, the plot might have succeeded.

Even so, Carter Sweeney was still very much on Mark's mind that morning as he sat reading the *Los Angeles Times* over breakfast at his kitchen table. The news of Sweeney's upcoming habeas corpus hearing had finally come out.

What surprised Mark was that the news was relegated to a mere paragraph on page 29, squeezed in between a paleobotanist's theory that figs were mankind's first cultivated crop and the discovery of a new species of crustacean in an underground lake in Israel.

The marginalization of Carter Sweeney to near obscurity must have been a great relief to both Neal Burnside and John Masters, but it troubled Mark.

Why hadn't Sweeney found a way to make his hearing front-page news? It was very uncharacteristic of him to let an opportunity for attention slip away. So it had to be a calculated move. To what end? Sweeney must have other plans to capitalize on his hearing. But what were they?

Mark was still pondering those questions over his Grape-Nuts and coffee when Steve came upstairs with Olivia, who'd obviously spent the night. They were both freshly showered and dressed for work.

It wasn't an awkward moment, at least not for Mark and Steve. Mark had long since reconciled himself to the fact that his son had a love life and, if they were going to live together, that meant inevitably bumping into some of Steve's lovers in the house. It was a small discomfort to live with for his son's company.

Not many fathers and sons enjoyed the close relationship that Mark and Steve had. But few of Steve's girlfriends were impressed by it. They wondered about the maturity and independence of a fortysomething man who still lived at home with his sixtysomething father. And many women didn't appreciate having to face their boyfriend's dad whenever they spent the night. It was, for most women, a relationship breaker.

But Mark got the sense that Olivia Morales wasn't looking for a relationship when she went home with Steve. She and Steve weren't sharing any furtive, flirtatious looks or stealing touches, strokes, and squeezes whenever they could. They appeared to be friends-with-benefits, which was an expression that perfectly described what Mark considered the fast-food attitude that people had towards relationships these days.

She got a bowl and a spoon, sat down next to Mark, and poured some cereal.

"Good morning, Dr. Sloan," she said. "You're up awfully early."

"Were you hoping I wouldn't be?" Mark asked.

"Of course I was," she said. "Seeing you gives me flashbacks to high school when I'd get caught sneaking out of my boyfriend's bedroom by his parents."

"Enjoy it," Mark said. "You don't get many chances in life to feel eighteen again."

"Seventeen," Olivia said.

"I didn't need to know that," Mark said.

"Sorry," she said. "I babble when I'm nervous."

Steve sat down next to her. "This Yokley case is turning into a full-time job for both of us."

It was an abrupt change of subject, almost a non sequitur, but Mark was thankful for it.

"With so many people and law enforcement agencies taking credit for the arrest, is there any official recognition or appreciation left for the two of you?" Mark asked.

"Neither one of us has received a promotion or a raise, if that's what you're asking, but we haven't been shoved to the sidelines either," Steve said. "This isn't a homicide case, so there's really no reason for us to be involved anymore. The fact that we still are acknowledges our contribution."

Olivia shook her head. "Boy, do they have you snowed. They just like having us around to do all the tedious legwork. Where else would they find detectives with our experience who'd be willing to do it?"

"Karen Cross knows who brought her into this," Steve said. "So do the agents at the FBI and the ATF and everybody else. Those are favors I can call in someday."

"You've already called in a few with me," she said with a sly smile.

"Is that what last night was?" Steve said playfully.

Mark cleared his throat to remind them that he was still there. "So where's the investigation heading?"

"Wherever the guns lead us," Steve said.

"And there are a lot of guns," Olivia added.

"We're trying to trace them from two directions," Steve said. "Where they were bought or stolen from originally and any past crimes in which they might have been used."

"That's going to take an enormous amount of time and manpower," Mark said. "What about the ROAR angle?"

"Nobody is taking that very seriously. ROAR went down with Carter Sweeney years ago," Steve said. "Gaylord Yokley is a one-man band."

Olivia nodded in agreement. "All that's left of ROAR is maybe half a dozen fat white guys with sixth-grade educations and Confederate flags in their garages who can't understand why they aren't running the world."

"But they managed to get their hands on fourteen hundred assault weapons," Mark said.

"Thank God for the Second Amendment," Steve said. "What would the terrorists and crooks do without it?"

CHAPTER TWENTY

As soon as Mark stepped into the hospital, his pager started vibrating on his belt. He glanced at the readout and saw that Jesse was paging him from the ICU. Mark headed straight there.

He found Jesse examining a set of chest X-rays up on the light box near the nurses' station. Mark looked over his shoulder.

"That was fast," Jesse said. "I didn't know you were in the hospital."

"I was walking in when you paged me," Mark said, studying the films. Both lungs were covered with diffuse patchy infiltrates—fluffy, white spots indicating inflammation caused by some kind of infection. "Who do these belong to?"

"Ken Hoffman," Jesse said.

Mark was shocked. He'd spoken to Hoffman, the heart-lung transplant patient, the previous night. Hoffman hadn't exhibited any signs of difficulty. In fact, he was doing so well that it seemed likely he'd be released in another day or two.

"What happened?"

"He woke up this morning lethargic, feverish, disoriented, and suffering from shortness of breath," Jesse said. "His breathing rate has gone from sixteen to forty breaths per minute. I listened to his lungs and they sounded wet. So I got him up here, ordered a chest X-ray and ran his blood gases."

"What are his O_2 sats?" Mark asked, referring to the amount of oxygen saturation in Hoffman's blood.

"They are on the way," Jesse said.

Mark went to Hoffman's bed and found the patient gasping hard, his skin sweaty, pale, and blue.

A nurse handed Jesse a piece of paper. Jesse glanced at the paper, then held it out to Mark. "I've got the blood gases. The O_2 sats have dropped from ninety-five percent to eighty-five percent."

"Let's get him on an oxygen mask," Mark said to one of the ICU nurses hovering nearby. "Fifty percent O_2 and run his blood gases again in an hour."

The nurse nodded and got to work. Mark stepped away to confer with Jesse out of Hoffman's earshot.

There were several explanations for Hoffman's rapid decline and none of them were good. It could be a bacterial infection, a viral infection, or his body rejecting his new organs.

If he was fighting a viral infection, the ordinary course of action would be to boost his immune system. But if it *wasn't* a viral infection, strengthening his immune system would turn his body against his new heart and lungs.

If the problem was organ rejection, they would boost his anti-immune drugs to stop the heart and lungs from being attacked by his immune system. But if it *wasn't* organ rejection, weakening his immune system would leave his body defenseless against a rampaging virus.

"I think we should play it safe and assume he's got it all," Jesse said, seemingly reading Mark's thoughts. "Let's bump up his anti-rejection drugs, the steroids, and cyclosporine, and put him on broad-spectrum antibiotics until we know exactly what we are dealing with."

"I was going to suggest the same thing." Mark glanced at his watch and saw that he was already late for a senior staff meeting on the annual budget. "I've got to go. Let me know right away if there's any change in his condition."

"Will do," Jesse said.

Mark hurried off to the third-floor conference room, where the tedious meeting had already been going on for ten minutes, though it probably felt like ten hours to the unfortunate department heads who were sitting through it.

Dr. Kerry Sakmar, the head of pediatrics, was giving a Power-Point presentation on his department's financial needs, justifying every dollar in his budget to stone-faced Janet Dorcott, as Mark slipped into the room.

Janet shifted her cold gaze to Mark as he took his seat. He felt like a high school student sneaking in late for homeroom and getting caught by his teacher.

"Sorry I'm late," Mark said. "I was checking on a patient."

"At least it was a patient and not a homicide victim this time," Dorcott said. "I suppose that's a small sign of progress."

Mark didn't bother to comment. Instead, he opened his copy

of the proposed budget and tried to concentrate on the pediatric presentation. But his mind kept wandering back to Hoffman's condition and his sudden, and disturbing, slide.

A half hour later, Janet was grilling Dr. Sakmar, making him justify every cotton swab and paper clip, line item by line item. It was like water torture, and every department head around the table had broken into a sweat, dreading his or her own presentation.

Except for Mark. He was calm. The other department heads were younger and more ambitious than he was, and they had more reason to play politics with Janet Dorcott. He wasn't interested in scoring points, nor was he intimidated by her authority. He had no intention of justifying his budget to a woman with no medical experience whatsoever. Hospitals weren't the same as discount superstores. He would present his budget as a package and she could take it or leave it. There weren't any cuts he was willing or able to make.

But he didn't get the chance to have that fight that morning. His beeper vibrated. It was a message from Jesse. Ken Hoffman's condition was deteriorating fast.

Mark left the meeting and didn't come back.

CHAPTER TWENTY-ONE

Over the next twenty-four hours, Hoffman's condition went up and down as Mark and Jesse struggled to stop his decline and diagnose the cause of his worsening condition.

They began by intubating him and putting him on a ventilator. At first the oxygen saturation in his blood increased, giving them cause for hope, but then a few hours later it plunged even lower than before.

Desperate to stop Hoffman's oxygen levels from plummeting further, Mark and Jesse increased the amount of oxygen he was receiving to eighty percent. His blood gases improved, but by the next morning, his O_2 sats had dropped to just seventy-two percent, their lowest level yet.

Mark had to see for himself what was going on in Hoffman's lungs. So he performed a bronchoscopy, sliding a specialized camera and catheter down Hoffman's throat and into his bronchial tubes.

He was looking for indications of a bacterial or fungal infection. Patients with repressed immune systems are prone to infections or possibly even the activation of tuberculosis that's been sitting dormant in their bodies for years.

Mark saw some nonspecific inflammation, which wasn't a surprise, considering Hoffman's breathing problems and cloudy chest X-rays. But he didn't see any bleeding or signs of infection. The sputum, the fluid in the lungs, appeared to be clear.

Except for the inflammation, which had to be caused by *something*, everything looked fine. The bronchoscopy didn't reveal a thing to Mark and only succeeded in adding to his growing frustration and infuriating sense of impotence.

He collected samples of the sputum and lung tissue and rushed them down to Amanda in pathology, hoping her tests would give them some answers.

Amanda called Mark and Jesse down to her lab a few hours later. Mark could tell from the scowl on her face as he walked in that the news wasn't good.

"I looked at his blood, and he's got an elevated white blood cell count, which is indicative of a virus, infection, or organ rejection," Amanda said. "I looked at his sputum and his lung tissue and saw no evidence of fungi or bacterial infection."

"You make it sound like there's nothing wrong with the guy," Jesse said. "He can't breathe. His last chest X-ray looked like a snowstorm. There's got to be *something* causing the inflammation in his lungs."

"I know, but whatever it is, it's not showing up on the slides."

"So we're back where we started," Mark said.

"Which is nowhere," Jesse said gloomily. "It's either infection or rejection and we're already treating both. The tests haven't told us a damn thing."

"All we can do is continue with the course we're on," Mark said. "Keep him on the ventilator and treat him with steroids and antibiotics."

"And hope for a miracle," Jesse said without much conviction.

"They've been known to happen," Amanda said.

But four hours later, it didn't look likely that there were any miracles in store for Ken Hoffman. His lungs looked like bones in the chest X-rays and his O_2 sats continue to drop even though he was breathing pure oxygen on his ventilator. His lungs were barely functioning.

It was a death sentence.

Mark had the grim task of informing Hoffman's wife and two young children that his prognosis didn't look good.

By midafternoon, two weeks after his transplant and a little more than a day after his breathing problems began, Ken Hoffman died of respiratory failure.

CHAPTER TWENTY-TWO

It became Dr. Amanda Bentley's job to discover exactly what caused Ken Hoffman's respiratory failure. She was getting just as frustrated as Mark and Jesse had been.

Mark tried to stay out of Amanda's way, but his curiosity kept getting the better of him. He found excuses to stop by her lab several times over the course of the next few days, and each time she had nothing new to tell him and she was awaiting various test results.

He thought about offering to help, but he realized his presence would only make her job harder. Amanda knew what she was doing and she would find the answer eventually.

Jesse was just as frustrated, but when he stopped by the pathology lab, Amanda wasn't nearly as polite to him as she was to Mark.

"If you come in here again, the next autopsy I perform will be on you," she said.

Jesse took the subtle hint and stayed clear of the lab after that, even when he had a justifiable reason to be there. On those occasions, he sent Susan instead, assuming that she would do her wifely duty and snoop while she was there.

But Susan respected Amanda's boundaries and didn't venture a single question about the status of the Hoffman autopsy. She simply picked up whatever test results she was after, traded a few niceties, and left Amanda alone.

"Would it have killed you to snoop just a little bit?" Jesse scolded Susan after one of her legitimate forays to the pathology lab.

"I'm not the snooping type," Susan said. "When Amanda has something to say, she'll tell us. You have to be patient."

"So how come you don't practice that same patience with

me?" Jesse said. "How come you're always asking me what I feel about everything?"

"That's different," Susan said. "She's performing an autopsy. I'm working on a marriage."

"It's the same thing," Jesse said, then scooted away to perform rounds before Susan could swat him.

Mark and Jesse happened to be meeting in the cafeteria for lunch, two days after Ken Hoffman's death, when Amanda paged them both.

They went down to the pathology lab, and this time Amanda greeted them with a look of satisfaction on her face. She'd solved the mystery.

"Do you know how he died?" Jesse asked, even though it was obvious that she did.

She nodded. "And you're not going to believe it."

"Tell me," Mark said.

"Not so fast," she said. "This was hard work and I want to enjoy the moment."

She started at the beginning, explaining each step of her investigation.

It drove Jesse nuts, but Mark was fascinated. Being a detective himself, he knew the pleasure of walking others through the clues before revealing his solution. He was the last person who was going to deprive Amanda of the same pleasure.

The upshot was that Amanda found viral antibodies in Hoffman's blood, lung tissue, brain tissue, and spinal fluid, which meant that whatever virus he had afflicted both his lungs and his central nervous system. And she'd managed to track that virus down.

"It was West Nile virus," she said.

That was the last thing Mark would ever have guessed, but now that he thought about the symptoms, it made some sense. West Nile virus was passed by mosquito bites and could, in extreme cases, cause encephalitis, paralysis, respiratory failure, and death.

Even so, it was hard news to accept. And Jesse couldn't. He shook his head and held up his hands in front of his chest as if holding the news back.

"Wait a minute," Jesse said. "You're telling me that an infected mosquito got into this hospital and bit the guy?"

"No," Amanda said. "West Nile doesn't incubate that fast. He must have been bitten before his transplant."

"Talk about bad luck," Jesse said.

But another chilling explanation occurred to Mark.

What if Corinne Adams was the one infected with West Nile? What if she'd passed it on to Ken Hoffman with her heart and lungs?

If that was what had happened, they were facing a major catastrophe. Her organs and tissues had been implanted in at least five other people, perhaps more by now.

Ken Hoffman's death would be only the first of many.

Mark was almost afraid to bring it up. "What if he wasn't bitten by a mosquito? What if he contracted the virus from the organ transplant?"

Amanda gave Mark a scolding look. "Do you think if that's how Ken Hoffman was infected that we'd be having this calm discussion right now? I'd be in crisis mode, calling every hospital that received her organs, the company that dispersed her bones and tissues, as well as the NIH, the CDC, and the PTL."

"Why would you call the Praise the Lord network?" Jesse asked.

"Because we'd need every prayer we could get," Amanda said. "As soon as I discovered the West Nile virus antibodies in Hoffman, I went back and checked the tissue and blood samples from Corinne Adams. I didn't find any trace of West Nile antibodies."

Unique antibodies are created by the body to defend against specific bacteria and viruses. If there weren't any West Nile virus antibodies in Corinne Adams's tissues or blood, it meant she wasn't fighting the disease when she died.

"Did Hoffman receive any blood transfusions?" Mark asked, remembering a case a few years earlier in which a dozen people were infected by West Nile–tainted blood.

She shook her head. "We're in the clear there, too."

"Which means Hoffman was infected on his own," Mark said, sighing with relief.

"The virus thrived, flaring up faster and deadlier than usual because of the anti-rejection drugs he was taking," Amanda said.

Only twenty percent of people infected with West Nile virus ever developed any symptoms, and even for them it was usually mistaken for a bad cold or flu. Just one percent of those infected with the virus suffered its most severe consequences. But Mark knew that organ transplant patients had a forty percent greater risk of developing serious illness from West Nile than anyone else, though the odds of their contracting it were astronomical.

Ken Hoffman was the exception.

"The poor guy. He was dead whether he got the transplant or not," Jesse said. "He never had a chance."

It was true.

If Hoffman hadn't received the transplant, he would have died from the atrial septal defect that doomed his own heart and lungs to fail. But because of the transplant, he died of a mosquito bite instead.

Fate.

It seemed to be stalking Mark Sloan lately. He hoped that didn't mean that they'd be meeting soon.

CHAPTER TWENTY-THREE

Amanda immediately notified the Los Angeles County Health Department of Ken Hoffman's death from West Nile virus. The LACHD informed the Greater Los Angeles County Vector Control District, the agency charged with wiping out disease-carrying insects and vermin. Within an hour of Amanda's alert, Vector Control's top man, Officer Lloyd Flegner, was on the case.

The bloodsuckers never had a chance.

Flegner was a retired LAPD detective who had spent twenty-five unremarkable years on the force, serving and protecting in virtual anonymity. So he gladly took his pension and went to work for Vector Control, where he put his unappreciated detecting skills to use finding mosquitoes, mice, bats, and rats and eradicating them.

To his awed colleagues at Vector Control, he was Columbo, Monk, and Gil Grissom all rolled into an authentic Members Only jacket, khaki cargo pants, and mud-caked Doc Martens. Flegner had an almost preternatural ability to read rat droppings. With one glance at a trail of excrement, he could assess the number of rats in the area, where they were hiding, and how long they'd been there.

If only the city's rapists, thieves, and murderers defecated constantly like rats did, Flegner's LAPD career might have been astonishing. He probably would have been chief of police by now.

His abilities also extended to mosquito tracking and abatement. Even in his off-duty hours, he liked to prowl roadside ditches, flood channels, and stagnant ponds, laying mosquito traps and looking for larvae.

He was the perfect man to investigate the Hoffman case. His

first stop was the Hoffman residence in Topanga Canyon to interview the grieving family about their movements in the week preceding the victim's admission to Community General Hospital. He needed to zero in on where Hoffman might have been attacked by that virus-carrying mosquito.

He learned that Hoffman, because of his deteriorating physical condition, rarely left their modest bungalow. And when he did go out, it was only for short walks in their secluded, woodsy neighborhood.

That made Flegner's job a lot easier. The viral hot spot was likely nearby.

So Flegner took a walk down along the narrow, badly paved road outside the Hoffmans' 1940s-era home. It was like discovering a lost civilization in a hidden valley.

In the 1960s and 1970s, Topanga Canyon was favored by hippies, poets, actors, lesbians, and folksingers. Flegner could see that some of those liberal, free-loving, pot-smoking, creative types still lived there, surrounded by a cloud of incense and the tinkle of wind chimes. He knew because he could see their droppings—the faded Clinton/Gore bumper stickers on their cars, the Trader Joe's grocery bags in their trash, the yellowed issues of *Rolling Stone* in their recycle bins.

But it wasn't the signs of survivors of a bygone era that Flegner was searching for. He was interested in standing water where mosquitoes could breed—empty pools and hot tubs, stagnant birdbaths, dormant fountains, and clogged catch basins. He found plenty of those and took samples from the puddles of green water for analysis.

Flegner was on his way back to his Vector Control vehicle, a decade-old Impala, to drop off his samples and grab some mosquito traps when he saw the dead bird. It was lying amidst a pile of leaves at the base of a tree.

He squatted down and examined the bird. He didn't know whether it was a mourning dove, a condor, or a baby pterodactyl. He wasn't an ornithologist; he was an ex-cop. He might not know a lot about birds, but he knew a thing or two about death.

Whatever killed this bird did it from the *inside*.

He knew something else, too.

Birds start dying of West Nile virus before people do.

Flegner put on a pair of rubber gloves, picked up the decomposing bird, and placed it in a plastic bag, which he dutifully labeled with the date, time, and location where it was found.

He wouldn't wait for the lab results before acting on his instinct. In the morning, he would order his troops to bug-bomb the entire neighborhood.

CHAPTER TWENTY-FOUR

Teeg Cantrell had given up any pretense of defiance. Either he'd resigned himself to his bleak future or he'd weakened under the hypnotic power of McDonald's Extra Value Meals. As long as Steve kept the chicken nuggets, Big Macs, and hot apple turnovers coming to the interrogation room, Teeg was happy to talk, describing in detail his various transactions with Gaylord Yokley.

Kirby Kirkland, Teeg's young, inexperienced public defender, was left with nothing to do but draw caricatures of celebrities in the style of *Simpsons* characters on his yellow legal pad. Steve thought Kirby had a brighter future as an artist than a lawyer.

"How did your gang get into the gun business with Yokley?" Steve asked, finally getting around to a question he probably should have started with.

"This homey who got out of Sunrise after doing a dime. He has a lot of juice, knew all about Yokley, said this dude could get us all the *quetes* we wanted," Teeg said. "If this homey hadn't stood up for Yokley, there was no way we would've been doing business in the burbs with some gringo."

Steve was amused when Teeg self-consciously peppered his speech with Spanish to give himself more street credibility. He wondered how that played for him outside of interrogation rooms.

But he got Teeg's point. The gang wouldn't have been talking to some white guy at all if it wasn't for the respected homey's recommendation. Steve knew better than to ask Teeg who the homey was. Ratting out Yokley was fine. No one was going to hold that against Teeg. Ratting out a homey, though, would get Teeg killed.

It wouldn't be too hard for Steve to figure out which one of Teeg's buddies had spent ten years at Sunrise.

Which was Carter Sweeney's home.

Ordinarily, that wouldn't have meant anything. Almost all the killers that Steve and his father had put away were spending their miserable lives at Sunrise. But given Yokley's ties to ROAR, and Sweeney's recent meeting with Mark, Steve couldn't ignore the connection.

"Have you ever heard your homey mention Carter Sweeney or ROAR?" Steve asked.

"I'm not talking about my homeys," Teeg said, slurping on a McDonald's shake.

"Okay," Steve said. "Did you ever hear Yokley mention them?"

"We weren't homeys, you know? We didn't kick it together."

"You never talked about anything besides guns?"

"We talked about Mariah Carey and Beyonce's asses," Teeg said. "Or maybe it was J-Lo's. Like which one was better, you know? And he's the one who told me about LaShonda."

"He knew LaShonda?"

"He knew how she was disrespecting me to my *gente*," Teeg said, color rising in his face.

"You mean by asking you for money to help raise your *niños*?" Steve said, tired of the Spanish shtick.

"How do you know they're mine? Yokley says she's been stepping out with those *pinchi putos* from the barrio the whole time I was with her."

Steve didn't see how a white racist in Palmdale could pick up street gossip like that or why he would pass it on to Teeg.

"When did Yokley tell you this?"

"The day that somebody took a shot at the bitch," Teeg said.

"That was you, Teeg."

"You don't know that," Teeg said, elbowing his lawyer.

"Actually, I do," Steve said.

"That's true," Kirby Kirkland said.

Steve noticed that the latest *Simpsons* character on the legal pad looked a lot like him. He wasn't sure whether to be offended or flattered.

"What kind of lawyer are you?" Teeg protested.

"The police have got you for this, no question about it," Kirby said. "The best we can hope for is a few good words to the judge from the prosecution on your behalf when it comes to sentencing and where you do your time. That's the reason we're cooperating."

At that moment the door opened and Tony Sisk strode boldly into the room, as if his entrance had been preceded by an orchestral fanfare. He wore his trademark double-breasted suit and, incongruously, enough bling to hold his own with any rapper.

Sisk was familiar to everyone in the room and anyone who'd watched Court TV. He was one of LA's more flamboyant and expensive criminal defense attorneys.

"Do not say another word, Mr. Cantrell," Sisk said, then pointed a finger accusingly at Kirby, which was pretty amazing, considering the heavy ring that was around his manicured digit. "This pitiful accident of human evolution is a servant for the jackals who've unjustly imprisoned you."

"Huh?" Teeg said.

Kirby was completely flustered in the face of Sisk's gale-force personality.

Sisk sighed, disappointed that his flowery oratory had been wasted on his new client. "This public defender isn't defending your interests. I will."

"You will?" Teeg's eyes widened in shock. "But I can't afford you."

"You don't have to worry about that," Sisk said. "Your good friend Gaylord Yokley is paying me."

"Why would he do that?" Teeg asked.

"Because he despises injustice and cruelty, Mr. Cantrell, as do I."

As much as Steve disliked Sisk's clients, he couldn't bring himself to dislike the man himself. He enjoyed Sisk's ridiculous bluster, even when it was directed at him.

"Isn't it obvious, Teeg? Yokley wants to shut you up before you can do him any more damage," Steve said. "The only interests he's looking out for are his own."

"He told me about LaShonda," Teeg said.

"And look where it's gotten you," Steve said.

"Mr. Yokley had nothing to do with your unlawful, disgraceful, and unconscionable detention," Sisk said, and then pointed his bejeweled finger at Steve. "Are you going to take the word of this sock-puppet of the ruling intelligentsia or are you going to listen to me, a man you know to be a champion of the oppressed? It's up to you, Mr. Cantrell."

Teeg turned to Kirby. "You're fired."

Kirby looked almost relieved. Sisk smiled victoriously and waved Steve and Kirby out of the room.

"Go throw yourselves on the mercy of your masters," Sisk said. "I need to speak in private with my very important client."

Steve and Kirby left the room without a word. Out in the hall, Steve turned to the public defender, who seemed to be in a mild state of shock.

"Do you think I could fit 'sock-puppet of the ruling intelligentsia' on a business card?" Steve asked. "It sounds a lot more impressive than 'lieutenant.'"

"If Sisk gets Yokley and Cantrell acquitted," Kirby said, "you'll have the chance to find out."

CHAPTER TWENTY-FIVE

Ken Hoffman's death from West Nile virus was the lead story on every local eleven o'clock news program and was even mentioned on CNN, Fox News, and most of the national newscasts. Mark figured it probably made the BBC and Al Jazeera, too.

It was a story no news director could resist. A man undergoes a heart-lung transplant, the operation is a success, but he dies from a common mosquito bite.

And wherever the story was told, one fact was sure to be mentioned: The man died at Community General Hospital.

The death was a tragedy and no one's fault, but Mark was sure that Janet Dorcott wouldn't see it that way. Once again, Community General was getting negative press and Mark was involved. It didn't matter than his involvement was tangential at best and that his name never came up in the news reports. He would still get nailed for it.

So be it.

Mark was switching off the TV when Steve came in, exhausted.

"Alone tonight?" Mark asked.

"Yeah," Steve said. "Relieved?"

Mark shrugged. "Just curious."

"It isn't serious between Olivia and me," Steve said. "It's just casual for now."

"Of course it is. I can't remember the last time you had a serious relationship."

Steve flopped onto the couch across from Mark, who sat in his favorite leather reading chair, his feet up on the ottoman.

"Fifth grade. Stacey O'Quinn. That was serious," Steve said. "She broke my heart and I've never recovered."

"Whatever happened to her?"

"It was thirty years ago," Steve said. "How should I know?"

"You're a detective," Mark said. "You could find out."

"God, how pathetic would that be?" Steve said.

Mark studied his son for a long moment. Steve couldn't meet his father's gaze.

"When did you find her?" Mark asked.

Steve grimaced with embarrassment. "Last year. She's living down in Costa Mesa with her second husband. She's got two kids from her first marriage and one from her second. She's a hairdresser."

"Sounds like you were better off without her," Mark said. "How's the Yokley case going?"

"Nowhere since Teeg lawyered up," Steve said.

"Didn't he have a lawyer already?"

"He had a public defender," Steve said. "Now he's got Tony Sisk, who also happens to represent Gaylord Yokley."

Mark felt a shiver on the back of his neck. He was suddenly and instinctively aware of danger all around him, as if he were walking down a dark alley in a very bad neighborhood.

"Those aren't his only clients," Mark said.

"I know he also represents that basketball player who raped a cheerleader and that sitcom star who got caught buying crystal meth on skid row. He's slumming with Yokley and Teeg."

"He's also Carter Sweeney's lawyer," Mark said.

Steve tensed up, undoubtedly feeling the same sense of danger that his father was.

"Since when?"

"I don't know," Mark said. "But Sisk is the one who called me with Sweeney's request for a meeting."

This wasn't good. Not at all.

"What the hell is going on here?" Steve asked.

"Carter Sweeney's grand plan," Mark said. "Whatever it is."

There was some ominous meaning behind these events, and whatever it was, Mark was sure it wasn't good for him, Steve, or anybody else.

"By getting his lawyer to represent Yokley and Teeg, Sweeney is virtually admitting to us that he's behind the plot to provoke a gang war to create anarchy in LA," Steve said. "Why would he want to do that?"

"Ego?"

"But he failed," Steve said. "Why take credit for a failure?"

"Perhaps to show us that even in prison he's still a force to be reckoned with."

"If Sisk has been relaying orders to Yokley on Sweeney's behalf in the furtherance of a criminal enterprise, we can arrest him."

"You'd have to prove it first," Mark said. "And you have nothing to go on but your suspicions and mine. There isn't a shred of actual evidence."

"So what do you suggest? That we should just be satisfied that we stopped Sweeney's plot?"

"What makes you think we've done that?" Mark asked.

Steve filled Mark in on everything he'd learned from Teeg. Mark was especially intrigued by Yokley's uncharacteristic tip to Teeg that his girlfriend was sleeping around with members of rival gangs. Did Yokley want to provoke the shooting? Or did Sweeney? And if so, why?

Sleep didn't come easily that night for Mark. He spent hours tossing and turning in bed, looking at the Yokley case from every angle, trying to discern the true shape of the plot and Carter Sweeney's actual intentions.

Was there more to it than stoking a gang war in the midst of a hotly contested mayoral election? Were anarchy and bloodshed Sweeney's genuine goals or had he always intended for the scheme to be revealed before it could be executed? What did Sweeney gain in either scenario? And how did Sweeney's meeting with Mark figure into all of this?

Coming up with questions was easy. What Mark was woefully short on was answers. He couldn't make everything that had happened fit into any kind of coherent strategy. Whatever Sweeney was up to, Mark simply couldn't see it.

And that scared him.

He knew Sweeney was a patient man and that his plans often took years to come to fruition. Were these the first steps in a long-term stratagem or was it the endgame finally unfolding in all its complexity?

But despite Mark's fear, and the blizzard of questions clouding his mind, his body finally overruled his intellect and he fell asleep.

The next morning he was no longer tormented by the questions and anxieties that had kept him up half the night. He was relaxed and letting his subconscious crunch the data.

Mark met Amanda and Jesse for cinnamon rolls and coffee in the Community General pathology lab. Although being surrounded by corpses waiting to be autopsied and bodily fluids to be tested didn't offer the warmest ambience for breakfast, Mark preferred it to running into Janet Dorcott in the hallways. He was tempted to hide here for the rest of the day.

"You can't avoid her forever," Jesse said.

"She's going to find some way to blame me, you, and Amanda for the bad press Community General is getting over Hoffman's death."

"Maybe not," Amanda said. "I heard from Vector Control on my way in today. They found a dead bird in Hoffman's neighborhood. It was infected with West Nile virus."

"That's the final piece of the puzzle," Mark said.

"It's also going to shift the media's attention away from us and onto the major mosquito abatement offensive the county is mounting in Topanga Canyon," Amanda said. "The county is spraying, removing sources of standing water, and doing whatever it is they do to kill mosquitoes. They're also telling everyone who lives in Topanga Canyon to wear long sleeves, long pants, and slather themselves with insect repellent."

"The people who live out there aren't going to be too happy about that," Jesse said. "A lot of those Topanga people don't even like to use deodorant."

"That whole hippie thing is a cliché," Amanda said. "Have you looked at what houses cost in Topanga? There are a lot of very wealthy movie stars, studio executives, and TV producers living in the canyon now."

"Okay," Jesse said. "Do you think *they're* going to like wearing long sleeves and reeking of bug repellent?"

"You have a point," Mark said.

"Community General isn't going to be the story anymore," Jesse said. "We can all relax."

The doors to the pathology lab swung open, and a dozen men and women marched in carrying computers, metal cases, and various pieces of medical testing equipment. They fanned out into the lab as if it belonged to them and began setting up their things. Before Amanda could say a word, a blond-haired man dressed entirely in black stepped forward, flashing his federal ID.

So much for relaxing, Mark thought.

"I'm Dr. Logan Sharpe with the Centers for Disease Control," he said. "This is my crisis team. We're going to be using this lab as our base of operations until the crisis is over."

"What crisis?" Amanda asked. "And what does it have to do with my pathology lab?"

"Jackie Blain, Bill Cluverius, Paul Bishop, Joel Goldsmith, and Victoria Burrows."

"Who are they?" Amanda asked.

"The people who received Corinne Adams's two kidneys and three liver sections," Jesse said, his voice heavy with dread.

"Right you are, Dr. Travis. Three of them are dead from encephalitis, two are in comas. Would you like to guess why?"

Mark thought he knew the answer. It sent a shiver of fear down his spine. The deadly catastrophe he'd envisioned the other day was coming true after all.

"The organs from Corinne Adams were infected with West Nile virus," Mark said.

"You just won the grand prize, Dr. Sloan," Sharpe said. "You get to be the middleman between my team and every other department in this hospital."

"How did you confirm it was WNV?" Amanda asked.

"We autopsied the brains of the dead victims. The brain tissue tested positive for WNV by PCR and by flavivirus immunohistochemical staining," Sharpe said. "The serum, plasma, and cerebrospinal fluid of the two comatose patients have all tested positive for WNV antibodies and RNA. We checked and double-checked the results."

Mark couldn't fault the science or the conclusions.

Polymerase chain reaction (PCR) is used to find the virus itself in blood and tissues. Routine tests locate viruses by isolating the antibodies that the body creates to fight the virus. PCR replicates any ribonucleic acid (RNA) that a virus leaves behind and reveals its identity, much the same way that deoxyribonucleic acid (DNA) left at a crime scene can be used to positively identify the criminal.

The immunohistochemical staining tags specific antibodies with a substance that makes the viruses glow under the electron microscope so they can be detected.

"But the county found a bird infected with West Nile right outside Hoffman's house in Topanga Canyon," Jesse said.

"It's a meaningless coincidence," Sharpe said, "but fortunate for the people who live in Topanga Canyon. Otherwise, WNV might not have been detected in their area until someone got infected."

"Someone *did* get infected," Jesse said.

"Corinne Adams didn't live or work near Topanga Canyon," Sharpe said. "So it's irrelevant in this case if there's a WNV hot spot there or not."

"This has to be a mistake. I've checked Corinne Adams's blood and tissues twice," Amanda said. "I can tell you with absolute certainty that there were no West Nile virus antibodies present."

"We're going to recheck everything and consider every possibility," Sharpe said. "And we're going to do it fast, before a lot more people die."

"We need to recall all of the donor's organs and tissues," Amanda said. "I'll get on the phone to MediSolutions International in Phoenix."

"We already have a team there, going through their records, tracking down every bone, tendon, fingernail, flake of skin, and lock of hair from her body. We also have people deployed to each hospital that received one of her donor organs. This is what we do, Dr. Bentley."

"Then what can I do?" Amanda asked.

"A cup of coffee would be nice," Sharpe said. "I take mine black."

CHAPTER TWENTY-SIX

Within an hour of the arrival of the CDC team, the entire hospital knew about the situation. And with the CDC chopper on the helipad atop Community General, it was only a matter of time before the press picked up on it, too.

Nobody was more aware of this than Janet Dorcott, who hunted Mark down and confronted him outside the pathology lab after he'd been running around the hospital, gathering the files and test results on Adams and Hoffman that Sharpe needed. Her face resembled a storm cloud, dark and angry, crackling with electric fury.

"Who is responsible for this?" she demanded, tipping her head towards the CDC team hard at work in the pathology lab.

"No one is," Mark said, balancing the heavy stack of files in his arms.

"Then why did a team from the CDC fly in from Atlanta and invade our hospital?"

"The organs harvested from Corinne Adams were infected with West Nile virus," Mark said. "They're looking for the cause."

"No, Dr. Sloan. They already know the cause. That's not why they are here. They want to know *how* it happened. Someone on your team screwed up. Didn't you test the donor for infectious diseases before the transplant?"

"Of course we did," Mark said, his own anger flaring now.

"Then why didn't West Nile come up?"

"It's not that simple."

"That's one explanation," she said. "The other is incompetence."

Mark wanted to slap her right across the face, but that would have meant dropping all the files. Instead, he lowered his voice and took a step closer to her. She held her ground.

"West Nile virus is exceedingly rare. Organ donors aren't routinely screened for it. Even if they were, the specific tests for the West Nile virus aren't always accurate and can't be completed in time for urgent transplant cases," Mark said. "If Corinne Adams was infected and it wasn't detected, it's not negligence or incompetence. It's bad luck."

"Bad luck seems to follow you and your close colleagues," Janet said. "If I was a member of the general public, I sure as hell wouldn't want to be one of your patients and I certainly wouldn't set foot in this hospital. In fact, I'd even think twice about driving near the building."

"If you feel so strongly about it," Mark said, "maybe you shouldn't be here."

"I'm not the one who should leave, Dr. Sloan. I strongly recommend that you consider our severance offer while it is still on the table," she said. "And while you're at it, you might also suggest to Dr. Bentley and Dr. Travis that they might be happier at other hospitals."

She turned and stomped off.

Mark wouldn't pass her suggestion along to Amanda or Jesse. He needed them focused on their work and not distracted by anger.

It had been his experience that chief administrators came and went. It was only a matter of time before Janet Dorcott left, too. The question was whether he would still be working at Community General when she did.

CHAPTER TWENTY-SEVEN

The Grand Majestic was a grandiose name for a grandiose hotel, an Art Deco monument to money and decadence, erected in downtown Los Angeles before the Great Depression as a place where high society could delight in their altitude.

But the market tumbled, and those who didn't fall from their great heights gradually moved their never-ending party west to Hancock Park and Beverly Hills.

The Victorian mansions they left behind on Bunker Hill were razed, and the hill itself was bulldozed, tunneled, and topped with office buildings.

The Grand Majestic remained, stripped bare of its elegance, slowly eroding from the inside out over the years, its once luxurious suites rented out by the day, and then by the hour, and then when even that pitiful business couldn't be sustained, abandoned altogether.

The building became submerged in a Dickensian mire of lawsuits and countersuits over ownership between banks, private investors, the city, and the historical society that lasted for decades. And while they fought, the Grand Majestic became a decaying, trash-strewn, urine-stenched shelter for junkies, whores, and drunks.

Now the Grand Majestic was being gutted for renovation into a dozen two-million-dollar town houses for the wealthy young professionals that police chief and mayoral candidate John Masters hoped would be filling the two soaring office towers that investors from Dubai were building downtown.

That's why the chief was at the Grand Majestic construction site, mingling with the workers and trailed by photographers. His shirtsleeves were rolled up and he wore a pristine hard hat, as if he might abruptly decide to pound some rivets.

Steve Sloan wondered if campaign protocol required that a candidate dress to blend in with whatever workplace he was visiting. If Masters made a campaign stop at a hospital, would he be expected to put on a lab coat so he could render a diagnosis? If he visited a university, would he be expected to lug a backpack full of textbooks around with him? It was ridiculous, but all politicians seemed to do it.

Maybe Masters realized how ridiculous it was, too. It seemed as though the former pro football player would have been more comfortable charging through the crowd of people and tackling them rather than shaking their hands and gifting them with a pained smile.

Masters wasn't a people person. He liked to control people, not move among them.

The chief toured the site, then gave a stump speech to the hundred or so construction workers on their lunch break about how the transformation of the Grand Majestic was symbolic of the rebirth of downtown. It was also indicative, he said, of the change he would bring as mayor to the most impoverished areas of the city. He promised to battle the blight of urban decay the way he'd battled crime. The weapons in his fight would be creating jobs by supporting more urban renewal projects. His dream, Masters said, was for Los Angeles "to truly be a City of Angels."

It was a catchy phrase, but Steve wasn't sure what it meant. In order for LA to be a City of Angels, wouldn't they all have to be dead? Wasn't "City of Angels" just a fancy name for a ghost town?

But the audience didn't seem to share Steve's confusion. They were stirred into enthusiastic applause, which Masters soaked up before retreating to his Lincoln Town Car and motioning Steve to join him.

They were alone in the car, sitting side by side in the backseat, sheathed in privacy behind glass tinted almost as dark as the chief's stony gaze. The chief locked the doors so they wouldn't be disturbed.

"I've been watching the Yokley case," the chief said. "Not much is happening with it."

"It's slow going," Steve agreed. "Tracing the guns back to their sources is tedious and laborious. The serial numbers were removed from most of the weapons, but it appears some of them may have come from—"

"I don't care about the guns," the chief said, interrupting Steve.

"That's the ATF's problem. I'm interested in Carter Sweeney. You should be, too."

"I am."

"Then why haven't I seen you following up on that?"

"There isn't anything to follow, sir."

Chief Masters grimaced. "Gaylord Yokley is aligned with ROAR, Sweeney's personal army of clueless morons, and he's represented by Tony Sisk, Sweeney's lawyer, who arranged for your father and Sweeney to meet for some goddamn reason. All of which just happens to occur weeks before the mayoral election. And right before Sweeney goes to court to argue that he should be released from prison because his rights were trampled in a gross miscarriage of justice, which, he says, was orchestrated by me and Neal Burnside. And you don't think there's anything to follow? Sweeney is plotting something."

Chief Masters had obviously been keeping a much closer eye on things than Steve had thought. Actually, Steve never thought about it. He tended to keep his attention focused on his work and not on the political machinations happening on the upper floors of Parker Center.

Big mistake.

"There's no evidence," Steve said.

"Get some," the chief said.

"The only people who can prove that Sisk is relaying messages of a criminal nature between Sweeney and Yokley are Sisk, Sweeney, and Yokley. And none of them are talking."

"Sure they are, Detective," Masters said. "Just not to us."

"Are you suggesting that we electronically eavesdrop on Tony Sisk?"

The chief sighed and looked out the window at the construction workers who were returning to their jobs, their lunch hour over.

"As of this moment, Detective, you are no longer on the Yokley investigation. You are now on special assignment to me."

"The last time that happened, I got shot. My father was framed for murder by Mob accountant Malcolm Trainor. And you withheld crucial information from me that nearly undermined the entire investigation."

"I've decided to overlook your mistakes and give you a second chance to impress me," the chief said. "I'm giving Lieutenant Tanis Archer the same opportunity."

Tanis had been Steve's partner in his previous stint on special assignment for the chief. Since then, her career had taken some serious body blows. Her lack of political prowess was even greater than Steve's. She'd arrested the son of a prominent politician for beating a woman, and then she personally gave him a taste of what it felt like to be the victim. Ever since then, she'd been shuffled from one terrible job to another in the hope that she would quietly resign. But she wouldn't. Giving up wasn't in her nature.

"She is presently assigned to an administrative position with the Anti-Terrorism Strike Force, where she will stay for the duration of this special assignment," the chief said. "The strike force has access to all the latest surveillance equipment as part of the war on terror. I think Carter Sweeney is suitably terrifying, don't you?"

"We don't have enough evidence, circumstantial or otherwise, to get a wiretap warrant," Steve said.

"Is that a problem?"

"What you're suggesting is illegal, sir."

The chief shrugged. "Don't tell me that it bothers you. I've seen how you operate."

"Maybe it doesn't bother me," Steve said, "but it should bother *you.*"

"Sweeney is a serial bomber who enjoys killing people," Masters said. "Is this really a man who deserves the protection of the law?"

"Doesn't everybody?"

"Carter Sweeney tried to humiliate your father, ruin his reputation, and destroy everything he held dear. And when that failed, Sweeney blew up Community General Hospital with you and your father in it, maiming and killing how many people? And you expect me to believe you're concerned about his civil rights?" The chief looked at Steve incredulously. "What kind of man are you? What kind of cop?"

Steve met the chief's gaze. "Does Carter Sweeney scare you that much?"

"My job is to protect and to serve the people of this city," the chief said. "I do it by stopping men like Carter Sweeney and making sure they never hurt anyone again. If you want to wear that badge, it damn well better be your job, too."

The chief hit the UNLOCK button on his armrest. There was nothing more to be said. The meeting was over.

CHAPTER TWENTY-EIGHT

Lieutenant Tanis Archer's LAPD career had hit rock bottom, a fact dramatically symbolized by the location of her office, which was a cement-walled cubbyhole in the subbasement of Parker Center. The air barely circulated there, and she could go months without seeing another person.

She didn't take it personally. Her rationalization was that the subbasement was the perfect place for the clandestine operations of the Anti-Terrorism Strike Force to be conducted without notice.

The room was lit by one bare bulb dangling from a wire that came from somewhere in the recesses between the pipes and ducts that ran across the ceiling. There was a trash chute in one corner with a laundry cart below it to catch the files and papers that were dropped down to her from her faceless, nameless superiors with data for her to input into the computer terminal atop the lone desk.

Her job was to coordinate requests from various agencies and then shred the original documents. When she wasn't doing that, she made balls out of rubber bands and bounced them off the walls.

Tanis had her feet up on her desk and was bouncing one of those balls when Steve came in. She was wearing a tank top, cargo pants, and Doc Martens.

"I see you're having another busy day," Steve said. He'd never been in Egypt when they opened a crypt that had been sealed for a thousand years, but he figured it smelled just like Tanis's office.

"The war on terror is brutal," she said.

"You and I are on special assignment to the chief," Steve said.

"Super Secret Special Assignment," Tanis said, tossing Steve the ball. He caught it. She swung her legs off the desk, opened a drawer, and pulled out a box. "The chief wants us to bug the conversations between a criminal defense attorney and his client. So you can bet that nobody but you and me knows we're doing it for him. If we get caught, we're on our own. We'll take the fall and Masters will do absolutely nothing to help us."

"And you're okay with that?" Steve asked.

"It's not like my situation could get any worse."

"You could go to jail," Steve said.

"At least those cells have windows, a bed, and a toilet," she said. "You know how far the nearest toilet is from here?"

"So that's how you're justifying this to yourself?"

"I don't feel a need to justify it. I don't have a problem with what I'm doing," Tanis said. "But I'm not as uptight and goody-goody as you think you are."

"We're breaking the law," Steve said.

"You've done worse than listen in on some private conversations. What bothers you now is that you're being ordered to do it instead of going rogue and coming up with it on your own," Tanis said. "It's okay to break some laws if it arises out of your righteous indignation—that way it's not the institution that's corrupt, you are. You see the LAPD the way Jack Webb did, as this noble bastion of truth and justice. But if the chief of police orders you to break the law, that undermines your faith in the institution. You can be bad, but the LAPD can't."

"Been watching a lot of Dr. Phil down here?"

"Wish I could," Tanis said, "but the reception sucks."

She opened the box. Steve peered inside and saw several business card–sized electronic devices that looked like ultrathin cellular phones with alligator clips attached to all four corners.

"We got these as a gift from our buddies at Homeland Security," she said. "You clip these gizmos to the phone lines. They are voice activated and the conversations they record are uploaded to a secure Web site that only you and I can access from anywhere on the planet."

Steve picked up one of the devices and examined it. "Why would I care about being able to get these recordings from somewhere else than right here?"

"Because if our off-the-books errand for the chief blows up in our faces, we could be on the run," Tanis said. "And these recordings might be the only leverage we have to keep our asses out of a Turkish prison."

"How could we possibly end up in a Turkish prison?"

"You're overthinking things," Tanis said. "The point is, the recordings are stored on a hard drive in some godforsaken corner of the former Soviet Union, and we are the only ones who can retrieve them. The chief may have given us this assignment, but we control the intel."

"What if Sisk is talking on a cell phone?"

"I've got gadgets that cover all of that. We can tap into his cell phone signal. But if he's using throwaway cell phones, we've got to bug his car, his house, and his office and hope we catch his end of the calls that way."

"I know where you got these goodies," Steve said, holding up one of the devices, "but how did you come up with the Web site and all of that?"

"I've made some sleazy friends working in anti-terror," Tanis said. "One of the few perks of this job."

Steve tossed the device back into the box. "I hate this."

"They why didn't you tell the chief to stuff it?"

"Because I'll do anything to make sure that Carter Sweeney can never hurt the people I love again," Steve said. "Chief Masters knows it, so he's using me. And I'm letting him do it because I can't think of a better way to stop Sweeney from doing whatever the hell it is that he's doing. What's your excuse?"

She shrugged. "I'm just bored out of my mind."

"This doesn't creep you out?" Olivia asked. She was lying naked beside Steve in his bed, looking up at the ceiling, trying to catch her breath.

"What part are you talking about?" Steve replied, pretty winded himself.

"Doing what we just did with your dad sleeping upstairs," she said.

"Not really," Steve said. "I'm an adult. He knows that."

"Well, it creeps me out," Olivia said. "Next time we're going to my place."

"As long as you keep your dog out of the bedroom," Steve said.

"But that's where Boris sleeps," she said.

"Not when I'm there," Steve said.

"Boris is just going to scratch at the door until I let him in."

"Then put him outside," Steve said.

"What's wrong with Boris being in the room?"

"I have a hard time concentrating with a dog staring at me."

She propped herself up on an elbow and looked at him. "Making love to me takes *concentration*? I'm not a problem to be solved."

"Of course you are," Steve said. "You're a woman."

She narrowed her eyes at him. "I'm not sure how I should take that."

"Would you prefer a guy who *wasn't* giving you his full attention?"

Olivia kissed him. "Nice save."

"Thanks," Steve said. "I've had some practice."

"Maybe you need more," she said with a sly grin.

"I wish I could," Steve said, "but I have to get up early tomorrow."

"Nobody is making us punch a time clock on this case," she said.

"I'm not on it anymore," Steve said. "I've been reassigned to another investigation."

"You saved that bit of news until now?" She studied his face. "Is this your way of breaking things off?"

"It's not my idea," Steve said. "It's orders from above."

"What's the case?"

"It's this one," Steve said. "Only I'll be working the Carter Sweeney angle."

"So take me with you," she said.

"I can't," Steve said.

"These orders from above," Olivia said. "How far above are we talking about?"

"The next step up is Bob Dylan," Steve said. "And then God."

She lay down again. "You're going to get burned. You know that, right?"

"Oh yeah," Steve said, rolling over on his side to face her. "Will you be there for me when that happens?"

Olivia didn't look at him. "Probably not."

Steve nodded and kept looking at her.

"You want me to go?" she asked.

He stroked her hair. "No."

"Even after what I just said?"

"I just wanted to know where you stood," Steve said. "You told me straight out. I respect that."

And to prove it, he gave her a deep kiss. She grabbed him by the shoulders, rolled on top of him, and pinned him down.

"You're getting some more practice whether you think you need it or not," she said.

"Yes, ma'am," he said.

CHAPTER TWENTY-NINE

Dr. Mark Sloan was awakened at five-thirty a.m. by a call from one of Sharpe's crisis team members. They were having a meeting in the executive conference room at Community General in one hour and Mark was expected to be there.

As much as Mark resented being awakened by a stranger and ordered on ridiculously short notice to attend a compulsory meeting, his curiosity about the status of the CDC investigation was stronger than his irritation. There was no way he was going to miss the meeting, and Sharpe knew it. So why the last-minute call? Why the power play?

There was no reason for Sharpe to play that kind of game, but Mark wouldn't put it past Janet Dorcott—which made him wonder what she was up to and why she wanted him rattled.

Whatever her reasons were, it couldn't be good for him, Jesse, or Amanda.

Mark dressed in a hurry, without showering or shaving. He grabbed a Coke for the caffeine rush, an untoasted bagel so he'd have something in his stomach, and got in the car.

Traffic was light, even for Los Angeles, at five forty-five in the morning, and Mark managed to make it to the hospital by a little after six.

Jesse was sitting alone in the conference room when Mark arrived. His hair was askew, his face was unshaven, and his eyes were bloodshot. He was eating handfuls of chips from a bag of Fritos and washing them down with gulps from a carton of Yoohoo. He looked miserable.

"That's a hearty and nutritious breakfast you've got there," Mark said.

"What did you have to eat?" Jesse asked.

"A Coke and a bagel."

"Health freak," Jesse said.

Amanda came in, balancing a cinnamon roll the size of a Frisbee on a too small plate on top of her extra-large coffee from Peet's. She sat down carefully beside Mark and managed not to spill anything on the table in the process.

She didn't seem the least bit rattled by her rude wake-up call. Then again, she didn't work the kind of shifts that Jesse did and, as an adjunct county medical examiner, she was used to being awakened at all hours and sent to homicide scenes.

"Why do I feel like this is my last meal?" Amanda asked, setting the plate with her cinnamon roll down in front of her.

"Because if you eat that by yourself," Mark said, "the fat, sugar, and calories will kill you faster than a firing squad."

"Is that your way of saying you'd like to share this with me?"

"Only as a humanitarian intervention to save you from certain death," Mark said.

"You want some chips, too?" Jesse asked, offering Mark the bag.

"No, thanks," Mark said.

"What about my certain death?"

"You're beyond saving," Mark said. "And I'm not suicidal."

Amanda broke her pastry in half and handed a piece to him. "I was frozen out of the CDC investigation. They said they wanted an entirely fresh set of eyes. They took all the files and samples I had and shoved me out the door."

"Same with me," Jesse said. "It was kind of nice having a day off."

"You don't look like you've had a day off," Amanda said.

"I've been sleeping," Jesse said. "For me, that's a vacation, which is good, since it's the only kind of vacation I can afford."

"Sharpe kept me busy running around the hospital getting him every scrap of paper, X-ray, and test result we had on Corinne Adams and Ken Hoffman," Mark said. "The CDC is creating a meticulously detailed time line, scrutinizing every action that was taken since both patients entered Community General."

"The implication, of course, is that somebody screwed up," Jesse said. "Gee, I wonder who they think that might have been?"

Jesse downed his Yoo-hoo, crunched the empty carton in his fist, and then tossed the carton towards the trash can across the room. He missed.

"They are just being objective and thorough," Mark said,

though privately he shared Jesse's misgivings. They weren't being told the whole story.

Mark's suspicions were confirmed when the door opened and Sharpe came in, accompanied by several of his team members whom Mark recognized and one man in a dull gray suit whom he didn't.

They were followed by Janet Dorcott, two of her assistants, and Clarke Trotter, Community General's rotund legal counsel. Trotter kept smoothing out his tie, revealing his nervousness. Mark knew that Trotter wouldn't be here unless the hospital felt that it was exposed to some kind of legal liability.

Sharpe and his team, and Dorcott and her team, took their seats at the table across from Mark, Jesse, and Amanda. The stranger did not. He leaned against the wall, his arms crossed over his chest, an unreadable expression on his pockmarked face. But his body language suggested to Mark that he was someone with some kind of official status who was passing judgment on them all. The fact that nobody sat on the side of the table with the three of them only added to Mark's feeling that he, Jesse, and Amanda were facing some kind of tribunal.

"Thanks for coming in on such short notice," Sharpe said, opening a thick file in front of him. "Our investigation has confirmed that Corinne Adams was infected with West Nile virus at the time that her organs were harvested."

Mark wasn't surprised, given what Sharpe had already told them and the deaths of the organ recipients from WNV-related encephalitis. The stranger didn't seem shocked either. But Janet Dorcott and her minions reacted as if they'd had ice water splashed in their faces.

"Then how the hell did we miss it?" Janet demanded. It was the same question she'd already asked Mark. Either she hadn't listened to the answer or hadn't believed what she'd been told.

"Excuse me, Janet," Clarke Trotter said, raising his pen to signal his interruption, "but I don't think we can or should suggest, even for the sake of argument, that an error was made by this hospital or any of its employees. I would suggest that we all be careful about how we characterize this unfortunate situation."

Spoken like a true lawyer, Mark thought.

"When I want your opinion, Clarke, I will ask for it," Janet said, then turned back to Amanda. "I'm waiting, Dr. Bentley, to hear your explanation."

Clarke blinked hard but otherwise maintained his composure.

The stranger in the back of the room cracked a thin smile. It seemed to amuse the guy to see the lawyer slapped down. Whoever this man was, Mark decided, he must not be all bad.

"Donors are screened for a range of infectious diseases in a manner consistent with established national organ-procurement standards," Amanda said in a matter-of-fact way. "We followed those standards and didn't find West Nile virus antibodies in any of our tests."

"Why not?" Janet said.

"It takes weeks for the body to manufacture antibodies against an invader," Sharpe said. "If Corinne Adams was infected within fifteen or twenty days of her accident, there might not have been any antibodies present in her system to see."

"Even if there were," Mark said, "it wouldn't mean she was fighting an infection at the time."

"I don't understand," Janet said, her tone implying that her confusion was due not to any lack of knowledge on her part but rather to someone else's ineptitude.

"Antibodies in the blood simply indicate that the virus was once in the body. It doesn't mean that the virus is *still* there," Mark explained, trying not to sound patronizing. "If you had mumps as a child, you will have antibodies against the virus in your body for the rest of your life to defend you if it ever comes back."

Janet turned to Sharpe. "Then how did you find the West Nile virus in the samples when Dr. Bentley couldn't?"

"We used PRC testing to reveal the presence of the viral RNA in the donor rather than the antibodies created by the body to combat it."

"Why didn't *you* do that?" Janet asked Amanda.

"It's not a required or routine test according to national organ-procurement protocols," Amanda said. "And it takes time, much more than we have in a typical organ-donation situation."

Mark had told Janet that, too, though not in so much detail. Either Janet hadn't listened to what he said or she didn't accept his explanation.

"If Corinne Adams was infected," Clarke said, "why wasn't she showing any obvious symptoms?"

"The incubation period for West Nile virus varies," Sharpe said, "but it's about fourteen days. If she was infected less than two weeks ago, she wouldn't have been showing any symptoms."

"If she had been, we wouldn't have done the transplant," Jesse said. "Though not everyone who is infected with the virus gets sick. So without symptoms to see or West Nile antibodies in her tests, we had no way of knowing she was infected."

"If she wasn't sick yet, why did the symptoms show up so fast, and to such an extreme degree, in the patients who received her organs?" Trotter asked.

"Because their immune systems were compromised by the anti-rejection drugs," Sharpe replied. "They were extraordinarily vulnerable."

Trotter sighed, visibly relieved. He almost smiled.

"So, if I understand you," the lawyer said, "the CDC has determined that Corinne Adams was infected with West Nile virus and, through no fault of ours, she passed the virus along to the recipients of her organs."

Mark had shared the same conclusion with Janet Dorcott yesterday. But the official CDC determination meant that the hospital would be free of any legal liability in the deaths, even if the media and the public might not immediately grasp the distinction.

However, neither the hospital's liability nor the possible negative publicity was on Mark's mind at the moment. He was thinking about fate, which was having a lot of sick fun messing with him lately.

Enough already, Mark thought. I get the point. There's no escaping you. Is it really necessary to keep reminding me?

"I advise you to start testing every prospective organ donor for West Nile virus," Trotter said to Janet.

"Then you might as well shut down our transplant unit altogether," Jesse said. "The odds of someone getting infected with West Nile virus from an organ transplant are right up there with getting hit by a meteor. There are only two recorded cases of West Nile being transmitted by organ transplant."

"I agree with our legal counsel on this," Janet said. "Better safe than sorry."

Mark spoke up. Her ignorance was getting harder and harder for him to take.

"It's already impossible to get donor organs for everyone who needs them. If you raise the standards for organ donation too high, you're going to reject a lot of viable organs, and people will die because of it," he said. "Any organ transplant carries a risk of fatal complications. But the benefits far outweigh the risks. Organ recipients, and those waiting for donor organs, will be the first ones to tell you that."

"We'll take this up at a later date, Dr. Sloan," Janet said, her face tight with anger. "I'm sure Dr. Sharpe and the CDC have far more important things to do than listen to us debate hospital policy."

But Sharpe and his team didn't seem ready to go anywhere. And neither did the unidentified man leaning against the wall.

"I agree with you, Dr. Travis," Sharpe said. "It's extremely rare for someone with an undetected case of West Nile virus to die of unrelated causes and then infect others with his donated organs."

"Great. Case closed. I'm glad that's over," Jesse said, getting up from his seat. "Now I can get back to work."

"So what do you think the odds would be of it happening twice in one month at the same hospital with the same surgeon?" Sharpe asked.

Mark had a terrible feeling that Sharpe wasn't posing a hypothetical question.

"It's never happened here before," Jesse said, standing at the table.

"Yes," Sharpe said. "It has."

CHAPTER THIRTY

Jesse sat down and glanced first at Mark and then at Amanda. They were every bit as startled by Sharpe's statement as he was. So were Janet Dorcott and her two assistants, who were rendered even more deeply speechless than they already were. Clarke Trotter began smoothing his tie, which apparently wrinkled at the slightest hint of liability.

"As part of our investigation, we reviewed the last half dozen organ-harvesting operations performed at this hospital and followed up with the recipients," Sharpe said, referring to the file in front of him.

He went on to explain that a week before Corinne Adams's operation, Jesse had removed two kidneys and a liver from Bruce Wethersby, a thirty-one-year-old bike rider who was hit by a car and left brain-dead. His organs went to three recipients, one in San Bernardino and two others out of state.

The recipient of the liver tested positive for West Nile RNA but hadn't shown any symptoms yet.

"Unfortunately, the kidney recipients weren't so lucky," Sharpe said. "One has developed acute flaccid paralysis consistent with West Nile–related encephalitis and is in a coma. The other kidney recipient died two days ago from brain-stem herniation. Both victims have tested positive for West Nile RNA and antibodies."

Mark noted that they weren't being called patients anymore; they had become victims. The distinction was significant and ominous.

"We tested the donor's tissue and fluid samples for West Nile," Sharpe said, "and they came back positive for the virus."

The man leaning against the wall stepped forward and began to stroll casually around the table. "It could be a big, tragic coincidence that these two organ donors were both bitten by virus-carrying mosquitoes before they showed up in this hospital and had their organs harvested by Dr. Travis. But we don't think so."

"Who are 'we'?" Mark asked pointedly.

"The FBI, Dr. Sloan. I'm Special Agent William Ort. I'm also an M.D. Some people in the bureau call me Special Agent Ort. Others call me Dr. Special Agent Ort. But they all call me when there's a federal crime of a medical nature."

"A doctor who likes to solve crimes," Amanda said, glancing at Mark. "Imagine that."

"You think somebody intentionally infected these donors with West Nile virus before or after they were admitted to this hospital," Mark said.

"I do," Ort said.

"You think it's me," Jesse said.

Ort shrugged. "You're certainly a person of interest."

"I'd have to be one dumb killer," Jesse said.

"I've seen dumber," Ort said.

Mark was sure that Jesse wasn't the only suspect. Amanda's pathology lab did all the testing of the donors' blood, tissue, and organs. There were also several interns, nurses, and orderlies who had worked with both donors in the ER, the ICU, and during the transplant surgery.

If someone outside the hospital was infecting donors, the question was whether he was doing so before or after the victims had their accidents.

Corinne Adams fell down a flight of stairs. But what if she was *pushed*?

Bruce Wethersby was hit by a car. But what if it was *intentional*?

That meant someone chose the victims, somehow injected them with the virus, and then engineered their accidents. It seemed like a massively complex undertaking. But it was doable.

If they were infected with the virus after their accidents but before they arrived at Community General, then the possible suspects would include the paramedics, the firefighters, and the police officers who arrived at the scene to treat the victims.

Whoever it was would have had to obtain a sample of West Nile virus from somewhere, and that wouldn't have been easy. But once he had the virus, keeping it viable would take only a freezer.

Whoever was doing it had come up with a chilling and

ingenious way to kill. He was letting the organs, bones, and tissues do the killing for him. There was no telling how many people he could murder from a distance, all over the United States, just by infecting one person.

It was serial killing by proxy.

Mark was still mulling over the implications when he noticed Ort studying him. Ort didn't look pleased with whatever he'd read in Mark's expression.

"This is now a federal serial killer investigation," Ort said. "The CDC is lending us their resources and expertise. Representatives from the National Institutes of Health and the Food and Drug Administration will also be involved."

"You're talking about a lot of people descending on this hospital from outside agencies," Janet said. "Things are going to get out of hand very quickly."

"By that, I presume you mean that the media will find out about our investigation," Ort said. "That's inevitable."

"There's no evidence that anyone at Community General Hospital is involved in this," Janet said, "but if word gets out before you have a suspect, the implication will be that we are responsible for these deaths."

"Murders," Ort said.

"The reputation of this hospital could be ruined," Janet said. "That's a crime, too."

"I can't be concerned about that," Ort said.

"You'd better be," Trotter said. "Need I remind you of past cases in which the FBI falsely implicated people in crimes and later paid out millions in legal judgments as a result?"

"That's not my problem," Ort said. "I expect nothing less than the full cooperation of everyone in this hospital. You will be receiving warrants within the hour compelling you to open specific patient records for our review."

"We need to shut down the transplant unit immediately," Mark said.

"I think that's a good idea," Sharpe said.

"It's a horrible idea," Janet said. "We do that and it's practically an admission of guilt—and a public relations nightmare for this hospital."

"If we don't," Mark said, "we run the risk that someone else will be infected and more viable organs will be ruined."

"Keeping the transplant program running will help the investigation conclude more swiftly," Janet said. "The FBI can catch whoever it is in the act."

"Unless it's me," Jesse said.

"Or me," Amanda said.

"Or me," Mark said. "Besides, I don't think you want the liability of using a donor as a guinea pig. If you're right, and someone outside Community General is responsible, by keeping the program open you are encouraging the killer to go ahead and infect, and perhaps murder, another victim."

"Dr. Sloan has a good point," Trotter said.

"Shut up, Clarke," Janet said.

"I agree with Dr. Sloan and Dr. Sharpe," Ort said. "If you don't close the transplant program down voluntarily, I'll see to it that the appropriate agency compels you to do it anyway. You won't like that publicity any better. We're done for now."

Everyone rose. Janet Dorcott pointed at Jesse.

"You're suspended until further notice. I don't want to see you in this hospital." She turned to Mark. "We have to talk. Now."

Ort stepped between them. "Me first."

The agent led Mark to the back of the room, where they could talk privately.

"Thanks for saving me," Mark said.

"When I said I wanted everyone's full cooperation, I wasn't talking about you," Ort said. "I'd like you to cooperate less."

"Meaning what?" Mark asked, genuinely confused.

"I saw the look on your face. You were already thinking about what investigative angles you and Scooby-Doo were going to pursue. Don't."

"I do have some experience at this sort of thing," Mark said. "I could be an asset."

"You're a suspect," Ort said.

Mark looked at him incredulously. "I've been a consultant to the LAPD for over forty years. My son is a homicide detective. I've worked closely with the FBI many times, and so have Dr. Travis and Dr. Bentley."

"I'm aware of all that," Ort said.

"Then how could you possibly believe that any of us would purposely infect an organ donor with West Nile virus?"

"I know cops and FBI agents who've turned out to be rapists, embezzlers, blackmailers, and killers," Ort said. "So do you, Dr. Sloan. We both know their badges and past achievements in law enforcement didn't make any difference. They still committed heinous crimes. I believe whatever the evidence tells me. And right now, it tells me that you are a possible suspect. Stay out of this investigation."

Ort held Mark's gaze for a moment to emphasize his point and then walked away.

Someone was using patients at Community General Hospital as guns, and their organs as bullets, to kill people. There was no doubt that these killings would go public, and when they did, the scandal would smear the hospital where Mark had spent his entire career and destroy the reputations of two doctors who were like his own children.

If Dr. Special Agent William Ort thought Dr. Mark Sloan was going to sit by and let that happen, then Ort wasn't much of a detective—and he needed all the help that Mark could give him.

Whether he wanted it or not.

CHAPTER THIRTY-ONE

Steve and Tanis showed up outside of Tony Sisk's house in the hills above Malibu shortly after the attorney left for work. They were driving a Pacific Bell truck and were wearing telephone technician uniforms.

It took them only a few minutes to attach the bugs to the phone lines at the junction box. They didn't need to break into Sisk's house and plant listening devices in order to eavesdrop on conversations in the rooms. They had devices that could do the job from outside.

The phone line bugs did double duty. Not only did they record incoming and outgoing calls, but when the phones weren't in use, they became voice-activated listening devices, capturing any conversations that were going on in the room.

Another device, hidden under the windows, picked up the sound waves in the room and transmitted them back to the secret Web site using the home's own satellite dish.

Steve and Tanis managed to thoroughly and efficiently violate Tony Sisk's civil rights in under half an hour.

From there, they moved on to Sisk's office building on Wilshire Boulevard in Beverly Hills. Still posing as telephone technicians, they were able to do all their work without leaving the garage.

While Tanis compromised the office's phone lines and surveillance system, Steve slipped underneath Sisk's Mercedes S-class and planted devices that would turn the car into a luxurious mobile recording studio.

An hour later, Steve and Tanis were at Starbucks having coffee and cake, their earphones plugged into their laptops, listening to Sisk discuss all the weaknesses in the DA's case against a famous basketball player accused of rape.

"Now this is what I call police work," Tanis said, smiling happily.

Steve wished he could share her pleasure, but uneasiness gnawed at him deep inside. He couldn't shake the feeling that something was very wrong.

Mark sat on his deck facing the beach, a notepad in his lap. It was a sunny, cloudless day, the sky a brilliant blue, the sea an emerald green. He watched the waves break and thought about murder.

As soon as he got home, he had set up his laptop on the kitchen table and searched the Internet for information about the car accident that left Bruce Wethersby, the first organ donor, brain-dead. He found a small news item in the *Los Angeles Times* and learned that it wasn't a hit-and-run accident. The distraught driver, forty-four-year-old Charlotte Unger, called 911 and stayed at the scene, comforting the victim until the paramedics arrived.

Unger told police that Wethersby crossed in front of her car as she was making a right turn. It was possible that Unger also pushed Corinne Adams down the staircase at UCLA, and the FBI was certainly going to look into it, but Mark was going to assume for now that the killer wasn't responsible for the initial accidents.

That meant the killer didn't enter the picture until Wethersby and Adams were already critically injured.

So were they injected with the virus at the scene or after their arrival at Community General?

Mark thought about both scenarios, playing them out step by step.

If the killer was one of the first responders, a cop or a paramedic, he had to carry a syringe of West Nile virus around with him until a potential organ donor showed up.

The killer would have to quickly determine at the scene if the victim was a registered organ donor and then gamble that the victim would end up brain-dead, as opposed to recovering or simply dying.

It was a big gamble.

If the killer guessed wrong, and odds were that he *would* most of the time, then Mark should be able to find some serious accident victims who later developed West Nile virus symptoms.

Mark made a note on his pad to check into it, but he had a hunch that he wouldn't turn up any cases that fit the description—because there was a safer and more dependable way for the killer to work. The killer could wait to strike until the accident victim was declared brain-dead and scheduled for organ harvesting.

And the killer couldn't get that information until after the victim had been treated at the hospital and a battery of tests had been done.

So Mark scratched the notion that the killer was one of the first responders.

The killer was at Community General.

No doubt Special Agent Ort had already reached the same conclusion, which was why Mark was considered a suspect, along with a couple hundred other Community General employees.

Anyone who had access to the ER or the ICU could be the killer.

But Mark was getting ahead of himself. He realized he'd skipped a crucial question in his thinking.

Where did the killer get his stash of West Nile virus?

Mark knew that the cultivation of viruses was a difficult procedure that required specialized knowledge, as well as expensive and highly technical equipment. But there was another, easier way to get the virus: Take it from someone already infected with it. The contaminated blood could be frozen or refrigerated for months without losing its infectivity. The killer would then have the means to infect more people.

It wouldn't take much blood.

Only one tiny vial.

The killer could easily keep the vial hidden on ice in one of the many refrigerators and freezers in the hospital until a brain-dead organ donor came along.

And then all he had to do was draw some of the infected blood into a syringe, creep into the ICU, and empty the syringe into the patient's IV a day or two before the organ harvesting.

No one would know what had happened until it was too late—when organ recipients all over the country began to die.

Even then, the deaths would most likely be written off as a freak occurrence, a terrible tragedy.

Which is exactly what the CDC, Mark, and everybody else would have done, if only it hadn't happened twice at the same hospital.

So why did the killer do it again? Didn't he realize that it was too big a coincidence to be ignored? Or was that the point?

Mark made a note on his pad: Was it an irresistible compulsion or did the killer *want* to be noticed? If so, *why*??

But there was a far more important question that needed to be answered first. He wrote it down, too.

Where did the killer get his vial of West Nile–infected blood?

The killer could have taken the blood from anyone with West Nile virus, regardless of whether they were suffering from mild or extreme symptoms.

And where was the killer most likely to find someone who had been positively diagnosed with the virus?

At a hospital.

And why should the killer look any farther than home?

Community General.

Mark got up, went back into the house, and sat down in front of his laptop computer. He logged on to the Community General computer system and began searching for any patients who'd been admitted with confirmed cases of West Nile virus. It wasn't a common affliction, so he didn't expect to find many.

He was right. He found only one.

Six months earlier, a fifty-five-year-old man had come into the ER suffering from what initially seemed to be a severe case of the flu. But he was soon diagnosed with West Nile virus. He was hospitalized for two weeks and then went home.

The man's nurse was Susan.

A quick check of the records confirmed that she'd also treated organ donors Bruce Wethersby and Corinne Adams.

And in both cases, Susan's husband, Dr. Jesse Travis, performed the organ-harvesting surgeries. Susan was right at the center of it all.

Mark didn't believe for a second that Susan was the killer, but the circumstantial case against her would be very convincing to someone who didn't know her as well as he did.

He could even see a strong case being made that both Jesse and Susan were involved in the tainting of the organs with the virus.

They both had the medical knowledge, the means, and ample opportunity.

And there was another fact in their pasts that made the case against them even more damning. They both knew how an organ could be used to kill . . . because they'd seen someone else do it before.

Jesse and Susan had helped Mark solve a homicide several years ago in which a patient consumed drugs to taint his kidney with a substance that would kill the intended recipient of the organ.

The case was hardly a secret. Clarke Trotter knew all about it and probably saw the same parallels between it and the current case that Mark did.

It could be argued that Jesse and Susan had merely improved on a technique that Mark had introduced them to—and instead of killing one person with a tainted organ, they'd found a way to murder many more.

Mark had no doubt that was exactly the argument that Special Agent William Ort would make.

Unless Mark caught the real killer first.

CHAPTER THIRTY-TWO

Mark called Amanda, Jesse, Susan, and Steve and asked them to come to the beach house right away. He didn't tell them why. He didn't have to. They were used to getting calls like that from him. It was his rallying cry, gathering them together to start another investigation.

What was unusual about Mark's call this time was that he made a point of asking Susan to come too.

Although she'd occasionally helped Mark before, homicide investigation wasn't something she was interested in. Susan only reluctantly got involved when either Mark or Jesse needed her for a specific task, but she was never asked to join in the early stages of one of Mark's investigations. It made her uneasy.

Susan shared her feelings with Jesse on their way to Mark's house. Jesse shrugged off her concern.

"It just means that Mark already has a plan," Jesse said, "and you're part of it."

She wanted to believe that Jesse was right, but when they got to Mark's place, Amanda was just arriving and she appeared startled to see Susan there.

"I know," Susan said to Amanda. "I think it's weird, too."

"What are you talking about?" Amanda asked innocently.

"Me being here," Susan said.

"You're my wife," Jesse said. "Why shouldn't you be here?"

"Because I'm not one of the Superfriends and I don't want to be," Susan said. "I don't usually get summoned with the Bat Signal by the Justice League of America to the big meeting at the Fortress of Solitude."

"You've got the superhero stuff all mixed up," Jesse said, shaking his head. "We're going to have to spend a lot more time watching Cartoon Network together."

"Lucky you," Amanda said to Susan.

At that point Steve pulled up in his truck, driving too fast and nearly rear-ending Amanda's Chrysler 300.

When Steve got out, everything about him seemed askew, as if he'd just emerged from a wind tunnel.

"What's the emergency?" he asked.

"Mark didn't tell you?" Amanda replied.

"I was on assignment," Steve said. "He left me a message on my cell and he paged me. All he said was that it's an emergency."

"Relax. It's no big deal. The feds are hunting for a serial killer," Jesse said. "And they think it's me."

"Or me," Susan said.

"Or me," Amanda said.

"Oh hell," Steve said with a grimace and led the others into the house.

They all settled in their usual places around the kitchen table, except for Susan, who waited for everyone to sit before taking a seat beside Jesse. She felt like an uninvited guest, despite everyone's best efforts to make her feel at home. But whatever discomfort she felt evaporated once Mark started talking. He gave her more important things to worry about.

Mark began by quickly explaining to Steve everything that had happened, beginning with Wethersby's bike accident and on through to the meeting that morning.

He did it for his own benefit, too. Starting at the beginning forced him to review the facts and events again. Sometimes, in the retelling, he saw things he'd overlooked before.

Unfortunately, that didn't happen this time.

When Mark was done, Steve looked slightly dazed by everything he'd heard.

"How did I miss all that?" Steve asked.

"You've been occupied with the Yokley investigation," Mark said.

"I live right downstairs," Steve said.

"Where you've been occupied with Olivia," Mark said. "I never found the right moment to talk to you. Besides, until this morning, it was just a medical mystery. There was nothing remotely criminal about it. I didn't think you'd be interested."

"Who is Olivia?" Amanda asked.

"Steve's girlfriend," Mark said.

"She's not my girlfriend," Steve said. "We've just been seeing a lot of each other over the last few weeks."

"How did I miss that?" Jesse asked.

"Because you've been occupied with becoming a suspect in a serial killer case," Susan said. She turned to Mark. "Do you have a plan?"

Mark shook his head. "I wish I did. At this point, all I really have are some working assumptions."

He explained his thinking on the investigation and shared the conclusions that he'd reached, including the likelihood that Jesse and Susan were going to be at the top of Ort's list of suspects.

Susan took Jesse's hand and squeezed it. "I had a feeling this was going to be bad news."

"I'm sure this guy Ort isn't half as smart as Mark," Jesse said reassuringly. "By the time he gets around to us, we'll be able to give him the killer. Case closed."

Mark appreciated Jesse's confidence in him, but he didn't share the young doctor's optimism or faith in his abilities.

"I wish you were right, Jesse. But my guess is that Special Agent Ort is already way ahead of me," Mark said. "We don't have much time, maybe a day at most, before the FBI comes for one of you."

"This is so wrong," Susan said. "How could the FBI think that we'd kill anyone? Or that we'd be stupid enough to do it in a way that points right back to us? Jesse has been helping you solve murders for years. If he wanted to kill someone, he knows how to do it without getting caught. And so do I."

"I don't think telling the FBI that we could be much better killers than they think we are is really our best defense," Jesse said. "We might want to come up with something else."

"The best defense is to find better suspects," Mark said. "Whoever we're after has free access to the entire hospital and can easily get into patient records."

"That narrows the field to every doctor, nurse, orderly, and file clerk at Community General," Amanda said. "The only people you're leaving out are the patients."

"I know," Mark said grimly. "We can begin by correlating the shift schedules of every employee in every department with the periods when the West Nile virus patients, Wethersby and Adams, were in the hospital."

"Getting the information shouldn't be hard," Amanda said. "It's all in the computer. The problem is that it's an enormous amount of data. We aren't going to be able to cross-reference everything in just a day."

"We have no other choice," Mark said. "We can log on to the Community General system from here and get right to work."

"We also have to find that vial," Jesse said.

"Do you have any idea how many refrigerators there are in the hospital?" Amanda asked. "It could take days—and that's assuming the killer hasn't removed it by now."

"We'll have to leave that to the FBI and concentrate on a task we have a chance at accomplishing. We're looking at an all-nighter," Mark said. "But by morning we should have at least a few possible suspects for Steve to check out."

"I can't," Steve said.

Everyone turned to look at him. Steve rarely refused to help Mark, and never on a case that involved someone close to them.

"This is a federal case," Steve said. "I have no jurisdiction."

It was a weak argument, and Mark didn't buy it. There was something more going on.

"You've got to be kidding," Amanda said. "Since when do you care about jurisdiction?"

"It's more than that," Steve said.

"It better be," she said pointedly. Mark was thinking the same thing, but he was glad she said it instead of him.

"This case is going to get a lot of attention from law enforcement and the media," Steve said. "I can't risk any of that attention shifting to me."

"Are you worried about your career now?" Jesse asked. "That's a first."

"I'm worried about going to jail," Steve said. He looked at their faces and grimaced. "I shouldn't be telling you about this, but you're family, and it's the only way you'll understand why I can't help you now."

With that preamble, he reluctantly revealed to them the details of his special assignment from the chief to illegally eavesdrop on Tony Sisk's telephone conversations relating to his client Carter Sweeney.

There was a moment of silence while the others processed what Steve had told them. Now they were the ones looking slightly dazed.

Mark was astonished at the enormous risk Steve was taking on behalf of the chief, a man his son didn't trust, respect, or particularly like. Then again, the chief was making it easier for Steve to take action against Sweeney, who posed a serious threat to every-one sitting in Mark's house that day. Steve was putting his career, and his liberty, at stake for them.

"We really have to talk to one another more," Mark said.

"That's an understatement," Amanda said, pinning Mark with her gaze. "When were you going to tell us about Carter Sweeney?"

Mark winced. He realized now that he and Steve had left Amanda, Jesse, and Susan completely in the dark about his strange meeting with Sweeney and the killer's possible scheme to ignite a gang war in Los Angeles.

"I didn't want to worry you," Mark said.

"The man dropped a hospital on top of us," Amanda said. "I think we have a right to decide for ourselves whether we want to worry about him or not."

"I've got so much to worry about now, I'm having a hard time picking one to focus on," Jesse said. "Maybe we should make a list."

Someone pounded on the front door, and pounded again two seconds later.

Steve glanced at Mark. "There was a certain urgent, law en-forcement authority to that, don't you think?"

"I have to agree, considering those Men in Black watching our back door," Amanda said, motioning behind Mark and Steve to the beach. "In case we try to escape by sea."

Mark turned to look. There were three men wearing sunglasses and dark suits standing on the beach behind the house.

He faced the others, the expression on his face conveying what they were all thinking. They had run out of time before they'd even had a chance to begin.

"I don't think I'm going to need that list after all," Jesse said glumly.

The pounding on the door got more insistent.

"I'll get it," Mark said, rising and crossing to the front door. He opened it, and Special Agent Ort marched in, followed by three other agents. "Come on in."

"Having a party?" Ort asked everyone at the table.

"It's book club night," Jesse said. "We're discussing *The Secret Life of J. Edgar Hoover*. Did you bring your copy?"

Susan gave him a scolding glance. His attitude wasn't helping either one of them.

Ort glanced at Steve. "Lieutenant Sloan, I'm afraid you are about to find yourself in a very uncomfortable position."

"Why?" Steve asked. "Am I under arrest?"

"No, but your friends are," Ort said, tipping his head towards Jesse and Susan.

"Oh my God," Susan said.

"Are you going to be a problem?" Ort asked Steve.

"You bet I am," Steve said. "But not here and now."

"Fair enough." Ort nodded. "Jesse Travis and Susan Travis, you are under arrest on multiple murder charges. Stand up and place your hands behind your backs."

They did as they were told. Susan shared a fearful look with Jesse. "I can't believe this is happening. I've never even had a parking ticket."

The two other agents stepped forward, patted Jesse and Susan down, and handcuffed them while Ort read them their rights.

Even though Mark had known this moment would come, it didn't make it any easier for him to take. He hated seeing his friends treated this way.

"You're making a huge mistake," he said. "All you have, at best, is circumstantial evidence against them. There are dozens of people at Community General with just as much access to all three patients as they have."

"But there are only two with their fingerprints all over the vial of West Nile virus–tainted blood that we found," Ort said. "It was hidden in a thermos in a refrigerator in the doctors' lounge."

The implication of that discovery for Mark went beyond the incrimination of Jesse and Susan. It meant that the killer was actively working to throw the investigators off track. The vial was definitely planted. But was it the killer's intention all along to frame Jesse and Susan? Or was it a desperate move that was improvised to buy time?

"Why would Jesse and Susan infect the patients they were treating?" Steve asked. "It doesn't make sense. They'd have to be incredibly stupid."

"Or arrogant," Ort said. "It wouldn't be the first time doctors and nurses have killed their patients. You've caught a few yourself."

"We couldn't have done it without Jesse and Susan's help," Steve said.

"Who better to flush out a medical murderer than two

health-care professionals with the same homicidal inclinations?" Ort asked, then motioned to his men. "Get them out of here."

"You're going to regret this," Steve said.

"Don't say a word," Mark said as Jesse and Susan were led out by the two agents. "We'll get you a lawyer and have you out on bail as quickly as possible."

Ort turned to Amanda. "You, too, Dr. Bentley. Stand up and put your hands behind your head."

"Who did I kill?" Amanda asked, getting to her feet and doing as he instructed.

"No one as far as we know," Ort said as the remaining agent patted Amanda down and handcuffed her. "Your crimes were committed against the dead. You're under arrest for the illegal procurement and sale of organs and body parts."

"There was nothing illegal about the harvesting of organs from Wethersby and Adams," Mark said. "Both patients were registered donors."

"Their organs were distributed by a reputable and legitimate biomedical company," Amanda said. "Everything was done in strict accordance with federal law."

"These charges have nothing to do with Wethersby or Adams," Ort said, "except that looking into those cases gave us the opportunity to dig deeper into the workings of your morgue."

"Then what is going on here?" Mark demanded.

"We've been investigating Dr. Bentley for months," Ort said. "We haven't found any skeletons in her closet, but we've found plenty of PVC pipe."

"What are you talking about?" Amanda asked.

"Deboning bodies and stuffing them with PVC pipes to cover your crimes. Ripping out eyeballs and selling them to the highest bidder. That sort of thing," Ort said. "You've been gutting bodies and selling the organs on the black market for years."

Mark had been expecting the FBI to come after Jesse and Susan, but he was completely blindsided by these charges. There was never a hint of impropriety surrounding Amanda or the adjunct county morgue. As far as he knew, not a single complaint had ever been filed against her by any individual or agency.

"You better have some damn good evidence to back this up," Steve said, "or she and her lawyer will debone you."

"We've raided the mortuaries Dr. Bentley has been working with in this scheme and exhumed a dozen bodies," Ort said. "It's all over for her. The best thing she can do for herself now, and for the families of the dead, is to cooperate."

"Whatever case you think you have is built on lies," Amanda said. "I'm innocent."

"And I'll prove it," Mark said. "That's a promise."

The other agent led Amanda out, informing her of her rights on the way to the door.

"You're going to want to rethink that promise," Ort said.

"You obviously don't know my father very well," Steve said. "Or what he's capable of."

"The evidence against all three of your friends is overwhelming and irrefutable," Ort said. "Once it all comes out, you will be convinced that they're guilty not only of the crimes that we've charged them with but also of betraying your trust."

And with that, Ort walked out.

CHAPTER THIRTY-THREE

Mark and Steve stood for a moment in shell-shocked silence. It was almost possible for them to believe that everything that had just happened had been a figment of their imaginations.

There were no signs that Amanda, Jesse, and Susan had been there or that the arrests had ever occurred. The Men in Black were gone from the backyard. Even Jesse's and Amanda's cars were gone, presumably towed away for forensic examination.

Mark didn't know what Ort hoped to find in the cars. Drops of West Nile virus–infected blood on the dashboard? A cooler full of body parts in the trunk?

This whole situation was unbelievable to him. And yet it had happened. Amanda, Jesse, and Susan were in FBI custody.

The enormity of the situation was almost too much for Mark to grasp. Were the murders and the organ-theft ring related? Or was it just a coincidence that the two investigations converged?

It had to be a coincidence, because Mark couldn't see how or why the two cases could be connected. But coincidences always bothered him, and this one certainly would.

He had to act. He had to do something. But where should he start? The obstacles in front of him at the moment seemed huge and insurmountable.

Mark began by prioritizing his goals and considering the most immediate and efficient way of achieving them.

"Forget what I said before about not being able to help," Steve said, interrupting Mark's thoughts. "The arrests have changed everything. I'll do whatever it takes."

Mark nodded. "Good. You can start by giving me the ownership papers to your restaurant."

* * *

Ort left Amanda sitting for hours in a windowless interrogation room at the federal building. She assumed he did it so she'd eat herself alive with anxiety and fear. But that only works if you're guilty. And since she wasn't, she was grateful for the solitude. It gave her time to calm down and think through her dire situation.

Once she got past her anger, she was able to look at her predicament objectively and methodically, approaching it as if she were analyzing a crime scene or conducting an autopsy.

The FBI believed she was using her morgue as a body farm, and according to what Ort had said at Mark's house, they had the documents and the corpses to prove it.

She didn't doubt that someone was stealing the body parts, most likely the mortuaries that Ort had raided. In order for the scheme to work, the mortician would need detailed medical histories on each donor, as well as death certificates and consent forms indicating that the harvesting was authorized. Her signature would be the natural one to forge. And since she worked closely with many of the funeral homes in the area, getting copies of her signature on similar forms wouldn't be difficult.

While it was against the law to sell body parts for profit, the middlemen between the hospitals, morgues, and universities and the end users of the organs and tissues could charge "reasonable fees" to cover processing, storage, and distribution. But nowhere in the law did it define what was "reasonable" and what wasn't.

There was also very little government oversight of procurement companies—the "body brokers"—to make sure that they were receiving their body parts from legitimate sources.

A human body, sold piece by piece, could be worth as much as $150,000 on the open market. A finger went for as little as $15, while a lower jawbone could bring nearly $4,000. Every body part had a price.

The demand for body parts far exceeded the supply, so the black market thrived and proved irresistible to people with easy access to cadavers, like those who worked at funeral homes, morgues, and the willed-body programs at universities.

If there were a hundred bodies involved, as Ort had suggested, then the funeral homes in the scheme were able to divvy as much as ten million dollars among themselves. Now that the FBI was on to them, the morticians were trying to make it look like Amanda was the criminal and they were the innocent victims.

To make that work, they would need more than forged documents with her name on them. There would also have to be a money trail that led to her. Amanda figured that they must have established some sort of offshore account in her name and regularly transferred money into it to make it appear that she was the ringleader.

What Amanda wondered was whether she was simply the convenient fall guy or if the point of the scheme all along was to frame her for a crime she didn't commit. If it was some kind of vendetta, someone had put an enormous amount of time and effort into it.

Who had such a deep and abiding hatred towards her? Whom had she wronged so grievously?

Amanda couldn't think of anyone.

So she decided that the frame wasn't personal, only practical. She expected the morticians would even offer to testify against her to lessen their own sentences or obtain immunity from prosecution.

Amanda had to admire their ingenuity, well aware that she was like a doomed fly marveling at the spider's intricate and inescapable web that ensnared her.

By the time Ort finally came to question Amanda, three hours after she was taken into custody, she may not have known the specific details of the case, but she had a pretty good idea exactly where she stood.

Which might as well have been in front of a firing squad.

Ort sat across the table from her and set a large file down in front of him. "Five months ago, a technician at MediSolutions in Phoenix was double-checking some of the medical history in the paperwork that came with a body part from your morgue," Ort said. "He tried calling one of the doctors listed in the documents and discovered no such person existed. That was odd, don't you think?"

Amanda didn't answer. Ort went on.

"So he called some of the other doctors in the documents. They were either fictitious or, if they existed, knew nothing about the donor of the body part. So this technician checked other documents from your office and found the same problems. That's when he called us."

Ort opened the file and passed some documents to Amanda. "Recognize these?"

"They are standard forms," Amanda said. "You can find them at any hospital or county morgue."

"But you can't find them with your signature on them."

"That's not my signature," Amanda said.

"It looks like your signature," Ort said. "And our handwriting experts say that it is."

"They're wrong," Amanda said.

"After we got that call from MediSolutions, we started looking into you. We discovered some interesting things. For instance, we learned that corpses were leaving your morgue gutted. Bones removed. Corneas removed. Muscle membranes removed. Just about everything was gone. The only way you could get away with that was if you were in collusion with funeral homes. We've exhumed several of those bodies. They were stuffed like scarecrows to make them presentable at funerals."

"I'm sure they were, because it was the funeral homes doing the gutting," Amanda said. "The only way they could get away with selling the body parts to legitimate procurement companies was to include convincing documentation."

Ort didn't acknowledge that he'd even heard her comment. Instead, he examined some of the papers in front of him.

"In the last year, you've removed one hundred twenty-eight corneas from bodies in your morgue without prior consent. Isn't that true?"

"Sounds about right," Amanda said.

"You were paid three hundred thirty-five dollars a pair for those corneas," he said.

"The county medical examiner's office was paid a small administrative fee," Amanda said. "MediSolutions will sell those same corneas for thirty-five hundred dollars a pair to cover their so-called reasonable costs."

"You say that like someone who thinks she deserves a piece of the action," Ort said.

"I say that because the middlemen in the human parts supply industry are violating the spirit, if not the intent, of the Uniform Anatomical Gift Act and the National Organ Transplant Act."

"Your righteous indignation would be a lot more convincing if not for your own actions," Ort said. "Claudia Grauman, the funeral director at Shreibman and Sons in Glendale, has given us a sworn statement that on more than a dozen occasions you gave her corneas that she then sold to buyers in Europe, splitting the profits with you."

"She's lying," Amanda said.

"Terence Winter, the funeral director at Schenck and Cardea in Chatsworth, has given us a sworn statement detailing several instances when you smuggled bodies of indigents and John Does out of the morgue to him, which he then sold to drug companies for the extraction of growth hormones and spinal membranes used in medications."

"He's lying, too."

Ort sighed and closed the file. "Do you deny that you routinely remove body parts without prior consent?"

"Under California law, I can remove body parts for medical training and other purposes after a reasonable effort has been made to locate family members and gain their consent," Amanda said. "I have the authority and the obligation to remove pituitary glands, corneas, and a number of other body parts under the Health and Safety Code so that they may be used to benefit others."

"'A reasonable effort' is what?" Ort asked. "Twelve hours?"

"According to the law, yes," Amanda said. "But you already know that."

"Is there anybody watching over you to make sure you are actively using those twelve short hours to find family members and get their consent?"

"No," Amanda said. "There is not."

"In fact, you're entirely on your own."

"Yes, I am."

"So if you spent no time at all, nobody would know. You could just start cutting the moment the body comes in, particularly when the corpse is an indigent or a John Doe, and fill out the documentation with fraudulent times and dates."

"I don't do that," Amanda said.

"But you *do* take body parts without consent from dozens of corpses every year."

"As I said before, I do so only as allowed by law," Amanda said. "And not for personal gain."

"So how do you explain the three-point-seven million dollars wired to your Cayman Islands account over the last two years by your funeral home partners?"

"The cost of doing business," Amanda said.

"So you admit they were paying you your cut?"

"They were paying insurance. They were establishing a money trail so that if you ever stumbled on their scheme they could point the finger at me and save themselves."

"You expect me to believe that criminals would throw away

three-point-seven million just to create the appearance that you were their ringleader?"

"It was an investment," Amanda said. "If they didn't get caught, they could always come back and get the money later. They still can, if I go to jail and you let them walk with short sentences or total immunity."

"You've got this all figured out, don't you?"

"Not as well as they do," Amanda said.

"It wasn't until the Community General morgue became an adjunct county morgue, and you were appointed as a medical examiner, that you had the opportunity to steal body parts with impunity," Ort said. "Your new role gave you an endless supply of bodies and virtual autonomy to do with them as you pleased."

"The only thing you said that's true is that I'm a medical examiner and Community General shares its morgue with the county," Amanda said. "The rest is pure fiction."

"Dr. Sloan was instrumental in creating the adjunct county morgue at Community General and getting you appointed as a medical examiner, wasn't he?"

"The medical examiner's office desperately needed additional manpower and morgue space," Amanda said. "Mark found a simple, fast, and inexpensive solution to that problem."

"And a way to make some money," Ort said.

"For Community General Hospital," Amanda said. "What are you getting at?"

"A way for you to shave a decade or two off your prison sentence," Ort said. "Testify against Dr. Sloan."

She shook her head. "I haven't committed a crime and neither has he."

Ort stood up and gathered his papers. "Everyone else has turned against you to save themselves. He's the only one who hasn't. *Yet.*"

The agent went to the door, opened it, and looked over his shoulder at her as he was stepping out.

"Think about it," he said.

She did. And the conclusions that she reached terrified her.

CHAPTER THIRTY-FOUR

The law firm of Tyrell, Dinino, and Barer specialized in representing very rich people who committed very sordid crimes. The firm's offices occupied three floors of a building at Wilshire Boulevard and Beverly Drive, the heart of wealth and power in Hollywood.

Successfully defending actors, supermodels, rock stars, and professional athletes for brazen acts of violence and depravity had turned founding partner Arthur Tyrell into a celebrity himself. Tyrell was a big man—in stature, girth, and personality—who commanded and enjoyed attention, whether in front of a jury or television cameras. In fact, he'd been spending more time lately on Court TV than in court, much to the consternation of his partners.

The problem was that much of Tyrell's reputation was based on an almost unbroken string of courtroom victories, which he doubted he could sustain.

It wasn't that he'd lost confidence in his legal and persuasive skills, but he knew a big reason for his success was that most juries would let celebrities get away with just about anything, regardless of DNA, fingerprints, eyewitness testimony, or even a signed confession. It wasn't the actor, singer, or quarterback on trial; it was all the unforgettable characters they'd portrayed, all the classic songs they'd sung, or all the incredible plays they'd made on the football field.

But that was changing. Thanks to the explosion of tabloid journalism in print, on TV, and all over the Web, as well as ubiquitous celebrity "reality" shows, the public was beginning to realize that stars weren't gods. The celebrities were just as lustful, jealous, petty, stupid, and greedy as everyone else, but they made a lot more money and were recognized on the street by strangers.

One of the major turning points in public sentiment came with the Lacey McClure case. She was the movie star Tyrell successfully defended against charges that she murdered her husband and his starlet lover. Those charges were built, in large part, on evidence gathered by Dr. Mark Sloan.

Tyrell put Mark, Steve, and Amanda on the stand and eviscerated them in front of millions of television viewers. And in doing so, he also castigated and embarrassed the LAPD, the district attorney's office, and the entire criminal justice system. He managed to get the case thrown out at the preliminary hearing, only to have his victory snatched away when Mark tricked Lacey into admitting, on live television, that she'd murdered someone else.

It shook the public's faith in actors, in the courts, and in celebrity criminal attorneys. Tyrell's caseload evaporated. He managed to get a gig for a few months as a commentator for Court TV during Lacey's subsequent murder trial, but after that his practice, and his TV career, suffered enormously.

Which was why he relished what he saw unfolding on the evening news that night on the sixty-five-inch flat-screen television in his office. Dr. Mark Sloan was getting his comeuppance.

According to the news, two of Mark Sloan's closest colleagues at Community General had been arrested by the FBI for intentionally infecting donor organs with West Nile virus, thereby causing five deaths and leaving three people in comas. It also sparked a frenzied nationwide recall of the skin, tissues, bones, and other body parts taken from two donors before they ended up in more people. The CDC, the NIH, and the FDA were coordinating that effort.

But the scandal didn't end there.

The FBI also arrested Dr. Amanda Bentley, the adjunct county medical examiner, for running a massive organ-theft ring out of the hospital morgue with the help of two local mortuaries. More than a hundred bodies intended for burial or cremation may have been deboned and gutted, the valuable body parts sold with forged documentation on the black market.

The Community General transplant program and the two local funeral homes were shut down. The FBI hinted that more arrests were in the offing.

DA Neal Burnside immediately spun the scandal to his advantage, making a statement to the press on the steps outside of City Hall.

"These horrifying crimes are a direct result of grossly irresponsible decisions by Chief Masters and his predecessors, giving unprecedented law enforcement authority to a civilian," Burnside said. "The chief has allowed Dr. Mark Sloan, and the two doctors charged with multiple counts of murder today, to enjoy unsupervised and unrestricted access to LAPD resources. It was Chief Masters who, among others, succumbed to Dr. Sloan's back-channel lobbying to have an adjunct county morgue set up in *his* hospital and run by *his* protégée, Dr. Amanda Bentley, who now stands accused of organ theft. It was Chief Masters's negligence and Dr. Sloan's hubris that created the lawless environment that made these tragic deaths and unspeakable desecrations possible."

Tyrell had leveled many of the same charges at Mark Sloan and the LAPD during the Lacey McClure case. Although Lacey turned out to be guilty, that didn't change the fact that the LAPD's relationship with Mark and his unrestricted access to the morgue were legally and ethically questionable.

But somehow that all got forgotten in the media frenzy that followed Lacey's second arrest for murder and the subsequent trial.

What people remembered was that Lacey was guilty, that Tyrell was wrong, that the DA's office bungled its case, and that Dr. Mark Sloan was right all along.

For those reasons alone, it was nice to see Mark getting trashed.

Even so, Tyrell had surprisingly mixed feelings after watching the newscast. For one thing, Tyrell intensely disliked Burnside and hated the idea that the DA had found a way to use the scandal to gain political points in his mayoral bid.

The scandal also promised to be the biggest story of the year in Los Angeles and was certain to garner national, if not international, attention for weeks.

The worst part was that the most Tyrell could hope to get out of it was a chance to give a sound bite to CNN about his experiences with Mark, Burnside, and Masters. If he was lucky, it would add up to thirty seconds on some late-night broadcast.

All of this was on Arthur Tyrell's mind when his secretary buzzed him on the speakerphone.

She informed him that he had an unscheduled guest outside his door who insisted on being seen immediately.

"Who is it?" Tyrell asked.

"Dr. Mark Sloan," she said. "He says you know him."

Arthur Tyrell smiled to himself, glanced up gratefully to the heavens, and said, "Send him right in."

CHAPTER THIRTY-FIVE

The Commons in Calabasas was a shopping center designed to look like a village in France, except for the Ralph's supermarket and Rolex clock tower.

Tanis Archer sat at an outdoor table in the shadow of the clock tower, a set of iPod earphones plugged into the laptop open beside her. She was sipping a latte and eavesdropping on Tony Sisk, who was having dinner at an Italian restaurant fifty yards away, when Steve sat down across from her.

"I never knew this corner of the Valley existed," Tanis said. "I'm still not sure that it does. Look at these people, Steve. They all look as if they were manufactured at a mannequin factory."

It was true. The people were too attractive to be real. But Steve wasn't in the mood for people-watching or idle chitchat.

"Has Sisk said anything about Sweeney?" he asked.

"Nothing besides having his junior lawyers file the necessary paperwork to keep the habeas corpus hearing on track for next week," Tanis said. "Are you ready to relieve me from this arduous duty?"

"We're done," Steve said.

"We're on assignment until the chief says we aren't," Tanis said.

"Not anymore," Steve said. "The Web site will tape every conversation whether we're here to listen to it or not. We have other priorities now."

"Like what?"

"Like getting Amanda, Jesse, and Susan out of jail," Steve said. "And catching a serial killer who has murdered five people already."

Tanis yanked the earplugs out of her ears. "You sure know how to get a girl's attention. Would it be asking too much for you to give me just a few more details?"

Steve told her everything. As he was getting to the end of his story, Tanis started typing something on her laptop.

"Am I boring you?" Steve asked.

"They've got free WiFi here," Tanis said.

"If you're checking your e-mail, I'm going to throw that laptop into the street."

"I'm logging on to the Anti-Terrorism Strike Force computer, tough guy. I'm going to get you the names of the funeral homes that were raided and find out everything there is to know about the people who own and operate them."

"You can do that?"

"It's what you wanted, isn't it?"

"Well," Steve said, "yeah."

"One of the few perks of working in Anti-Terror is that, in the wake of 9/11, law enforcement agencies are supposed to be sharing intel. We do it mostly by sharing databases. It makes it easier to identify possible terrorist cells and for unscrupulous cops like me to snoop where I don't belong."

"Can't you get caught?"

"Getting caught is inevitable," Tanis said. "If that wasn't true, we'd both be out of a job."

"We may be anyway," Steve said.

"Your doom and gloom are distracting me." Tanis held out her empty cup to Steve without taking her eyes off her screen. "Get me a latte and a raspberry tart. This may take a while."

Tyrell listened to Mark's story as if he were hearing it for the first time. It was different from what he'd learned from the newscast, and a bit more detailed. Tyrell made a few notes, but mostly he studied Mark, taking his measure.

Did Mark Sloan meet the criteria for being a client of Arthur Tyrell's?

First and foremost, a client had to be well-known and well-off.

Mark wasn't a celebrity in the usual sense, but people certainly knew who he was. And if they didn't before, they knew now. At this isolated moment in time, Mark Sloan was poised to be the most famous man in Los Angeles. It was a title he could easily hold, in the absence of another major scandal or a Tom Cruise movie, for weeks.

As far as wealth, Tyrell assumed that Mark was a man of some means, though hardly at the same level as his previous clients. Could Mark Sloan afford him? Probably not. Ordinarily, that would be the end of any consideration for clienthood. But these weren't ordinary times.

"I've used my home and Steve's restaurant as collateral to secure their bail," Mark said, passing some papers to Tyrell from the bail bond company. "As long as the bail amount for Amanda, Jesse, and Susan combined doesn't exceed three million dollars."

Tyrell set aside his legal pad and pen. "Why me, Dr. Sloan? After what I did to you, your son, and Dr. Bentley, I should be the last attorney you'd ever want to hire."

"It's precisely because of what you did to us that I want you to represent them," Mark said. "The case against Lacey McClure was as strong as any I've ever made. The preliminary hearing should have been a mere formality, the first step on her journey to prison. If she'd had any other defense attorney, it would have been. But you tore the case apart. You put me on trial instead and you won. I need that brilliance on my side this time."

"You're just appealing to my ego because you can't afford me," Tyrell said.

"Is it working?"

Tyrell looked Mark in the eye. "You don't like me, do you?"

"Not much," Mark said.

"Just so we understand each other, I believe everything I said in court about your hubris," Tyrell said. "It's amazing to me that you've been able to get away with dabbling in homicide investigations for as long as you have, and set up that little crime lab for yourself at Community General, without anyone noticing how outrageous it is."

"This could be that moment," Mark said.

Tyrell smiled. "I can't have you second-guessing me or my strategy. We do everything my way or I walk."

"Fair enough," Mark said.

"No one talks to the press but me. Too often my clients try to convince the public through the media that they are innocent. That's not what the media are there for."

"What are they there for?"

"To be used, Dr. Sloan. They are there to be manipulated as necessary to achieve whatever goals I may have at any given time," Tyrell said. "Do I have your word that your friends will agree to my terms?"

Mark nodded.

"I'll need a $150,000 retainer," Tyrell said. "But with three clients and two complex cases, I will go through that pretty fast."

Mark took out his checkbook, made out the check, and handed it to the attorney. "You haven't asked me if they're guilty."

"I never will. It's a meaningless question. My clients know if they are guilty or not," Tyrell said. "All that matters to them and to me is that I win."

CHAPTER THIRTY-SIX

At first Amanda was shocked when Arthur Tyrell walked into the interrogation room, introduced himself to Ort as her lawyer, and sent the FBI agent out of the room.

Tyrell was the man who had eviscerated her on the witness stand, on live television, during Lacey McClure's preliminary hearing. But then, remembering that, she was able to see the perverse logic behind Mark's thinking in hiring the man.

It didn't stop her from hating Tyrell, though.

"Are you sure you've got the right person?" she asked. "I'm not rich, famous, or guilty."

Tyrell took the seat that Ort had vacated. "On the contrary, Dr. Bentley. You have a sizable trust fund and, if the government is to be believed, millions in an offshore account. I should also inform you that in the short time you've been in custody you have become, if not a celebrity, certainly widely known and notorious. As far as guilty goes, who really cares?"

Tyrell proceeded to lay out the ground rules that Mark had agreed to on her behalf, got her promise to follow them, and told her what he saw as the weaknesses in the government's case.

There was only one.

"Reasonable doubt," he said.

"That's it?"

"The evidence against you appears to be voluminous, detailed, and convincing," Tyrell said.

"It's all fake," Amanda said. "The morticians are lying to save themselves, my signatures were forged, and money was transferred to an account I never opened."

"Then that is what I will make the jury believe," Tyrell said. "Or at least accept as being possible."

She told him about Ort's interrogation, and what she'd learned from it, and what she'd said. Tyrell made some notes and kept shaking his head disapprovingly as she spoke.

"You shouldn't have said anything," Tyrell said. "You didn't help yourself."

"I didn't hurt myself either."

"Don't say another word to anyone but me," Tyrell said. "Remember, every word you say damages your case. The less they know, the better. From now on, I will do all the talking. Is that clear?"

Amanda nodded. "I think I know why I was framed."

"You were a convenient scapegoat for their crimes," Tyrell said.

"That's only part of it," she said. "It's much bigger than that."

Tyrell glanced at his watch and got up. "We'll have plenty of time to discuss it all. But first, I'd like to get you, Dr. Travis, and his wife out of here, and I still have to meet with them. Your arraignment is at eight a.m. tomorrow."

"I'll try to make it," she said.

CHAPTER THIRTY-SEVEN

Mark spent the night slogging through the Community General employee shift schedules covering the days when the West Nile virus patient and the two donors were being treated.

There was nothing else for him to do. Steve was investigating the funeral homes that were supposedly conspiring with Amanda to sell body parts. Arthur Tyrell was busy advising his new clients and preparing to argue for their release on bail in front of the federal magistrate in the morning. That left Mark all by himself in the beach house, hunched over his laptop and tanked on coffee, toiling to find whoever had infected the organ donors with the virus.

The name of the killer was on the screen in front of him—he knew that. He just didn't know which name it was. But he would find out. Mark wouldn't stop until the real killer was behind bars and Jesse and Susan were cleared.

This could be that moment.

His own words kept ringing in his ears as he worked, and he didn't know why. Was it his fear of personal ruination bubbling to the surface? He couldn't let Burnside's speech get to him or allow his own selfish anxieties to distract him now. He needed to devote all his energy and attention to proving his friends innocent.

They deserved nothing less than that.

For years they had risked their careers and even their lives helping him solve homicides. They didn't have to do it. Chasing murderers wasn't part of their jobs, at least not until Amanda became a medical examiner, which she did at his friendly urging. Did she really want it? Or did she do it to please him?

Amanda and Jesse assisted in his unofficial investigations out of loyalty and respect. Susan did it out of love and devotion to her husband. But he knew he could always depend on them to put his investigations before everything else in their lives.

How often had he taken advantage of that? What had he ever done for them besides use them as his field investigators and players in his cons?

Now he was going to pay them back for everything they had done for him. For once, he wouldn't think about himself. He was going to be as devoted to them as they were to him. His own fate didn't matter.

This could be that moment.

Okay, so what if it was? Even if he wasn't doing anything to defend himself, it wasn't as if helping his friends was an entirely selfless act. Their fate was his own. If they went down, he was sure to follow. So the harder he worked for them now, the more he did for himself.

But that rationale didn't silence the voice in his head.

This could be that moment.

Mark pressed on despite the nagging echo from his conversation with Tyrell. He would confront his fears or his guilt or whatever the hell was bothering him later. The phrase became the elevator music in his head as he worked.

He printed out the work schedules and the lists of employees on them. He copied the information by hand to the three dry-erase boards, one for the initial virus patient and one for each organ donor, that he'd set up on easels in the living room.

By dawn, out of all the names that intersected across the three boards, a dozen stood out to Mark as the likeliest suspects. It had more to do with gut instinct than tangible clues, but he was willing to take the gamble that he was right.

The twelve people he selected were nurses, doctors, orderlies, and technicians who wouldn't create any suspicion if they were seen at the bedsides of any of the three patients. But either by chance or by premeditation, there were some last-minute changes in their usual schedules that put them in the hospital when there was little likelihood that they would be seen with the three patients.

Mark needed more information to narrow the field of suspects even further. He would check their personnel files to learn more about them and then talk with their supervisors to find out why their schedules had been rearranged.

He was attempting to pull up the personnel files when he abruptly lost his connection. He tried to log back on, but when he typed his user name and password, he was sent to an error page that read:

Access denied. Contact the system administrator for further information.

Mark tried again and got the same message. Either his forays through the Community General database had been discovered or Janet Dorcott was simply taking preemptive measures. Either way, his task had just gotten a lot more complicated.

This could be that moment.

He glanced at his watch. It was 6:20. He doubted that either Janet or her minions were in the hospital yet. Whoever had locked him out of the system probably got an angry call from Janet this morning and booted him off from home. It left him no choice but to go to the hospital to look at the hard copies of the personnel files.

But to play it safe, he wouldn't walk in through the main lobby, the ER, or the employees' entrance.

He had a key to the loading dock. From there, it was only a short walk to the personnel department file room.

Mark had a key to that door, too. He had a key to every door in the hospital—a fact that, if he hadn't been the one investigating the crimes, would have made him a pretty good suspect for the killings.

CHAPTER THIRTY-EIGHT

The personnel files weren't giving Mark much hope until he opened the one for Mercy Reynolds, the utilization nurse. She was in the hospital at all the right times and could wander freely into every department. But that was true of the other eleven suspects, too. What made Mercy especially interesting was the name of her previous employer.

She'd worked for MediSolutions International, the organ-procurement company that distributed the tainted organs from Wethersby and Adams and many of the body parts that Amanda was accused of illegally harvesting from corpses.

Of course, it could just be a coincidence.

MediSolutions had been distributing body parts harvested from donors at Community General for a decade. There was nothing unusual about the company's handling of the organs in both cases. It was one of two companies that distributed organs, body parts, and tissues from almost every hospital, morgue, and mortuary in Southern California.

But where crime was concerned, Mark believed that one coincidence was suspicious and two were evidence of a plan set in motion.

All of which led to one irrefutable truth for Mark.

Mercy Reynolds was the killer.

She was the one who had injected West Nile virus into Bruce Wethersby and Corinne Adams as they lay brain-dead in the ICU.

She was the one who had framed Jesse and Susan.

Mark didn't have any evidence, but he knew he was right. He could feel it, as if she were standing right behind him, breathing on his neck.

It's me, Mark. I did it. Catch me if you can.

He copied all of Mercy's personal information from the file, put it back where he'd found it, and left the room, his heart racing. As soon as he stepped into the corridor, he saw Janet Dorcott marching his way, flanked by two security guards.

"I knew after we shut you out of the computer system that we'd find you either here or in the patient records room," she said. "You can't resist violating the rules, can you?"

"Amanda, Jesse, and Susan are innocent," Mark said. "The sooner I can prove it, the better it will be for them and this hospital."

"You astonish me, Dr. Sloan. I can't decide if you're playing dumb or if your arrogance and sense of entitlement have blinded you to reality."

"The reality is that there's a killer still stalking the halls of Community General," Mark said. "And until she's caught, patients are in grave danger."

"*You* are the danger, Dr. Sloan. Everywhere you go, people die. That's not good for a hospital. That's not good for anyone," she said. "You're fired. Get out and don't come back."

This could be that moment.

The voice in his head this time wasn't his. It was Mercy, whispering in his ear. He actually turned to look for her. No one was there, of course, and it left Mark feeling naked. He shivered.

"You have no grounds to fire me," he said.

"There are so many to choose from," she said. "Let's start with gross incompetence, violation of patient privacy, and criminal malfeasance. Two doctors and one nurse under your direct supervision are in jail for crimes committed at this hospital. We are cooperating with local, state, and federal authorities investigating your supervision of the adjunct county medical examiner's office and your use of hospital resources for personal purposes."

"The board will never stand for this," Mark said.

"It was a unanimous vote, and the severance offer is rescinded," Janet said. "You get nothing. We're finished with you."

"I haven't done anything wrong," Mark said. "Neither have Amanda, Jesse, and Susan."

He felt he had to say it, even though it didn't matter and wouldn't change anything.

His forty-year career at Community General was over.

Although he'd been ready for a change for some time, he didn't want to be forced out under a cloud of scandal. He wanted to leave on his own terms, with his reputation and legacy intact, his family and friends happy and safe.

Apparently it wasn't going to happen that way.

"You will find your personal belongings in boxes on the loading dock. Pick them up by five o'clock today or they'll go in the Dumpster." Janet motioned to the guards. "Show Dr. Sloan out. If he ever enters this hospital again, even if it's on a gurney with his brains spilling from the back of his head, drag him out of here."

Mark turned and walked out, the guards following behind him. And as he went, the voice whispered to him again. Only now it wasn't Mercy's voice, and it wasn't his own. But it was familiar nonetheless. He didn't so much hear the words this time. He felt them.

The moment has come.

CHAPTER THIRTY-NINE

Mark couldn't fit all the boxes in his car, so he found the few personal items that were important to him, consolidated them into one box, and stuck it in his car with his framed degrees and commendations. The rest could be trashed, along with what was left of his career and his reputation.

It seemed that the unrelenting loop in his head was right. His moment had come. But even more troubling than that was what he'd learned.

Mercy Reynolds was the killer.

And the murders she'd committed and the organ-theft scandal were somehow linked. But how?

Only Mercy Reynolds knew.

He looked back at the hospital, wondering if she was in there, looking out at him through one of the windows, laughing to herself.

She'd beaten them all. Amanda, Jesse, and Susan were in jail. Mark's career was in ruins.

Why did she do it? Was it self-preservation, her way of covering her crimes, or was it something more?

Mark took out his cell phone and called Steve, who answered on the first ring.

"Where are you?" Mark asked.

"Back at the house, looking at your boards," Steve said. "You've been busy."

"You need to find Mercy Reynolds, a utilization nurse at Community General. She's the killer." All Mark heard in reply was the hiss of static. "Steve? Are you there?"

"Yeah," Steve said. "You found the killer in one night?"

"I actually saw her with Corinne Adams once," Mark said.

"For all I know, Mercy had just finished injecting her with the virus."

"What proof do you have?"

"None at all," Mark said.

"Did you sleep last night?"

"Did you?" Mark asked.

"I'm just saying you may be exhausted and it may be affecting your judgment."

"Find her, Steve," Mark said and gave him her home address from her personnel records.

"Okay, I will," Steve said. "Don't you want to know what I've found out?"

"Of course," Mark said, pacing beside his car.

"There's an organized-crime connection to the two funeral homes in this body-parts ring," Steve said. "They were both owned by Gordon Ganza. The funeral homes were investments made on Ganza's behalf by Malcolm Trainor."

Mark stopped in his tracks, stunned by the news.

Ganza was a major figure in organized crime in Southern California who was killed a few years back. Mark knew that only too well, since he'd been the one framed for the killing by Malcolm Trainor, Ganza's accountant. Trainor engineered the frame from prison, where he had been serving a life sentence for the murder of his wife, a crime that Mark had solved.

"After Ganza's murder, his sons sold off everything but the funeral homes," Steve continued. "I guess they knew better than anyone that death is a booming business."

Could Trainor be responsible for what was happening to Amanda, Jesse, and Susan? Mark wondered. It certainly wouldn't be the first time Trainor had managed to pull off a complex criminal conspiracy from within his cell at Sunrise Valley.

This could be that moment.

There was a reason why those words had haunted him all night.

It was his subconscious screaming the answer to the puzzle to him, over and over and over again.

And yet he still didn't hear it.

Now he did.

He knew why Mercy Reynolds tainted the organs with West Nile virus.

He knew why the funeral homes claimed Amanda was supplying them with body parts.

The only thing he didn't know was how it was all done.

But he knew *why*.

When Mark spoke, he tried to keep his voice even and calm. If he told Steve what he was thinking, his son would think he was crazy. He had no proof at all to back up his conclusions.

Not yet, anyway.

There was still one common element of the two cases left to explore.

"Steve, what do you know about MediSolutions International?"

"I was just getting to that," Steve said. "They're based in Phoenix. The guy who runs it is Noah Dent. Wasn't he once the chief administrator at Community General?"

One coincidence is suspicious. Two coincidences are a plan. Three are a conspiracy.

In his short time at Community General, Noah Dent had closed the adjunct county medical examiner's office, laid off half the nurses, and tried to fire Mark.

But then, without explanation, Dent abruptly reversed all his actions, quit his job, and disappeared. Mark never looked into Dent's sudden change of heart and mysterious resignation, though he suspected that Jesse had motivated it in some way. Dent left, and that was all that mattered to Mark. Good riddance.

Now Dent had reemerged at MediSolutions and at the center of the two scandals that plagued Community General, leading to the morgue's being shut down and Mark's getting fired. Had Dent somehow achieved what he'd set out to do at Community General after all?

Whatever the explanation, it was clear that Mark's lack of interest in pursuing the mystery was coming back to haunt him.

Like everything else.

"Find Mercy Reynolds," Mark said.

"I told you that I would," Steve said.

"Find her fast, Steve. She's the key to it all. The body-parts ring. The murders. Everything."

"The two cases are connected?"

"If we can get Mercy to talk, we can clear Amanda, Jesse, and Susan."

"Where are you going to be?"

"Pursuing another angle," Mark said. He hung up before his son could press him any further.

CHAPTER FORTY

Steve hurried out of the beach house and was surprised to see Chief Masters's Lincoln Town Car parked out front, at the edge of the private road that ran parallel to the Pacific Coast Highway. The tinted rear window slid down as Steve approached. Masters sat in the backseat, scowling.

"Get in," the chief said.

"I'm in a hurry." Steve stood outside the door and didn't make a move to open it. "Can we make this quick, sir?"

"Have you made any progress on your assignment?"

"Everything is in place, but we haven't learned anything yet," Steve said. "We'll let you know when something comes up."

"Then what's your rush?"

"I have work to do," Steve said.

"Not if it involves the trafficking of stolen body parts from the adjunct county morgue or the two doctors accused of infecting organ donors with West Nile virus," the chief said. "They don't concern you."

"My friends are in trouble, and Burnside is using the bogus charges against them to smear my father," Steve said. "I'm concerned."

"Let me rephrase that," the chief said. "We're talking about federal cases, which are outside the jurisdiction of the LAPD. And even if they weren't, you have a conflict of interest that would exclude you from being part of either investigation."

"You've ordered me to eavesdrop without a warrant on the private conversations between a defense attorney and his client," Steve said. "You are in no position to lecture me on jurisdiction, ethics, or the finer points of the law."

"I'm the chief of police," Masters said, his face taut with anger. "I'll lecture you on whatever the hell I want to, and you'll do as you are told. Burnside is using your father and these arrests to attack me. If you and your dad start investigating, you will be playing right into Burnside's hands."

"You expect me to turn my back on my father and abandon my closest friends?"

"If Burnside discovers that Dr. Sloan is using LAPD resources for his own purposes, it will confirm all the allegations that he's made. It would be disastrous."

"For you," Steve said.

"For everyone," Masters said. "Stay out of it and let the FBI investigation run its course."

"Even if it means my friends are imprisoned and my father's reputation is ruined."

"Yes," the chief said.

"I can't live with that," Steve said.

"Too damn bad," the chief said. "You have no choice."

"Sure I do," Steve said. He reached into his jacket, took out his badge, and tossed it into the limo. "Problem solved. I'm a private citizen now."

"You don't want to do that."

Steve stood up straight. "I want to do whatever I can to help my father and my friends."

The chief picked up the badge. "Without this, you're no good to them anyway."

"It's nice to know you think so highly of my detective skills."

"Have you forgotten about Carter Sweeney?" the chief said.

"He's your problem now," Steve said.

"You're deluding yourself if you honestly believe that," the chief said and nodded to his driver.

The Town Car pulled away.

Steve watched as the vehicle drove up the driveway to the Pacific Coast Highway. As it surged forward into the traffic, the chief threw Steve's badge out the window into the plants along the shoulder.

The badge glinted in the morning sun. It could have been a crushed beer can, a shard of glass, or some other piece of glittering trash.

Steve walked over and picked it up. The badge was dented. Somehow, that seemed fitting. He brushed the badge off on his pants leg and put it in his pocket.

His cell phone rang. He took it out and glanced at the caller ID on the readout. It was Tanis Archer.

"What's up?" Steve asked.

"Tony Sisk just got a very interesting call at his house," Tanis said. "You'll never guess who is demanding an immediate face-to-face meeting with Carter Sweeney."

Oh hell, Steve thought.

"Erase the recording," Steve said.

"The chief is going to find out that your father is meeting with Sweeney," Tanis said. "He'll probably get a call the moment Mark shows up at the prison gates."

"That's not why I want you to delete the recording. I don't want my father tied in any way to these illegal wiretaps," Steve said. "He's got enough problems."

"And he thinks that seeing Carter Sweeney is going to make things better?" Tanis said. "If your dad was smart, he'd run off to a secluded beach somewhere until after the election. Why does he want to see Sweeney?"

That was a good question. Steve didn't have the answer, and he was angry with his father for not confiding in him.

He could understand why his father might want to confront Malcolm Trainor. At least there was a strand that connected Trainor in some way to the players in the body-parts case.

But why Carter Sweeney?

Did his father think that Sweeney was responsible for what was happening to Amanda, Jesse, and Susan?

If so, based on what? There was nothing tying Sweeney to those cases.

It was insane. And that, Steve realized, was probably why his father didn't tell him anything about his suspicions.

"I don't want to get into it now," Steve told Tanis. "I'll tell you all about it later."

"You don't know, do you?"

"I need you to find out everything you can about Mercy Reynolds, a nurse at Community General."

"Does she have something to do with Sweeney?"

"I'm hoping you can tell me," Steve said.

"Oh, boy," Tanis said. "This is bad."

"Frankly," Steve said, "I think you're being overly optimistic."

CHAPTER FORTY-ONE

Amanda slept soundly on the hard cot in her cold, miserable jail cell. She could sleep anywhere, regardless of whatever discomfort or stress she was experiencing.

"It's like a superpower," Jesse had once told her.

It wasn't quite that great, but it was a handy skill nonetheless. She was sure it was what allowed her to juggle two demanding jobs and not collapse from exhaustion.

She was awakened by a guard at six a.m., given a tray of dry toast, scrambled eggs, and a lukewarm cup of horrible coffee. For her appearance in court, the guards let her change out of her yellow county jail jumpsuit into the clothes she was arrested in. She was handcuffed and escorted to a van, which took her to the federal courthouse a few blocks away.

Arthur Tyrell was already in the courtroom, as were Jesse and Susan, a prosecutor, and several reporters, who had notebooks ready, pens poised for action.

Tyrell was immaculately dressed in a tailored suit. He exuded power and confidence.

Jesse and Susan were both disheveled and pale, with dark circles around their eyes. They stood with their shoulders touching, the only reassuring physical contact they could manage to give each other under the circumstances. They seemed relieved to see Amanda, a familiar and rested face.

"How are you holding up?" Amanda whispered as she stepped up beside them.

"Better now that I've seen the two of you," Jesse said with a smile.

Amanda found herself warmed by the smile, which she returned with one of her own.

"I'm finally past being terrified," Susan said. "It took too much energy. I'm so tired now that all this seems surreal."

"It's having Arthur Tyrell represent us that makes it feel that way," Amanda said. "Our world has definitely tipped off its axis."

"I just want to go home," Susan said.

"That's our next stop," Jesse said.

The federal magistrate came in through a back door and took his seat at the high bench. He was in his sixties and tried to hide his enormous bald spot by combing over a few strands of hair from either side of his head. It was a wasted effort.

The federal prosecutor, a stick figure of a woman in a dark suit that made her skin appear white as chalk, spoke first, laying out the charges against Jesse and Susan.

Tyrell spoke up. "My clients are upstanding members of the community who have saved countless lives. Not only that, but they have aided law enforcement on many occasions. To accuse them of these crimes, on entirely circumstantial evidence, is an affront to justice as well as to basic common sense. There are more than a dozen other people you could arrest at Community General using the same circumstantial evidence."

"Susan Travis treated the West Nile virus patient as well as the two donors. Her husband, Dr. Travis, was the surgeon who supervised the testing of the donors and harvested their organs," the prosecutor said. "And the fingerprints of both of them were on the vial of the patient's virus-infected blood hidden in the doctors' lounge refrigerator. The only thing missing here is a signed confession."

"Which is what the prosecution would need to convince any jury on such preposterously thin evidence," Tyrell said. "Dr. Travis and his wife are innocent."

"Save the drama for the trial, Mr. Tyrell," the magistrate said, turning to the prosecutor. "What is your recommendation?"

"These are two cold-blooded thrill killers who preyed on the vulnerable and the sick. They represent a grave danger to society if they are released," the prosecutor argued. "We oppose bail and ask that they be held in custody pending trial."

"That's ridiculous," Tyrell said. "These are two upstanding professionals with no priors who have dedicated their lives to the betterment of their fellow man. We ask that the court release them on bail pending trial."

The judge didn't take even a moment to consider the arguments.

"Given the heinous nature of these allegations, I share the government's concerns. Bail is denied, and the accused are remanded pending trial." The judge banged his gavel. "Next case."

Tyrell blinked hard, surprised. He wasn't used to losing. He didn't know what to say to his clients, not that he had much of a chance to speak. The guards were already stepping forward to take them away.

Jesse and Susan looked at each other in shock. Realizing that they had only a few more seconds together, they leaned toward each other to kiss, but before their lips could touch, they were pulled away by the guards and taken out the back door.

"I love you," Jesse called out.

"I love you, too," Susan replied, her chin trembling.

And then they were gone, on their way back to their cells to ponder their uncertain futures.

Amanda stepped forward, shaking more with rage than fear.

"That went well," she said to Tyrell. "Should we bet on my chances now?"

Tyrell didn't look at her.

The prosecutor informed the court of the charges against Amanda and the evidence that backed them up.

"Given her considerable financial resources here and overseas, we believe Dr. Bentley presents a significant flight risk," the prosecutor concluded. "We therefore ask the court to keep her in custody pending trial."

"Once again, the government is overreacting and overreaching. Dr. Bentley is a respected pathologist and has served with distinction as an adjunct county medical examiner, working hand in hand with law enforcement," Tyrell said. "She has deep roots in the community and is eager for her day in court. She will gladly surrender her passport and even submit to wearing a tracking device. Given these facts, there is no reasonable argument for keeping her in custody. We request that she be released on bail immediately."

The prosecutor opened her mouth to speak, but the judge held up his hand to halt her.

"I don't need to hear any more. If the charges are valid, there is no telling how much money Dr. Bentley has squirreled away in off-shore accounts to aid any possible evasion of justice. I agree that she presents a considerable flight risk. I am denying bail and remanding the accused to the county jail."

Once again the gavel fell. Amanda wasn't surprised at the outcome, but Tyrell looked dumbfounded.

"I have a message for you to give Mark," she said to Tyrell as the guards approached her. "Tell him it's Sweeney."

CHAPTER FORTY-TWO

Carter Sweeney and his attorney, Tony Sisk, were waiting in the visitors' room when Mark arrived. Sisk looked uncomfortable, his brow dappled with sweat, but his client was almost giddy, a big smile on his face.

"This is an unexpected treat, especially after our last meeting. You seemed a bit peeved when you left," Sweeney said. "I honestly didn't expect to see you again until our lunch."

Mark tipped his head towards Sisk. "What is he doing here?"

"His presence makes this conversation an attorney-client meeting, which is protected from eavesdropping," Sweeney said. "Not that I don't trust my jailers to respect my civil rights."

Sisk cleared his throat. "I want to say, for the record, that I am very uncomfortable with this."

"There is no record," Sweeney said. "That's the beauty of it, Tony. You can say whatever is on your mind."

"This is a mistake," Sisk said. "*That's* what's on my mind."

"Duly noted," Sweeney said, turning to Mark. "Please, have a seat. Relax. Tell me the latest gossip. What's Lindsay Lohan's weight these days? What country will Angelina adopt from next?"

Mark took a seat across from the two men. "Since you went to such pains to establish that we can speak freely, I'm assuming that you know why I'm here."

"Because you like me," Sweeney said. "You really, really like me."

"Amanda has been arrested for illegally procuring and selling body parts through the morgue," Mark said. "Jesse and Susan have been charged with murder. They're accused of infecting organ donors with West Nile virus, causing the deaths of several organ recipients."

"How awful," Sweeney said.

"They're innocent," Mark said.

"Aren't we all?" Sweeney said.

"They've been framed. It's a plot that's probably been years in the making and the execution, and you're behind it," Mark said. "That's why you called me here before, to give me a little preview of what was coming."

"Let's say, for the sake of argument, that I am the mastermind behind this ingenious plot," Sweeney said, winking at Mark.

"Oh please," Sisk said. "Let's not."

"It seems to me that your past has finally caught up with you," Sweeney said. "That's what this is all about. It's time for you to atone for your sins, my friend."

"I haven't committed any," Mark said.

"We're all sinners, Mark."

"Not on your scale."

"Come now, you're being modest. This facility is full of people that you have deprived of life, liberty, and everything they hold dear."

"They have no one to blame but themselves."

"The same could be said of you and your present worries," Sweeney said. "These people that I'm talking about are a very clever, charming bunch. I really like them. We've become quite close over the years, particularly Malcolm Trainor and myself. And we all share one thing in common. You, Mark."

"I'm touched," Mark said.

"One of the problems with prison is that it doesn't offer a very rich artistic or cultural environment. There isn't anything to really engage our intellectual curiosity and keep our minds occupied," Sweeney said. "The fact is, those of us who haven't been executed yet don't really have anything better to do with our time than think of ways for you to experience some measure of our living hell."

Mark thought of all the murderers he knew who were contained within these prison walls. They certainly had the combined knowledge, experience, contacts, and resources to pull off the audacious, meticulously planned, and undoubtedly expensive criminal plot that had ensnared his friends.

"Thinking is not the same as acting," Sisk said. "For instance, you might imagine strangling your nagging wife, but that doesn't mean you've done it or that you will ever do it. Conceding that you may have certain thoughts is not to be construed, in any way, shape, or form, as an admission of having committed criminal acts."

"Thank you for that ponderous and pointless clarification," Sweeney said.

"Why are you admitting to this?" Mark said.

"He's most emphatically *not* admitting to anything," Sisk stammered, his face turning red. "Didn't you hear a word I said?"

Sweeney ignored Sisk and smiled thinly at Mark.

"There would be no pleasure in pulling off a scheme like this if the victim didn't know who was doing it and why."

"Amanda, Jesse, and Susan haven't done anything to you or the others in here."

"They've assisted you in your investigations," Sweeney said. "But, more importantly, you care about them. You are feeling their pain. You are feeling their helplessness."

"If you hate me so much, why go after them?" Mark asked. "Why don't you just kill me?"

"Carter Sweeney is not a killer. He would never hurt anyone," Sisk said. "This is a hypothetical discussion about an alleged conspiracy that is merely a product of your irrational paranoia, arising from your complicity in what you know to be the unjust, cruel, and inhuman incarceration of my client."

"Now *that* was good stuff," Sweeney said, nodding with approval. "You should come see Tony's show in Los Angeles Superior Court tomorrow, Mark. I'm sure he'll be even better."

"You haven't answered my question," Mark said.

"You're an old man. Your life doesn't mean as much to you as the lives of those you care about. Besides, killing is quick. The people in here are suffering. You should suffer, too," Sweeney said. "The idea is for you to lose everything and everyone that's important to you, to leave you alone and miserable for the rest of your long life in a prison of our making. You don't have to be in here to be imprisoned."

"Now that I know what you're doing," Mark said, "I can stop you."

"This has all been hypothetical, right, Tony?" Sweeney said.

"Absolutely," Sisk said. "A wild flight of fancy to engage the imagination and pass the time."

"And even if it wasn't, there's nothing you can do," Sweeney said. "The job is done, and the people who are responsible for it are already serving life sentences or facing execution. In a sense, they've attained a state of absolute freedom to do as they please."

"You say that as if you're not one of them," Mark said.

"I'm not," Sweeney said. "I'm getting out soon. I don't want to miss our lunch date."

CHAPTER FORTY-THREE

Mercy Reynolds lived in a tiny bungalow that had halfhearted Spanish intentions and was crowded amidst other similar bungalows north of Hollywood Boulevard, close enough to the Hollywood Bowl to hear the music on a warm summer night.

These were the kind of bungalows that shouted "Los Angeles" to location managers trying to re-create the 1940s for movies and TV shows. Steve felt like he should be wearing a fedora and smoking a cigarette as he approached Mercy's front door.

He'd called Community General Hospital first and was told that Mercy hadn't shown up for work or called in sick. Steve took that as a hint that she'd fled while the attention of the FBI was still focused on Jesse and Susan.

She had an overly ornate wrought-iron knocker on her door. Over the years, the knocker had chipped away at the paint underneath it. The wear and tear of popularity.

He used his ornate knuckles to announce himself instead of the knocker.

There was no answer.

He knocked again. Still there was no answer.

Steve tried the doorknob. The door was unlocked.

He had mixed feelings about unlocked doors. On the one hand, it saved him the trouble of either breaking and entering or having to summon the manager to unlock the door for him. On the other hand, nobody left their doors unlocked in Los Angeles. It wasn't safe, especially in this neighborhood.

So the unlocked door either meant that she'd left in a hurry and didn't care about locking up after herself—

Or it meant something bad had happened.

Being cynical, pessimistic, and a police officer, Steve assumed the worst.

He took out his gun, stepped to one side, and eased the door open with his left hand. The door had opened only a crack when he caught the scent.

It was the acrid, stomach-churning smell of death. His nose was attuned so well to the nuances of the foul scent that he could almost peg the time of death without even seeing the body.

What he was smelling now was not so much the decomposition of flesh but the evacuation of bladder and bowels that inevitably follows the sudden loss of life.

Whoever was dead hadn't been dead very long.

He opened the door the rest of the way and saw a woman he assumed to be Mercy Reynolds lying on her back in the entry hall, a bullet hole in her chest and another in the center of her head.

Steve could tell from the position of her body and the blood spatter on the walls what had happened.

Her murderer was a professional. That was obvious from the coldly efficient way that he worked.

The killer knocked on the door. Mercy opened it. The killer was holding a silenced gun. He shot her once in the heart and once more between the eyes after she fell, to be sure that she was dead. He closed the door and left. The whole thing probably took less than thirty seconds.

Steve quickly walked through the seven-hundred-fifty-square-foot bungalow to make sure there was no one else around, alive or dead, then holstered his weapon, put on a pair of rubber gloves, and rummaged through the purse on the table beside the door.

He pulled out a wallet, checked the ID, and confirmed for himself that the dead woman was, in fact, Mercy Reynolds, the key figure in the entire case, the one person who could tie everything together.

Someone clearly didn't want that to happen.

But Mercy was talking anyway, even in death.

She was saying to Steve that her violent demise proved that she wasn't just some lone, drooling psychopath who got her thrills injecting patients with West Nile virus.

Her corpse was stating, quite eloquently in fact, that her actions were in the service of a greater goal, one that would be compromised if she ever revealed what she knew.

The two bullet holes suggested that still at least one other person, who had more than a passing familiarity with murder, was involved in all of this.

Perhaps two people, if Malcolm Trainor was involved. Or three, if Steve threw Carter Sweeney into the mix too.

Steve's head was starting to ache.

He went into the kitchen and noticed a light blinking on Mercy's answering machine. He hit PLAY. The robotic male voice that was programmed into the machine announced that Mercy had three messages and that the first one was left at 11:10 p.m. the previous night. The caller was a man. He sounded scared.

"Get out. You aren't safe. They're going to kill you. They're going to kill us all."

Steve listened to Mercy's two other messages. They were both calls from her increasingly pissed-off supervisor at Community General, wondering where she was and why she wasn't at work.

While he listened to the messages, Steve picked up Mercy's portable phone and was pleased to see it was one of the newer models with a digital display and caller ID recognition. There was a rocker button on the receiver that allowed him to toggle through the last fifty calls she'd received.

There was only one number he was interested in, and that was the one warning her, too late, that her life was in danger.

The number showed up, saving Steve at least one investigative step.

His cell phone rang. He set Mercy's phone down and answered his own. It was Tanis.

"I know some things about Mercy Reynolds," Tanis said.

"So do I," Steve said. "You first."

"She studied nursing at UC-Berkeley," Tanis said. "Her boyfriend at the time was David Vogt."

"Should that mean something to me?"

"He was killed in a bank robbery in Pacoima a couple years ago," Tanis said. "He was a member of ROAR."

Steve glanced down at Mercy's corpse.

She'd worked at MediSolutions, which was run by Noah Dent, who used to be an administrator at Community General.

She'd had a boyfriend who was a member of ROAR, the revolutionary idiots Carter Sweeney manipulated into doing his bidding.

And she'd infected two organ donors around the same time that Gaylord Yokley, a ROAR member and black-market gun dealer, was arming the gangs in hopes of sparking a street war and plunging the city into anarchy.

And she worked at the same hospital where two funeral

homes, with ties to Malcolm Trainor and that did business with MediSolutions, were stealing body parts from corpses and selling them.

Connections. Coincidences.

And more connections. And more coincidences.

Steve couldn't put all the pieces together to make a clear picture. It was a muddle. But he knew they fit somehow. The more he tried to sort it out, the more confusing it became.

"What have you learned about Mercy?" Tanis asked, interrupting his thoughts.

"She's dead," Steve said. "I'm at her place."

"Suicide?" Tanis asked.

"Her body is in the entry hall," Steve said. "She was shot once in the chest and once in the head."

"Summary execution," Tanis said. "I guess Mercy must have misbehaved."

"Or someone was concerned that she might."

"Someone who either is a professional killer or knows how to find one," Tanis said. "This changes things in a big way."

"It certainly does," Steve said.

CHAPTER FORTY-FOUR

It wasn't fate that had been pursuing Mark Sloan. It was Carter Sweeney. Mark knew that now, but it gave him very little comfort. In some ways, fate and Carter Sweeney were one and the same for Mark.

On the long drive back to Los Angeles, Mark thought about his encounter with Sweeney, who'd basically admitted to conspiring with other murderers inside Sunrise Valley State Prison to frame Amanda, Jesse, and Susan for crimes. And all to get back at Mark for what he'd done to them.

Somehow Carter Sweeney, Malcolm Trainor, and perhaps everyone else Mark had ever convicted had pooled their intellect and resources to come up with a plan. And then they'd managed to oversee the funding and execution of their plot from within the prison walls.

It was truly an audacious undertaking. There were so many elements that had to be controlled, so many contingencies that had to be anticipated, and so much groundwork that had to be done in order to pull it all off.

But their plan was only as good as the people who actually carried it out. And for that, Sweeney and his fellow prisoners had to rely on people on the outside.

The only name Mark had was Mercy Reynolds, but surely she wasn't working alone.

Where did they find Mercy Reynolds and how did they get her to do their killing?

Did Noah Dent hire her at MediSolutions and did he have anything to do with her getting a job as a utilization nurse at Community General? Did Dent know what Mercy was planning to do? Was Dent part of the conspiracy or was he simply being manipulated?

Mercy knew the answers, but Mark didn't think she'd tell him unless he could apply some pressure.

He didn't have any leverage against her. But with what little knowledge he had, and what he could guess, perhaps he could play Dent and Mercy off one another.

Mark decided to try Dent first. It would be easier to break Dent than a stone-cold killer who'd calmly injected helpless patients with a deadly virus.

Unless Dent was every bit as cold as Mercy was.

It was a chance Mark would have to take. As soon as he got back to LA, he would book himself on the first flight out to Phoenix, which was where MediSolutions was based. And while he was there, he would also find out how closely involved Dent was with the funeral homes that were part of the body-parts scandal.

Somehow Sweeney, Trainor, and company had managed to get some Mob-controlled funeral homes into the body-parts business and to forge Amanda's name on key documents.

Mercy probably had something to do with the forged documents. She might even have been the one funneling cadavers and body parts to the funeral homes.

But why, Mark wondered, would the funeral directors be willing to face possible jail time for the sake of a bunch of imprisoned killers seeking revenge? What was in it for them?

Perhaps they didn't know they were being used and ultimately set up. Perhaps they were just in it for the money and really believed they were working with Amanda the whole time. It would certainly make their testimony more convincing.

The more Mark thought about it, the more he saw the cunning logic in setting up the funeral directors that way. It also meant one less link to Sweeney and company.

So, somehow, Trainor had conned his former associates into getting into a body-parts business with Amanda—only it wasn't really Amanda they were dealing with. If they were dealing with anyone, it was probably Mercy acting as an intermediary.

Mark wondered what Mercy's motivation was. He doubted it was money. It had to be something personal. Whatever it was, it placed her in the center of the conspiracy.

But as far as Sweeney knew, Mark didn't know anything about her. That gave Mark a slight edge and some time.

But Sweeney wasn't a stupid man, and neither were the people he was working with. They knew how persistent Mark could be. They knew he'd eventually find her. And they knew the damage she could cause if he did.

They would take precautions.

If they had some kind of strong personal connection with her, they would make her disappear, creating a new identity and life for her somewhere far away from Los Angeles.

Or they could kill her.

The thought terrified Mark—without Mercy, he was lost.

And so were Amanda, Jesse, and Susan.

He couldn't worry about that now. It was out of his hands. He hoped Steve would find Mercy before she either disappeared or was silenced.

In the meantime, something else troubled Mark. It was the timing of the scandals, which became public at the height of the mayoral race and right before Sweeney's habeas corpus hearing.

The scandals had already worked in Burnside's favor, though Mark couldn't see what Sweeney and his friends gained from his becoming mayor. Burnside was the DA who'd put most of them behind bars. Sweeney and company couldn't be any fonder of Burnside than they were of Chief Masters. Nor could Mark see how either Burnside or Masters as mayor bolstered Sweeney's bid for freedom.

So what was the point? And why time the scandals to break now?

And where did Gaylord Yokley's little gang-war plot fit in? Somehow, it did, because the arrest happened about the same time that the Community General scandals were revealed.

Mark wondered what would have happened if Teeg Cantrell hadn't tried to shoot his girlfriend, Yokley hadn't been arrested, and the gang war had erupted as planned, turning Los Angeles into a battleground.

It would have been a national story, perhaps even international news. Neither the media nor the public would have paid much attention to the scandals at Community General, despite the lurid nature of the crimes.

Mark considered the ramifications of that scenario for a few minutes and then looked at the Yokley case from another angle.

Why did Yokley tell Cantrell that his girlfriend was cheating on him? How did Yokley find out and why did he care?

Mark decided to turn the Yokley case inside out and see what possibilities it raised.

What if Cantrell was set up? What if Sweeney had always intended for Yokley to be arrested, his weapons seized, and the gang-war plot to be revealed?

What if things had actually turned out exactly the way Sweeney had wanted them to?

If so, how did the arrest help Sweeney and his fellow killers at Sunrise Valley?

Mark didn't know.

There were hundreds of different ways to look at everything that *had* happened, what *didn't* happen, and what *might* have happened, but he still couldn't see the shape of Sweeney's plan.

Rather than try to figure it out, Mark decided to take an easier approach. He would start with Sweeney's goals and work backwards from there.

There was no confusion about what Sweeney's intentions were. He wanted to destroy Mark Sloan and get out of prison.

What had Sweeney said?

The idea is for you to lose everything and everyone that's important to you, to leave you alone and miserable for the rest of your long life in a prison of our making.

Sweeney had already made significant progress on that goal. Mark had lost his job, his reputation was in ruins, and his closest friends were in jail for crimes they didn't commit.

Everything and everyone.

But the one person in the world who mattered most to Mark was his son.

It was Steve who'd arrested Sweeney, Trainor, and the others.

It was Steve who'd cracked the Yokley case.

There was no way Sweeney was going to let Steve go unscathed.

Mark had to warn Steve—but what could he tell him? Be careful? It seemed woefully inadequate. How could Steve protect himself without knowing what form the threat might take?

For all Mark knew, the plan was moving inexorably forward and Steve was ruined already, but it just wasn't obvious yet.

And when it was, it would be far too late for Mark to do anything to save him.

CHAPTER FORTY-FIVE

Before leaving Mercy Reynolds's apartment, Steve gave Tanis the phone number from Mercy's caller ID. Tanis told Steve the name, Rusty Konrath, and the address in West Los Angeles that went with it.

Then Steve called the LAPD dispatcher to report the murder. He waited for a couple of uniforms to show up at Mercy's apartment to secure the scene for the CSI guys and then he left.

It probably wasn't the smartest career move he'd ever made, but Steve figured that sticking around would be a waste of his time. He would learn more about who'd killed Mercy Reynolds by visiting Konrath than he would by hanging out at her bungalow while the crime scene mice dusted and photographed everything.

Rusty Konrath lived in a neighborhood of bland apartment buildings and condos west of the San Diego Freeway, south of Wilshire Boulevard and north of Santa Monica Boulevard. It was a neighborhood favored by UCLA students for its proximity to the Westwood campus, just a mile away.

Konrath's apartment was on a gentle slope overlooking a high school built in the late 1940s in the Italian Romanesque style, all brick and arched windows. It was one of many old, overcrowded, and decaying Los Angeles schools in desperate need of earthquake retrofitting, which the city couldn't afford to do.

That was the gist of the campaign stump speech Neal Burnside was making at a podium on the front steps of the school to a crowd of parents, students, and teachers when Steve arrived.

Steve parked in front of a fire hydrant and walked up to the apartment building, Burnside's speech echoing up and down the street. Burnside was vowing that when he was elected mayor, he would march to Sacramento and demand the funds necessary to keep the community's children safe.

Burnside was the last person Steve wanted to see right now. He was afraid he might slug the guy for making Mark a campaign issue. So Steve didn't hang around to listen to the speech or say hello. He had more important things to do.

The door to the apartment building lobby was propped open with a bent piece of torn cardboard to prevent it from closing and locking, which completely undercut the whole point of the security buzzer system.

He checked the mailboxes to see which apartment was Konrath's, then slipped into the lobby, wedging the piece of cardboard back in place.

He took the stairwell and was only one flight up on his way to the third floor when he heard the crack of a rifle shot. It came from at least one floor above. He could hear screams and pandemonium outside.

He drew his gun and raced up the stairs. He paused at the door to the second floor, pulled it open, and swung into the hallway in a firing stance.

The corridor was empty. Everyone must have been outside listening to the speech, attending classes at UCLA, or at work.

He waited a moment to see if anyone came running out, then moved up two flights to the next floor, glancing below every few seconds in case anyone came charging into the stairwell.

Steve paused at the third floor, opened the door slowly, and looked down the hall. An apartment door was ajar at the far end.

He moved cautiously down the hall, his heart pounding, his ears attuned to the slightest sound. He reached the half-open door.

It was Konrath's apartment.

Another coincidence.

There were too damn many of them, and this one gave him a dull ache in the pit of his stomach. It was the same ache he felt whenever he went to get a cavity filled. He knew he was going to get his teeth drilled, something no amount of Novocain could make endurable for him, and yet he walked into the dentist's office anyway.

Because he had to. It was the right thing to do. But at least it was his decision to face the nightmare.

This was worse.

He was caught up in a series of events that he couldn't undo. It would be like trying to reverse the course of a river.

It was like fate. Just as inescapable, just as certain, driving him relentlessly forward towards a predetermined outcome. Only it wasn't some unknowable cosmic force shaping these events.

It was a person.

These thoughts passed through Steve's mind in the nanosecond between when he recognized Konrath's apartment number and when he kicked open the door.

Steve swung low into the room, ready to shoot anything that moved.

Nothing did.

It was a one-bedroom apartment, furnished on the cheap with thrift-store finds and snap-together Ikea sale items. There was a smear of blood on the entry hall floor, and it led to the kitchenette.

Steve peered around the corner into the kitchen area. The body of a young man, perhaps in his late teens or early twenties, was on his back on the floor, his arms raised above his head. He wore cargo shorts and a T-shirt. Rusty Konrath had been shot once in the chest and once in the head and dragged by the arms into the kitchen.

Steve knew what he was going to find next. He knew it as if he'd lived this moment before or had been given a script in advance.

But he had to see it anyway.

His heart was pounding so loudly it felt to him like someone was hitting the side of the building with a battering ram.

Steve stepped into the living room. One of the windows was open. A rifle with a scope sat on the floor in front of the window, along with a pillow where the shooter had rested his knees.

He peered out the window. He had a direct, unobstructed view of the high school steps.

Of course.

There was a crowd around Neal Burnside's body behind the podium. People were screaming and pointing in the general direction of the window where Steve now stood.

Someone had shot Neal Burnside. And if the shooter was the same professional who'd killed Mercy Reynolds and Rusty Konrath, then Neal Burnside was almost certainly dead.

Steve had shown up within seconds of the shooting. The killer hadn't fled into the stairwell and probably didn't take the elevator. Which meant the killer was still in the building. Or at least he was until Steve entered Konrath's apartment.

But it was too late for Steve to start searching now. Officers were undoubtedly swarming around the building and charging up the stairs. Whether they found Steve in the hall, the stairwell, or the elevator, the outcome would be the same.

Steve holstered his gun, took out his badge, and clipped it to his jacket so when the cops came rushing in they wouldn't shoot him.

He raised his hands, too, just to be safe.

Two uniformed officers and one detective burst into the room, their guns aimed squarely at Steve's chest.

The detective was Olivia Morales. She didn't seem very happy to see him.

"He's one of us. I know him," she said, but she didn't lower her gun. "What are you doing here, Steve?"

"I didn't shoot Burnside, if that's what you're asking, Olivia. I was in the building running down a lead in a murder case. I heard the shot and ran up here, hoping to catch the shooter. It's just a co-incidence."

But even as he said it, he knew that it wasn't.

Mercy's murder, the message on her tape machine, all of it was intended to bring him right here, right now. Things were only going to get worse for him from this point on. He was certain of that.

"I'm going to need to take your gun," she said.

Given their relationship, there were a lot of cute ways he could have answered that question to ease the tension in the room. But this wasn't the time for cute. He simply nodded.

She motioned to one of the officers, who stepped forward, patted Steve down, and took his gun. The officer placed it in an evidence bag.

"You two secure the floor," Olivia said, holstering her weapon and taking the evidence bag from the officer. "I'll stay with Lieutenant Sloan."

He knew that he had to be treated like a suspect. He didn't resent Olivia for it. He would have done the same in her position.

And then it hit him.

Olivia's being here was yet another coincidence. She was working the Yokley case. Her presence was every bit as strange and convenient as Steve's arrival on the scene.

It wasn't the hand of fate, but someone's hand was involved. He had no doubt about that.

"It was a big surprise seeing you come through the door," Steve said.

"It was a bigger surprise seeing you standing where the sniper should be."

"You know why I'm here," Steve said.

"I'm still vague on the details," she said.

So he told her, from the beginning. And when he was done, he said, "What's your story?"

"Mine's a lot simpler. Burnside called me an hour ago, said he needed to see me right away. He told me to meet him at the high school," Olivia said. "I guess I'll never find out why now."

"So he's dead."

"As can be," she said.

CHAPTER FORTY-SIX

The narrow street in front of Mark Sloan's beach house was clogged with police cars. Mark's first, horrifying thought as he drove up was that Steve had been killed, but that quickly passed when he saw that there were no vehicles from the medical examiner's office or the morgue.

He was so relieved he almost didn't care what the police were doing at his house.

Mark parked on the shoulder of the Pacific Coast Highway, waited for traffic to pass, then opened his door and got out. He was heading for his house when one of his neighbors, walking a wonderfully coiffed poodle, stopped him.

Prentiss Cloud was a jeweler in his fifties with tanning-parlor skin and a head of white hair that rivaled his poodle's. Cloud seemed to be wearing the entire inventory of his Malibu store on his neck, ears, and fingers at all times.

"Enough is enough, Dr. Sloan," Cloud said. "Your home is a magnet for crime and disaster. We've seen it all at your house. Bombings, murders, robberies, shootings, kidnappings, plagues, and rapes."

"There's never been a rape," Mark said.

Cloud glared at him. So did the dog. "Do you know why the police are here this time?"

"No," Mark said.

"Maybe it's rape. Or a beheading. Or perhaps they've finally found Osama bin Laden," Cloud said. "Anything is possible at the Sloan residence."

"I'm sorry for the inconvenience." Mark started to go past him, but Cloud blocked his way.

"This is where we live, Dr. Sloan. This is where we seek peace, comfort, and security. Maybe even a little privacy," Cloud said.

"But that's not possible with you as a neighbor. Do us a favor and move. Do the world a favor and go somewhere remote where you can't make life miserable for your neighbors."

Cloud marched off with his poodle, their gaits almost matching. Mark wasn't angry at Cloud. He'd been expecting his neighbors to show up outside his house with torches for years.

Mark approached the house but was intercepted by a uniformed police officer, a woman who looked like she could bench-press a Toyota.

"Hold it," she said. "You can't go in there."

"I'm Dr. Mark Sloan and that's my house," he said. "What's going on? What's happened?"

She spoke into her radio. "I've got Dr. Sloan out here."

"I'll be right out," a male voice crackled back.

"Stay here," she said.

He looked over her shoulder and saw a crime scene tech walk out of the house carrying a clear plastic evidence bag that contained several handguns.

Mark had never seen the guns before. Steve had only three, but one was always on him and another was in the lockbox in his trunk at all times.

The tech was followed out a moment later by Lieutenant Sam Rykus, chewing on a fat cigar, his belly straining against the buttons of his shirt.

"Sam," Mark called out. "What's going on?"

"We're searching the place," Rykus said. "You want to see the warrant?"

"I want to know why you're doing it," Mark said.

Rykus stared at him. "You're joking, right?"

"Do I look like I'm joking?"

"The DA was assassinated an hour ago," Rykus said. "He was shot while giving a speech at a high school."

Mark was stunned by the news, but he tried to stay focused on the situation at hand.

"You think that I did it?" Mark asked. "You think that because he criticized me on TV I'd shoot him?"

"No," Sam said.

"I've just returned from a visit to Sunrise Valley Prison. They must have me on a hundred cameras," Mark said. "Alibis don't get much better than that."

"You don't need one, Doc."

"Then why are you searching my house?"

"Burnside was shot from an apartment building across the street," Rykus said. "We found Steve in there with the sniper rifle."

Everything and everyone.

"You know Steve," Mark said. "You know he would never do something like this."

"That's what I thought," Rykus said, then jerked his head back towards the house. "But we found an arsenal hidden in there and a rifle just like the one at the apartment."

"Then they were planted," Mark said.

Rykus shrugged. "We're gonna be here for a few more hours. Any minute now, the media is gonna start showing up here. Maybe you want to be somewhere else."

Mark nodded, grateful for the advice, and walked back to his car, lost in his thoughts.

He knew with absolute certainty that the rifle used to kill Burnside and the guns Rykus found in their house were going to be linked to Gaylord Yokley's weapons cache.

Because it all fit.

Everything and everyone.

Mark could finally see how the plot Sweeney and his friends had concocted worked. All the pieces were falling into place so rapidly in his mind that it was dizzying.

That's when he was yanked backwards, nearly off his feet, as a car whizzed by, so close he almost felt the metal brushing his legs.

It snapped him out of his daze and he realized that he'd stepped out onto the Pacific Coast Highway without even bothering to look for traffic first.

How stupid.

He knew the highway was there. He'd even faced the traffic before, and he still didn't see what was coming.

It was the past few weeks of his life, neatly summed up in one near-death moment.

He turned to the female officer who'd saved him.

"Be careful," she said.

Mark nodded and said that he would, but it was far too late for that.

Steve leaned against his car outside of Konrath's apartment building. He was waiting to be questioned by whoever the lead investigator in the case turned out to be.

For the moment, the lead investigator was Olivia, the highest-ranking officer on the scene who wasn't caught practically holding the murder weapon.

There were two officers standing a polite distance away from Steve, pretending to be disinterested but in fact watching to make sure he didn't flee for the Mexico border.

Which was a good thing, because he was tempted.

But like the generally law-abiding citizen that he was, he stayed put and watched Olivia work.

She'd confiscated the film from the cameramen who'd been covering the speech, an act that was bound to raise all kinds of screaming about First Amendment rights. But it was worth the legal risk to secure the footage before it could be edited and any potential clues lost. She then moved the reporters and all the other media who'd since swarmed to the scene two blocks back behind a police barricade.

Steve would have done the same things in her position, freedom of the press be damned.

Meanwhile, the apartment building and the entire neighborhood were being searched, inch by inch, for any evidence or witnesses that could lead them to the assassin.

LAPD helicopters and a horde of news choppers buzzed loudly overhead, making it necessary for everyone on the street to shout in order to be heard.

Steve's cell phone vibrated in his pocket. He took the phone out and answered it.

It was Tanis, but he could barely hear her.

"You're in big trouble," Tanis said.

"Believe me, I know."

"It's worse than you know," Tanis said. "All of our bugs on Tony Sisk just went dark."

"They've been discovered," Steve said.

"Gee, you think? And within minutes of Neal Burnside's assassination," Tanis said. "Am I the only one freaked out by the timing?"

He glanced at Olivia, who was conferring with Chief Masters, who'd just arrived on the scene. He wondered if Masters knew the surveillance on Sisk had been compromised or if he'd pulled it himself when he learned where Steve was when Burnside was killed.

But what about Olivia? What was she doing there? How did she get in the building so fast? There was one explanation that came to mind, one he didn't like very much. It put their whole relationship in a disturbing new light.

"I need you to run a check on all of Olivia Morales's phones," Steve said. "I want to know when, and if, she got a call from Burnside's office today."

"I can't do that," Tanis said.

"We're talking about a few keystrokes on that supercomputer of yours."

"I'm nowhere near my supercomputer."

"Where are you?"

"Where I can't be found," Tanis said.

"I need you."

"I can't do you or me any good if I'm in jail," Tanis said. "We've been set up and we're both going down."

"So you're going to run?"

"Hell yes."

A car pulled up a few yards away and Special Agent Ort got out, followed by two other agents.

Steve got a beep from call-waiting. He glanced at his cell phone readout. The caller was his father. He put the phone back to his ear.

"I have to go," Steve said. "Good luck, Tanis."

"You too."

Steve disconnected from Tanis and switched over quickly to Mark. He assumed his father knew about Burnside's murder, and he didn't have time to give him the details of his own plight.

"I only have five seconds, Dad. Mercy Reynolds is dead. Her boyfriend was a member of ROAR who was killed in a bank holdup."

"Carter Sweeney is behind it all," Mark said. "He told me."

"I don't suppose he signed a confession," Steve said.

"No," Mark said.

"Then I'm going to need a lawyer," Steve said and hung up, sticking the phone in his pocket as Ort approached.

"Lieutenant Sloan," Ort said, shouting to be heard over the noise, "you're under arrest for the assassination of Neal Burnside."

Chapter Forty-seven

The interrogation room at the Federal Building looked a lot like the interrogation room at police headquarters. The same paint color. The same lighting. The same hard, uncomfortable furniture. Steve wondered if there was some obscure law somewhere that dictated exactly how interrogation rooms had to be designed and furnished. Or maybe they'd just used the same interior decorator.

"Daydreaming, Lieutenant?" Ort asked, holding a file under his arm and pacing in front of Steve.

"I have to entertain myself somehow," Steve said.

"You find this funny?" Ort said. "The DA was assassinated and you were found in the sniper's perch."

"No, I don't think it's funny," Steve said. "I think it's infuriating. You're wasting valuable time questioning me when you should be out there looking for the assassin. But I've come to expect this from you, Ort. This is the second time you've bungled a murder investigation."

"The second?"

"You arrested Jesse and Susan for the West Nile virus killings," Steve said. "You let the real killer go free, long enough for someone to silence her."

"And who might that be?"

"Mercy Reynolds, the utilization nurse," Steve said irritably. "I explained that to Detective Morales and I'm sure that she told you. I was investigating a homicide and that's what led me to Konrath's apartment."

"At the precise moment that Burnside was shot," Ort said.

"I told you why I was there," Steve said. "There was a message on Mercy's answering machine. I ran the number, and the address that came up was the apartment building."

"There is no message on the tape machine," Ort said.

"Then it's been erased," Steve said.

"Of course it has," Ort said. "When you say you 'ran the number,' what you mean is that you got the information from Tanis Archer, who is presently assigned to the Anti-Terror Strike Force."

"Yes," Steve said.

"Is Mercy Reynolds a terrorist?"

"Ask the next of kin of the people she killed."

Ort smiled. "Why did you have Tanis Archer get you the information rather than calling your office or your contact at the phone company?"

"She happened to call me at the right moment," Steve said.

"From her desk in Anti-Terror."

"She has quite a computer system there."

"Yes, she does," Ort said. "We traced an unauthorized incursion into our FBI database to her computer. She accessed information on our case against Dr. Amanda Bentley."

"I wouldn't know anything about that."

"You're a lousy liar. Tanis Archer discovered that Mercy Reynolds was a government witness, that she'd agreed to testify against Dr. Bentley and her coconspirators," Ort said. "Archer discovered that arrangements were being made to place Ms. Reynolds in the Witness Protection Program. So you had to act fast. That's why you killed her last night and then pretended to discover her body this morning to deflect suspicion from yourself."

"That's ridiculous," Steve said.

Ort pulled out a chair and took a seat across from Steve. He placed a file on the table and removed two pieces of paper from it for Steve to see. It was a ballistics report and a fingerprint analysis.

"The sniper rifle came from Yokley's house," Ort said. "It was one of the weapons that you recovered that you neglected to log. The rifle was wiped clean, but you missed a spot. We found a partial print of yours."

"It doesn't make me the shooter," Steve said. "It just means I touched the rifle in Yokley's house or afterwards when we were tracing the weapons. Do you think if I killed Burnside I would have just stood there with the rifle, waiting around to be caught?"

"You've had a stormy relationship with Burnside for years. And then he went on television and trashed your father, ruining his reputation. That must have infuriated you."

"Not enough to kill him," Steve said.

"Maybe you were ordered to do it."

Ort opened the file and spread out a series of eight-by-ten glossy photographs on the table in front of Steve. They were grainy surveillance shots of Steve and Tanis in phone company uniforms planting bugs outside of Tony Sisk's house and in the garage of his building.

Steve felt like he'd taken a gut punch, delivered by Carter Sweeney himself. The scope of Sweeney's machinations and manipulations over the last few weeks was becoming clear to him now.

"How many years have you been violating civil rights, planting evidence, and committing murders as the chief's covert operatives?" Ort asked. Steve remained silent. "Killing Burnside was just one more mission, wasn't it? You knew that after you shot Burnside there was no way you could get away in time, so you concocted this story about a call to Ms. Reynolds from Rusty Konrath, an innocent victim whose fatal mistake was having an apartment with a clear view of the high school. You remained at the scene because you knew it was the one thing no assassin would ever do. You were essentially hiding in plain sight."

Ort had the facts right, but they didn't point to Steve. They pointed directly at someone else.

"It wasn't me. It was Olivia Morales. She didn't get a call from Burnside asking her to come meet him at the high school. She was in the building already because *she* was the shooter," Steve said. "She knew I was coming. Olivia shot Burnside and hid somewhere on the third floor until I went into Konrath's apartment. Then she waited in the stairwell for the officers, fooling them into thinking she'd run into the building moments ahead of them. She probably killed Mercy Reynolds and Rusty Konrath, too."

Ort shook his head and sighed. "Why would she do all that killing?"

"I don't know," Steve said. "But it involves Carter Sweeney."

"Why stop there?" Ort asked. "Maybe I was involved. And the Vatican. And SpongeBob SquarePants."

"Olivia Morales and I worked the Yokley case together from the start," Steve said. "We became lovers. She knew everything I was doing. She had access to my home. She was setting me up the whole time."

"The reason Burnside called her was because he had these pictures," Ort said. "Someone slipped them to him. He knew you and Olivia Morales had become intimate. He was hoping she could give him more information about your covert ops for Chief Masters."

"Did Olivia tell you that?"

"ADA Karen Cross did," Ort said. "If you really want to bring someone else down to save yourself from death row, don't waste my time with this crap about Morales. Get serious and start cooperating. Testify against Masters and everyone else involved in this conspiracy."

"There is no conspiracy," Steve said. "Except the one perpetrated by Sweeney, Mercy Reynolds, and Olivia Morales."

Ort motioned to the photos and reports on the table. "The evidence says otherwise. This is a limited-time offer. Because once we apprehend Tanis Archer, we're going to make her the same offer, and you know she'll take it. Sure, she'll do some time—but you'll die."

Steve met Ort's gaze. "We're done talking. Let me know when my lawyer gets here."

Ort got up and headed for the door.

"You must be awfully devoted to Chief Masters to sacrifice yourself for him," Ort said. "I'm sure he appreciates it."

CHAPTER FORTY-EIGHT

It was a nightmare that kept getting worse. Mark's son was in jail for murder. The only hope Mark had left was that Amanda, Jesse, and Susan would be released on bail soon so they could somehow help him find the proof to clear them all.

But Arthur Tyrell had just taken that slim hope away from him. Mark sat down slowly on the couch in Tyrell's office and tried to absorb this latest body blow.

"Would you like a drink?" Tyrell asked, strolling over to his wet bar.

"I don't drink," Mark mumbled.

"This would be a good time to start," Tyrell said.

"I don't think so," Mark said. "I need a clear head."

"The problem is that you're seeing things too clearly, and so am I," Tyrell said, mixing himself a martini. "You need to blur the picture a bit so you can relax."

"My son has been arrested for murder and so have Jesse and Susan. Amanda is imprisoned for looting bones and organs from the dead," Mark said. "How can I relax? I have to get them all out and prove that they are innocent."

"You can't," Tyrell said.

"But you can," Mark said hopefully.

Tyrell picked up his drink and took a seat in an overstuffed easy chair facing Mark.

"I can't either," Tyrell said.

"You're being modest," Mark said.

"I told you I'm seeing things very clearly," Tyrell said. "I can't represent them or your son."

"You're quitting?" Mark asked in disbelief.

Tyrell nodded. "These are unwinnable cases, and you simply

can't afford to pay me what it will cost to defend the four of them."

"They're innocent," Mark said. "Doesn't that mean anything to you?"

"I don't practice law to seek justice. I practice law to make a living. I can recommend a lot of other criminal defense attorneys. But I'll be honest with you, Doctor. Whoever is foolish enough to take the cases will lose on every front. Bail will be denied for Steve. And in the months leading up to the trial, the media will publicize the damning evidence against all four of them, so it will be impossible to find a jury that hasn't been tainted. The jury will convict your son, Amanda, and the Travises on all counts. The defense attorney will then face the eternal wrath of the DA's office and the LAPD, which will make it brutally difficult for him to work in this city, since he will be unable to cut any deals for his clients. He might as well take the bar exam in another state, because he will be finished in California."

"It sounds like the perfect case for you," Mark said without a trace of sarcasm in his voice.

"What I've just described is a lawyer committing career suicide. I don't want that pitiful schlub to be me."

"For someone who says he's seeing clearly, your vision is awfully muddy," Mark said. "You're already that pitiful schlub. The only reason Amanda, Jesse, and Susan were denied bail was because you've lost your pull."

"The evidence against them was too strong," Tyrell said, downing the rest of his drink. "No lawyer could have done any better."

"Before the Lacey McClure case, you would have gotten them out on bail," Mark said. "But McClure ruined you. The DA and the police hate you. The public hates you. You and I both know that there's no celebrity case that's going to come along and revive your career. Because nobody wants to be associated with failure. Judges, juries, and reporters look at you and see the McClure case all over again. If you don't take these cases, you're done. I'm the only one who sees you for the lawyer you once were."

"Because you're desperate," Tyrell said.

"Of course I am," Mark said.

"And you know that nobody else has the stones to represent your son and his friends."

"Neither do you," Mark said. "The old Arthur Tyrell didn't

scare so easy. The fact that you do now should tell you something about how far you have fallen."

"These are no-win cases, not just for the defendants but for me too. I'll be crucified in the press, and for what? The money?" Tyrell laughed ruefully. "I'll eat through every penny you and my four clients have in the first month. After that, you'll all be destitute and I'll be defending four people pro bono."

"But if you win, it will be an audacious, high-profile victory, one that will totally eclipse the embarrassment of the McClure case forever. You will be revived and reinvigorated, coming back onto the legal scene even bigger and more powerful than you were before. And the big-ticket cases of clients who will come to you then will more than make up for your financial gamble."

"And what happens when I lose?"

Mark sighed. "Look at yourself, Arthur. What are you really risking? You can't be any worse off than you are right now. This is your last, best chance to save your career. You need Steve, Amanda, Jesse, and Susan as much as they need you."

"I wish you drank," Tyrell said and made himself another martini.

CHAPTER FORTY-NINE

Arthur Tyrell hadn't lost all his influence, at least not at the Los Angeles County Jail. He was able to arrange for him and Mark to meet with Steve, Amanda, Jesse, and Susan in a large holding cell late that night.

Steve was the first to be brought in by the guards. He was in a jail jumpsuit, his arms and legs in chains. Mark embraced him.

"I am so sorry," Mark said.

"It's not your fault, Dad. Carter Sweeney has every reason to hate me, too. I was the guy who arrested him."

"It's not just Carter Sweeney," Mark said,

"It's not?"

"I'll explain everything when the others get here," Mark said.

"Fair enough." Steve looked past Mark to Arthur Tyrell. "I never thought I'd be glad to see you. What are the odds of getting me out of this?"

"A million to one," Tyrell said.

"Are you good enough to beat those odds?" Steve asked.

"Probably not," Tyrell said. "But I'm closer to it than most."

"At least you're honest," Steve said.

"I wouldn't make that assumption if I were you," Tyrell said. "But if I am going to be your lawyer, you will have to trust me anyway and do exactly what I tell you. Can you live with that?"

"Easier than I can live with the idea of spending my life behind bars."

Jesse was brought in next. He was clearly startled to see Steve in the same jumpsuit and chains that he was in.

"I don't suppose you're dressed like that in a show of sympathy for my plight," Jesse said.

"I'm afraid not," Steve said. "They didn't tell you what happened today?"

"For some reason my room here doesn't have a TV, radio, or telephone," Jesse said. "I've been meaning to talk to the concierge about that. So, who did you kill?"

"The district attorney," Steve said.

Jesse grinned. "No, really, what happened?"

"Burnside was assassinated this afternoon," Mark said. "Steve was caught three minutes later in the sniper's perch with the murder weapon at his feet."

"And my fingerprints were on the rifle," Steve said, "which was one of the weapons recovered when I raided Gaylord Yokley's compound."

"And there's photos of Steve engaged in illegal eavesdropping and surveillance activities for Chief Masters," Tyrell added. "Burnside was killed within hours of receiving them."

"Oh boy," Jesse said. He turned to Steve. "You're so competitive, you just had to get yourself arrested for a bigger murder than I did."

"You're accused of serial killing," Steve said. "I think that's bigger."

"No, assassinating a public figure is much bigger," Jesse said. "You win, buddy. But I look better in this jumpsuit than you do."

"The hell you do," Steve said. "You've got no shoulders. This looks tailored on me."

Seeing them joking like that, in the midst of the worst adversity they'd ever faced, gave Mark some hope. It proved to him that, no matter what, they hadn't given up.

Tyrell leaned towards Mark. "What is wrong with them?"

Mark smiled. "Nothing. Besides being charged with murders they didn't commit and facing possible execution."

Tyrell shook his head. Jesse and Steve abruptly stopped talking, the words catching in their throats when they saw the guards bringing Amanda and Susan to the cell.

Jesse's eyes immediately welled with tears. The moment Susan was let in, Jesse shuffled over to her and they pressed against each other, face-to-face. With their wrists chained, they were unable to embrace. But they kissed, and rubbed their faces together, their tears intermingling.

Mark hugged Amanda. She and Steve exchanged kisses on the cheek.

It was a bittersweet reunion. Although they hadn't been separated long, the gulf between Mark and his loved ones had grown wide and deep. Mark was free and they were imprisoned, and were likely to stay that way, for many, many years to come.

Susan and Jesse sat close together, clutching each other's hands as if that was all that was keeping them tethered to this earth.

She looked plaintively at Mark. "What is happening to us?"

"Vengeance," Mark said.

"Who have we wronged?" Susan asked.

"You haven't," Mark said. "I have. And this is how they are making me pay—by taking away everything and everyone that I care about."

"They?" Amanda said. "I thought it was Carter Sweeney."

"It's him and it's everyone else I've put in that prison," Mark said. "They've teamed up and pooled their resources under Sweeney's leadership. They're making you suffer so that I will."

"How do you know?" Jesse asked.

"Because Carter Sweeney told me," Mark said.

CHAPTER FIFTY

Mark shared with them everything he'd learned from Sweeney and what he'd manage to figure out on his own.

He told them that the guns-to-gangs plot, the West Nile virus killings, the body-parts ring, and the murder of Neal Burnside weren't individual events but parts of a larger plot.

All of them, including Burnside and Masters, had acted exactly the way Sweeney knew they would and, in doing so, had engineered their own doom.

And now all the people responsible for sending Carter Sweeney to prison were ruined, publicly exposed as greedy, corrupt, and murderous right on the eve of his habeas corpus hearing.

Even Los Angeles was paying for its crimes against the Sweeneys. With the DA and the police chief embroiled in scandal, and no mayoral candidates left, the city would be plunged into anarchy.

"Let me see if I've got this straight," Tyrell said. "You're saying the four of them have been framed in a vast conspiracy concocted by a dozen murderers currently incarcerated at a maximum-security prison?"

Mark nodded.

"And you expect me to convince a jury that this insanely farfetched conspiracy is for real?" Tyrell asked.

"It's what happened," Mark said.

"I don't see it," Tyrell said. "More importantly, I don't know how to make a jury see it as anything but a paranoid fantasy."

"Let's start with Teeg Cantrell," Mark said.

"Who the hell is he?" Tyrell asked.

"A gang member who tried to kill his girlfriend in a drive-by shooting," Steve said. "He missed, but managed to kill an innocent bystander anyway."

"Typical," Tyrell said. "And tragic."

"It was an incident that Sweeney had Yokley intentionally provoke at that particular time and place," Mark said. "Sweeney knew that Steve would get the case, discover that Yokley was dealing guns, and then lead a raid on Yokley's home."

"What was the point?" Tyrell asked.

"To tie me to the weapon Olivia was going to use to murder Neal Burnside," Steve said.

"The same evidence that links you to the guns also links her," Tyrell said, making notes on his legal pad. "Okay, I can use that."

"You'll have to establish a motive for her," Steve said. "And we haven't figured that out yet."

"I only have to establish reasonable doubt," Tyrell said. "Motive doesn't matter. She's not going to be on trial. You are."

"Speaking of motive," Amanda said, "I'd sure like to know why Noah Dent helped Mercy Reynolds kill all those people and frame us."

Mark looked at Jesse. "I think you can answer that."

"You knew?" Susan said. "All this time?"

"I suspected Jesse had something to do with Dent's sudden departure from Community General," Mark said. "I just never bothered to ask."

"It all went down during that terrible week when Tyrell was ripping you apart in the Lacey McClure case," Jesse said. "I thought I was helping out. And now look what's happened."

"What did you do?" Mark asked.

"It goes back a few years. There was this medical student working as a paramedic. She responded to a bad bus accident and recognized one of the victims as the man who'd raped and beaten her in college. He'd never been caught," Jesse said. "She killed him and made it look like he died as a result of his injuries. But you saw through it."

"Tanya," Mark said, remembering. "She was a wonderful young woman with such a promising future ahead of her. Turning her in for the murder was one of the toughest decisions I've ever made. She was tried and convicted. What does that have to do with Noah Dent?"

"I went to Toronto, visited Dent's childhood home, and saw pictures of him and Tanya together. I found out that she was Noah Dent's first and only true love," Jesse said. "I used that information to make him undo all the damage that he'd done at Community General."

"What leverage did you have to make Dent do that?" Amanda asked.

Jesse swallowed hard. It was an unpleasant memory. "I threatened to go to the media and tell them everything Dent had done and why he did it. Tanya would be raped again, only in the media this time, and it would be his fault. Did he really want to put her through that again just to get back at Mark?"

It was an ugly threat, one that Mark knew must have sickened Jesse to make.

"Would you really have done that?" Steve asked.

Jesse nodded. "I would have done it for Susan, for Mark, for Amanda, and for myself. I was defending my family. I blackmailed Dent into setting things right, and then he left. I guess all I really did was delay the inevitable and make things much worse."

"You did all that detective work on your own?" Steve asked him.

"I had some help," Jesse said, glancing at his wife.

"I'm surprised you didn't tell Mark about it at the time," Amanda said.

"He was going through hell as it was," Jesse said, giving Tyrell a nasty look. "I didn't want him to have to relive what happened with Tanya, and I didn't want him to feel guilty for something that I did."

Mark didn't know what to say. Jesse had taken on a big emotional burden to spare him pain and to fix a problem that Mark had created. Hearing this admission only added to the enormous guilt Mark already felt for the misery he was causing Jesse and Susan now. Once again, the ones he loved were paying for his choices and his actions.

"I get why Dent would go after Mark, you, and Susan, but why would he help kill innocent people?" Amanda asked. "And why frame me for a crime? How does it all fit into Sweeney's grand plan?"

"I don't know how much Dent knew or didn't know about what Mercy Reynolds was doing, but I can guess at Sweeney's reasoning," Mark said. "The goal for him wasn't only to frame the three of you for crimes but to create a scandal that would destroy my reputation, get me fired, and that Burnside would use to attack Masters. Sweeney was establishing a motive for Steve to be angry enough with Burnside to want him dead."

"But it would take a lot more than that to make the frame

against me stick, which takes us back to square one and Gaylord Yokley," Steve said. "Sweeney used him and his ROAR buddies to make it look like I foiled a plot to spark a gang war on the streets of LA."

"You've been giving this a lot of thought, too," Mark said.

"From the moment I walked into that apartment and saw the rifle on the floor," Steve said.

"Using Yokley served another purpose," Mark said. "Sweeney sent his attorney, Tony Sisk, in to represent Yokley and Cantrell because he knew it would play on the chief's paranoia and provoke him to do something radical."

"Like ordering me and Tanis to bug Sisk's phones. And we walked right into the trap," Steve said, shaking his head, frustrated with himself. "They had cameras in place, just waiting to catch us in the act. I gave Sweeney the evidence he needed to make it look like I killed Burnside for the chief. I'm a damn puppet. The clever bastard played us all."

"No worse than I have," Mark said.

"You've never manipulated us," Amanda said.

"Of course I have," Mark said. "And I have been doing it for years. Carter Sweeney didn't put you here. I did."

CHAPTER FIFTY-ONE

There was a shocked silence in the cell, everyone staring at Mark. He waited a moment, letting his words sink in, and then he continued.

"I have an obsession with solving homicides and I've used each one of you to satisfy it. You are doctors. You didn't come to Community General to investigate murders. But you each had something I needed. Talent, energy, specialized knowledge. Under the guise of offering you guidance and friendship, I selfishly manipulated you in every way I possibly could to get you to help me, even though it might cost you your careers or your lives."

"We wanted to help," Jesse said. "That's why we did it."

"You only think you did. After Jack Stewart left Community General, I didn't have anyone I could use to do all my legwork. I got Jack into it because he came from a Mob family and was eager to do anything he could to prove he wasn't like them. Controlling Jack was easy. But you, Jesse, were even easier," Mark said. "Your father was absent in your life. You were hungering for a father figure to take his place. It was obvious the day I met you. So I became that father figure, the better to use you. I even got you to believe that you wanted to be me. And really, who would want that?"

"I would," Jesse said.

"Really? After what I've done to Susan? I played on her love for you to get her to take ridiculous risks she never would have contemplated otherwise." Mark met Susan's gaze. "You never wanted to be a part of any of it. But your devotion to Jesse forced you to keep your profound misgivings about me to yourself and accept the unreasonable sacrifices he was willing to make to please me. Tell me that isn't true. No, better yet, tell Jesse."

Susan stared at Mark, tears streaming down her cheeks. But she didn't say a word.

"Susan?" Jesse said, squeezing her hand. "I know that isn't true and so do you."

But she couldn't look at Jesse. It felt too much like a betrayal. Mark smiled at her and kissed her gently on the forehead.

"It's all right," Mark said, then turned to Amanda. "You were the easiest to turn of all. Doing autopsies was part of your job. It didn't take much to nudge you into getting involved in my homicide investigations. I played on your energy and ambition to pressure you into becoming an adjunct county medical examiner. You took on two full-time jobs at once, just so I could have unfettered access to the morgue. Did I care that it drove you to exhaustion, took you away from your son, and destroyed every romantic relationship you tried to have? No. Because I got what I wanted."

"That's hardly a revelation," Tyrell said. "I proved that in court during the Lacey McClure case."

"You were wrong, Tyrell," Amanda said. "And so are you, Mark. I've always wanted to be a medical examiner. Your interest in homicide investigation and your connections with the LAPD made it absurdly easy for me. If anyone took advantage in this relationship, it was me. I manipulated you into thinking it was your idea to put a county morgue in the hospital, and the worst thing about it is that you still believe it."

Mark shook his head. "You're incapable of using anyone like that."

"I used you," Amanda said. "I don't deserve to be on your conscience. I'm here because of the decisions I made in my life. This is as much about my past catching up with me as it is yours."

"Me too," Jesse said. "This is Dent getting back at me for something I did."

"Something you did for me, for an investigation I got you involved in," Mark said. "Open your eyes. All of you. See me for who I am and what I've done."

"Okay, Dad. What about me?" Steve asked. "Are you going to take responsibility for me being a cop, too?"

"I've used you most of all," Mark said. "I made you think the only way to win my love and respect was to become a cop. Look at you. You're in your forties and you're still living at home. Because I won't let you go. Because I've sabotaged you. I routinely intruded on your investigations, undermining your authority and making it impossible for you to establish a career separate from mine. Worse than that, I competed with you. I was afraid that if you succeeded without me my worst fear would come true—I'd be alone."

"What a load of crap," Steve said.

"What did you say?" Mark asked.

"You heard me, Dad. It's crap. Psychobabble garbage. Meaningless drivel. Melodramatic swill. And none of it's true."

"I meant every word of it," Mark said.

"I'm sure you meant every excruciating, cringe-inducing word," Steve said. "And you proved your point."

"That Carter Sweeney is right," Mark said. "That he and I aren't so different."

"You've proved just how thoroughly we've been manipulated by Carter Sweeney. You most of all," Steve said. "The reason he invited you out to see him in prison wasn't to taunt you about what was coming. He wanted to plant the idea in your head that you're some kind of mirror image of him, to make you wallow in self-pity and despair when his plans finally came to fruition. It wasn't enough for him to frame us for crimes and put us behind bars. It wasn't satisfying. Something was still missing. In order for him to truly enjoy it, he had to get you to destroy your family yourself. He wanted you to shoot your children and blow your brains out afterwards. And that's what you just tried to do. God, I bet he would have given anything to have seen it. Then he would have known that he'd truly broken you."

"You may be right," Mark said. "Or maybe he just made me see the truth."

"Everybody uses everybody," Steve said. "Everybody manipulates everybody. That's just a cruel way of saying that we need each other, we rely on each other, and we make sacrifices and compromises in our lives for the people we care about. Relationships are about give-and-take, and believe it or not, Dad, you're allowed to take, too."

"I've taken more than my share," Mark said. "Look at what I've taken from all of you."

"We are a family," Susan said. "That's what you've given us. What have you taken from it? No more and no less than each of us has. Yes, you've asked a lot from Jesse and me, maybe too much, and maybe I'm not always happy with it, but that's what happens in every family."

"You're not perfect, Mark. Far from it," Amanda said. "Believe me, we know that. We talk about it all the time."

"You do?" Mark said.

"Of course we do," Amanda said. "Your outrageous demands on our time and your irritating habits are among our favorite topics of conversation."

"They are?" Mark said.

"That and Lindsay Lohan," Jesse said.

"We don't talk about Lindsay Lohan," Susan said.

Jesse gestured to Steve. "We do."

"So stop feeling sorry for yourself," Steve said. "And get us the hell out of here."

"I wish I could," Mark said. "But I've got nothing left. Everything I've relied on before has been taken away from me. I don't have you. I don't have access to any medical or law enforcement resources. I don't even have the money to hire anyone. Every asset I have is going to your legal defense."

"If this meeting drags on much longer," Tyrell said, "you'll have spent it already."

"You've still got what counts the most," Steve said. "You're Dr. Mark Sloan."

"Damn right," Jesse said. "That's all we need."

CHAPTER FIFTY-TWO

The vote of confidence was momentarily inspiring, but Mark left the jail feeling no less guilt-ridden, and no better about his chances of prevailing, than he had when he went in.

Tyrell urged Mark to leave matters to him now, to let the battle move to the courtroom.

"There's no battle to move," Mark argued. "Up to now, we've been attacked. It's time for us to fight back, and the only weapon we have is the truth."

"The truth isn't all that convincing, and it's going to take too much work to change that."

"Are you telling me you don't want to make an effort?"

Tyrell sighed wearily. "Let me explain how this works, Mark. It's the prosecution that has to do all the hard work. As a defense attorney, my job is to sit there and poke holes in their case, to create a hint of confusion here, a possibility of a mistake there, and throw out a dozen other explanations for every fact they present. Pretty soon all that's left of their case is a lot of doubt. That's all it takes to set a guilty man free."

"They aren't guilty," Mark said.

"I keep telling you that it makes no difference," Tyrell said.

"If my son, and the people I care about, are going to get out of jail, you have to convince the jury that Carter Sweeney and every other murderer I sent to Sunrise Valley are behind this."

"I'm not saying one word about that conspiracy theory in the courtroom."

"You don't believe it?"

"It doesn't matter whether I do or not. The jury never will. A vast conspiracy of supervillains? It sounds like something out of a comic book. It would take way too much work and destroy whatever credibility I have left trying to get them to believe it. Because it's unbelievable, even if it is true."

"What other choice do we have?"

"There's a much easier way. The key to most defense cases is simply finding fault with everything the other side presents, to keep them scrambling to erase the doubt you're creating."

Mark had certainly seen Tyrell do that before. In fact, Tyrell had done it exceptionally well in the Lacey McClure trial. But even so, Mark didn't think that it was going to be enough this time.

Somehow, Mark had to find some evidence that proved his elaborate conspiracy theory. As things stood now, there wasn't a single shred of proof to back up any of his claims.

The scariest thing of all, though, was that he had absolutely no idea how to fight back or where to begin his investigation.

He went back to his car and just sat in the driver's seat, trying to figure out where to go next.

The press would be camped out around his house, so there was no point in going back there. The place would be a mess from the police ransacking and he'd get no peace to think about his next move. And he'd also have the press dogging him from the moment he left the house again.

He couldn't check into a hotel either. Most of the hotel workers in Southern California were media-savvy and supplemented their incomes by tipping off the tabloid magazines, newspapers, and TV shows whenever a celebrity, no matter how minor, was around.

And there were no friends he wanted to impose on. He didn't want any more people close to him to get hurt simply by being associated with him.

There was only one option left.

He had to go away.

As he pulled onto eastbound Interstate 10 and left downtown Los Angeles behind him, he couldn't help feeling like he was being exiled and that his life as he'd known it was over.

It was only when he was a couple hundred miles outside Los Angeles that he realized he was heading towards Phoenix and Noah Dent, though he wasn't sure what he intended to do once he got there.

He stopped for gas and a hamburger in Quartzsite, Arizona, a bleak desert truck stop about twenty miles east of the California border. It was almost midnight and it was still a hundred degrees outside.

Mark wanted to keep going, but he was too tired and was afraid he'd fall asleep behind the wheel. So after eating at the Carl's Jr., he drove down the barren, dusty road to the Super 8 Motel, where he checked in for the night.

The room was colorful and yet, in its own way, every bit as bleak as the desolate desert landscape off the highway.

Mark undressed, yanked off the flowered bedspread, and got under the scratchy sheets, resting his head on the thin pillows, which smelled like they'd been soaked in chlorine.

He was asleep within seconds and didn't wake up until almost eleven the next morning. The sheets were on the floor and he was soaked with sweat. The air conditioner was whining in a painful, losing struggle against the intense heat outside.

Mark showered but didn't realize until he got out that he had no toiletries or fresh clothes. So he smoothed his hair as best he could and tried not to look at his unshaven face in the mirror. He got dressed in his dirty clothes and went down to the lobby, where he snagged a free copy of *USA Today*.

The big story, of course, was the assassination of LA district attorney and mayoral candidate Neal Burnside, presumably by a cop acting on orders from the LAPD police chief, the opposing mayoral candidate.

Mark stuck the newspaper under his arm and decided to put off reading it until he'd had breakfast. He stepped out into the blazing sun and looked across the flat, rocky landscape, the only sound the passing of cars on the interstate behind the motel. The only hint of green he saw was the occasional cactus, all of which seemed to have been gnawed apart by birds or other animals.

The few buildings, spaced widely apart on the street, were mostly boarded up and abandoned until winter. There were a few fast-food franchises that were open, serving the travelers on the interstate, and a small market up the street.

Mark walked to the market and scrounged up all the toiletries he needed. There wasn't much clothing to choose from, so he bought a multipack of generic boxer shorts and tube socks, two pairs of shorts, and a couple of I GOT MY ROCKS OFF IN QUARTZSITE T-shirts in different colors.

For breakfast, he decided to stay away from the national fast-food places, mostly to avoid any travelers from LA who might recognize him, and wandered into a ratty diner instead, where he and the horseflies were the only customers. He devoured a heaping portion of scrambled eggs and a tall stack of pancakes, washed them down with several cups of coffee, and then returned to his dreary room at the Super 8.

Checkout time at the Super 8 was noon, and since it was well past that now, he bought himself the room for another day, which was fine by him. He was in no hurry to go anywhere. He brushed his teeth and changed into his new clothes while watching the latest news out of LA on CNN.

The present mayor, who'd chosen not to run again for health reasons, had fired Chief Masters with the unanimous backing of the city council and appointed deputy chief Stephanie Craft to take his place as interim chief.

Chief Craft immediately placed the city on high alert, putting every available cop on the street to quell any possible civil unrest in the wake of the assassination and subsequent revelations of police corruption. Plainclothes detectives were being put back into uniform and assigned to patrol in order to create a "strong and visible law enforcement presence" in the city.

She said her number one priority was to maintain order and keep the city from erupting into the widespread rioting, looting, and arson that had followed the Rodney King verdicts. The National Guard was mobilized and ready to assist the LAPD in quelling any civil unrest.

ADA Karen Cross announced that "serious charges" would be filed against Masters "imminently" and that his arrest could come "in the very near future." Meanwhile, police were searching for Tanis Archer, whom Cross described as a "key figure" in the spying scandal and who could have "vital information" on Burnside's assassination.

Masters hadn't dropped out of the mayoral race, but local pundits were expecting the announcement to come at any moment.

Mark was about to switch off the TV when he saw a report that made him freeze. It was from a correspondent with capped teeth and a square jaw stationed at the LA courthouse.

"In the midst of this crippling scandal, the worst that this city has ever faced, convicted killer Carter Sweeney walked into Superior Court for his habeas corpus hearing, accompanied by Tony Sisk, the famed criminal defense attorney whose home and office were allegedly bugged illegally by Chief Masters's covert operations unit. It is expected that Sweeney's legal team will argue that his conviction violated due process because of prosecutorial misconduct and fabricated evidence, charges that are likely to seem a lot more credible after the events of the last few weeks. Most of the key investigators and witnesses in the case against Sweeney are now facing corruption and murder charges themselves."

The footage showed Carter Sweeney walking into the courtroom, accompanied by Tony Sisk and several armed marshals. Sweeney was wearing a suit and tie, his arms handcuffed behind his back.

Just before Sweeney stepped into the courtroom, the camera zoomed in on him. He turned towards the lens, looked directly at Mark, and smiled.

Everyone and everything.

CHAPTER FIFTY-THREE

Mark didn't leave Quartzsite that day. He wandered the dusty streets, his mind as desolate and empty as the desert around him.

He stopped at an outdoor rock market, the agates and quartz spread out on sheets of sagging, sunbaked plywood supported by rusting barrels. The rocks resembled colored glass, were sold by the pound, and were too hot for Mark to touch. They felt like burning embers.

Farther down the road, there was a bookstore that was little more than a collection of tents and camper shells filled with yellowing paperbacks. The proprietor, a scrawny man with crooked teeth and a shaggy beard, was unabashedly naked, wearing only flip-flops to protect his feet.

On any other day, and in a different state of mind, Mark would have found the situation odd or amusing. But he felt disassociated from the world around him, as if he were simply passing through not just Quartzsite but life itself.

He was adrift.

Mark bought a map and a brochure about Quartzsite from the naked bookseller and wandered off to explore his new surroundings. He hadn't given it any thought; he was just doing it, without any purpose or desire. Perhaps it was merely an excuse to be actively doing something, anything.

He didn't think about the end of his career at Community General. He didn't think about his son, who was facing murder charges. He didn't think about Carter Sweeney, the mastermind behind the destruction of his life.

Instead, he visited the grave of Hadji Ali, a Syrian drover who helped lead the seventy-seven camels that made up the U.S. Army's ill-fated experimental Camel Military Corps that patrolled the sandy frontier before the Civil War. The camels were ultimately abandoned in the desert to fend for themselves. Ali's grave was a pyramid of rocks topped with a camel-shaped iron weather vane. The drover had died at age seventy-three, broke and depressed, chasing the last surviving camel into the seemingly endless, rocky desert. Legend has it that they found his body amidst the hardscrabble, his withered, sunbaked arms wrapped around the neck of the dead camel.

Having sampled all the cultural riches Quartzsite had to offer, Mark returned to his room at the Super 8 and sat on his bed, staring at the TV for hours, the stories of scandal and murder in LA blowing over him like a hot desert wind.

It was eight o'clock at night when Mark awoke, his sunburned arms clutching the thin pillow to his face. He didn't know when he'd fallen into his dreamless sleep or exactly how long he'd been out of it. But his throat was as scratchy as the sheets and his stomach was growling for food.

He sat up and saw his face staring back at him on the TV screen like a reflection in a mirror.

It wasn't a reflection. CNN was broadcasting a picture of him taken several years ago at the podium during a medical conference.

A reporter was speculating on where Mark had gone and what had happened to him.

"Some are calling him a tragic figure," the reporter said. "But others are now questioning his accomplishments as a homicide investigator, wondering if those astonishing successes were built on a foundation of lies, corruption, and fabricated evidence."

Mark switched off the TV and left the room.

It was a dark, dry night. The street was empty. The only traffic was a mile away, at the off-ramp, where cars stopped at the Carl's Jr. and the gas station and then continued on their way.

He walked back to the ramshackle diner where he'd had breakfast. There was only one other customer, an obese naked woman eating a large slice of banana cream pie. She was in her fifties, her hair almost as white as the whipped cream around her mouth. The tired waiter/cook/cashier didn't give the woman a second glance as he filled her coffee cup and handed Mark a greasy laminated menu.

Mark sat in a booth with his back to the naked woman, ordered a grilled cheese sandwich and a chocolate milk shake. While he ate, he looked out at the interstate, the cars lost in a blur of streaking light.

The vast conspiracy had worked flawlessly because Mark, and everyone else around him, had acted exactly the way Sweeney knew they would.

They were pitifully predictable.

There was no doubt that Sweeney had considered the options Mark had left and was already five steps ahead of him. Sweeney was depending on Mark Sloan to be unerringly himself.

So Mark would have to change.

He would have to behave completely contrary to his nature, to who he was, what he believed, and how he thought, or Sweeney would continue to accurately second-guess him.

But was that, too, part of Sweeney's plan for his destruction? If Mark stopped being who he was, what did he have left?

It didn't matter. He didn't have any choice. It wasn't about *his* survival anymore anyway.

It was about saving the people he loved.

So Mark gave it some thought.

How would a different man handle this situation, a man not bound by Mark's experience, morality, and ethics?

Someone who didn't care about others and, in fact, took pleasure in their suffering?

Someone who put his own needs first and did whatever it took to get what he wanted, when he wanted it?

Someone who didn't care about obeying any law except the ones he created for himself?

Someone like Carter Sweeney.

After a time, Mark finally got up and turned towards the door.

And stopped cold.

The naked woman was gone. There was another woman sitting in the booth. She wasn't naked and she was smiling right at him.

He knew her.

"How's the pie here?" Tanis Archer asked.

CHAPTER FIFTY-FOUR

Mark slid onto the bench opposite Tanis.

"It's not bad," he said.

"Did you see the naked lady who was sitting here before?"

"I did," he said.

"Good," she said. "I thought I was hallucinating. I've been under a little stress."

The waiter came. Tanis ordered a slice of pie and a cup of coffee. She and Mark didn't speak until she had been served and the waiter went back into the kitchen.

"How did you find me?" Mark asked.

Tanis frowned at him. "Don't tell me you were making an effort not to be found."

"Not really," he conceded.

"That's a relief, because I didn't think you were that dumb. You used credit cards to pay for your gas and motel room, which isn't something you do if you're trying to disappear. Take it from someone who is on the run and doesn't want to be found. But even if you'd used cash, I would have found you."

"You put a tracking device on my car," Mark said.

"It's how I show that I care," Tanis said. "What are you doing out here, Mark?"

He picked up a fork and took a bite of her pie. Stress was making him crave sugar. "I don't know. I thought at first I was on my way to see Noah Dent, but I'm not."

"Maybe you just needed some space."

"Maybe I did," Mark said.

"I have presents for you," she said. "Some are in your room."

"You broke into my motel room?"

She shrugged. "The other present is information. I know why

Olivia Morales framed Steve and killed Burnside. It wasn't for Sweeney."

"Was it for someone else at Sunrise Valley?"

"Yes and no," Tanis said. "Do you know who Harley Brule is?"

Brule had been in charge of the Major Crimes Unit in the Valley, which, ironically, had been responsible for most of the major crime in the Valley. Private investigator Nick Stryker found out about it and was blackmailing Brule. Mark found out about it while investigating Stryker's disappearance and gave the evidence to Steve, who in turn gave it to Burnside. Steve arrested Brule and his men. Burnside prosecuted them in a highly publicized police corruption trial that made him a viable mayoral candidate.

"Yeah," Mark said, "I know him."

"Olivia's fiancé was Larry Landvik, one of the MCU guys that got nailed. Landvik was the detective who blew his brains out instead of going to jail for a ten-year stretch. Guess who she blames for that?"

"I can imagine," Mark said.

"There's more. From what I can tell, she was helping the MCU guys make their scores, but she managed not to get caught, so there's some survivor's guilt going on there, too. Brule knew it and probably played on those feelings to get her to set up Steve."

"And murder Mercy Reynolds and Rusty Konrath," Mark said.

"Revenge is a cruel business." She started to get up.

"That's it? You're going already?"

"I've been here too long as it is," Tanis said.

"What are you going to do?"

"Run," she said. "You?"

"Fight," Mark said. "I might need your help."

"I might show up again," Tanis said. "Then again, I might not. I have to help myself right now."

"I understand," Mark said. "I'll keep that tracking device on my car."

Tanis smiled. "That's the nicest thing any man has ever done for me."

"It's how I show that I care."

She gave him a kiss on the cheek. "Be careful, Mark."

"You too," he said.

"I like the T-shirt," Tanis said, then turned and walked out. It wasn't until she'd been gone a few minutes, and he'd finished her pie, that he realized she'd stuck him with the bill.

He paid the check and left, walking slowly back to the motel.

When he got to the door of his room, he examined it to see if he could find any sign that indicated that Tanis had broken in. There wasn't any. He figured that she must have fashioned some kind of card key like his own.

Mark went in.

The TV was on, only now it was tuned to HBO and an episode of *The Sopranos*. The minibar was open and cleaned out. No wonder Tanis wasn't hungry. She'd even taken the alcohol. He'd probably saved her a trip to the market, which meant one less opportunity for her to get caught.

She'd left a black gym bag for him on the bed. He unzipped it. The bag was crammed full of audio and video surveillance equipment of all shapes and sizes. She'd even printed out some instructions for him on how to use the stuff.

It was a thoughtful gift, one he hoped he'd find a way to put to good use.

Mark zipped up the bag, set it on the floor, and sat on the bed, his back against the headboard. He'd never watched *The Sopranos* before. It was unlike any depiction of organized crime that he'd ever seen.

The violence was vicious and shocking, but, at the same time, it seemed almost mundane because it was deftly woven into the familiar world of suburban family life.

Mark understood the way Tony Soprano used violence to simplify complex situations and overcome the obstacles to his goals.

It was something Mark could never do.

Revenge is a cruel business.

But Mark didn't want revenge. He wanted justice. Then again, Mark wasn't going to be Mark anymore.

He couldn't be.

So what did he want and how was he going to get it?

The phone rang, startling him.

Mark hit the mute button on his remote and answered the phone with a cautious "hello."

"Hey, Mark, how's it going?"

It was Carter Sweeney.

Mark didn't ask Sweeney how he'd found him. Maybe Sweeney had assumed that he would head for Phoenix. Maybe it was the credit cards Mark used to pay for things. Or maybe there were two tracking devices on his car.

It didn't matter.

"I've had better days," Mark said.

"I'm sorry to hear that. Maybe I can brighten things up for you. I was wondering if you're available for lunch tomorrow," Sweeney said. "Because I am. We can go anywhere that you'd like."

Carter Sweeney was free.

CHAPTER FIFTY-FIVE

Mark hung up the phone without a word, released the mute on the TV, and channel-surfed until he found what he was looking for on Court TV. There was an entire program devoted to Sweeney's habeas corpus hearing and the startling outcome.

He learned that Judge Robert Lisker, who'd presided over the murder and kidnapping trials of Carter Sweeney, presided over the habeas corpus hearing as well.

Sweeney's lawyers went over every detail of the charges against him, arguing that Sweeney wasn't a serial bomber, as Mark had claimed in the first trial, and that the evidence in Sweeney's tool shed linking him to the explosives was planted by Mark and Steve. Sweeney shot Steve with a nail gun and fled because he reasonably feared for his freedom and his life.

That trial, his lawyers argued, was compromised by Sweeney's preexisting romantic relationship with ADA Sharon Ellison, who, he later learned, was sharing privileged information about him with DA Burnside, which amounted to prosecutorial misconduct. Ellison was later killed in a bombing that was among the murders Sweeney was charged with.

Sweeney was convicted on murder charges related to the bombings and sentenced to prison, but his bus was hijacked on the way to the penitentiary by his sister, Caitlin, who'd aligned herself with ROAR, a radical military group. Sweeney claimed that he was abducted by ROAR and that he was threatened with death if he didn't engineer the robbery of an armored car.

Contrary to Mark's fraudulent testimony in court, Sweeney wasn't fleeing with a hundred million dollars in stolen money when he was caught, but rather he'd escaped from captivity in the only vehicle available to him and was going for help.

Some of those arguments had been introduced during

Sweeney's two trials, but in light of recent revelations regarding the conduct of Dr. Mark Sloan, Lieutenant Steve Sloan, Dr. Amanda Bentley, the district attorney, and the chief of police, the allegations seemed far more credible and disturbing now.

The prosecution argued in the hearing that current events had no impact on the evidence presented in the previous trials and that, in fact, nothing had changed in Sweeney's case. The evidence against Sweeney was overwhelming, convincing and irrefutable when it was originally presented in court, and it remained so today. The actions of both the police and the prosecution were lawful and beyond reproach. None of Sweeney's constitutional rights were violated in any way and there was no cause for reconsidering his incarceration.

Judge Lisker shocked both parties by returning his verdict a few hours after the hearing concluded. He ruled that Sweeney's constitutional right to due process had been violated and that he'd been denied a fair trial as a result of the most egregious example of police corruption and prosecutorial misconduct that the judge had ever seen. On the basis of the evidence presented at the hearing, Judge Lisker was convinced that "no reasonable juror" would reach a guilty verdict if the trial were held today.

The judge set aside Sweeney's conviction and ordered that he be released immediately from custody.

A spokesman for the district attorney's office, which was still reeling from Burnside's assassination, said the office was reviewing the ruling and considering the options.

So, for the moment, Carter Sweeney was a free man. Comparing himself to Nelson Mandela and other political prisoners, he reaffirmed his love "for this great city" and vowed to find the bomber who was responsible for the crimes for which he had been falsely imprisoned. There was even talk that he might consider running for mayor, given what he called "the present lack of worthy candidates."

Mark switched off the TV in disgust. This time it really was his own reflection that he saw staring back at him in the screen.

But it wasn't the Mark Sloan he'd known before.

He was staring at a new man, with a new way of thinking and a new approach to dealing with his problems.

If the TV hadn't been bolted to the table, he would have picked it up and thrown it out the window.

Instead, he turned it back on and watched another episode of *The Sopranos*.

* * *

Mark stayed up all night, forcing himself to view his problem from an entirely new perspective. But he was locked into his usual ways of thinking.

So he tried a creative exercise that an actor or writer might use to get into character. He imagined how Tony Soprano might deal with the same situation that Mark was facing.

It opened up many possibilities, all of which required a cold heart, total disregard for the law, and lots of violence.

And that exercise allowed Mark to see a possible course of action, one that was completely out of character for him and would require him to do things that violated the principles he'd lived by.

He was okay with that.

His plan was risky, and relied on a lot of people behaving exactly the way Mark expected them to. But what he was counting on the most was that they were expecting the same from him.

And he wasn't that man anymore. They had seen to that.

But Mark still couldn't pull off what he had in mind alone. He'd need help.

To get it, he would have to pressure one person to gamble his career and his freedom and manipulate another person into risking his life. And all to serve Mark's selfish needs. There was little, if any, possibility that there would be any benefits at all for the others.

It was probably a lose-lose proposition for them.

So be it. He'd make them do it anyway.

Because he could. Because this Mark Sloan didn't give a damn.

At daybreak, he used a pay phone to call Special Agent Barton Feldman at the Chicago office of the FBI. Feldman had once been a low-level agent on the retirement track, exiled to the Denver office. But all that had changed a few years ago during Mark's investigation of the Standiford kidnapping. Mark gave Feldman the opportunity to make an arrest that revitalized his career and vaulted him to the top ranks of the bureau.

Now it was payback time.

Mark and Feldman spoke for nearly two hours. Feldman whined and complained. Mark connived, threatened, and made promises he couldn't keep.

Ultimately, Feldman gave in and agreed to do what Mark asked.

If Mark failed, Feldman could lose everything he'd gained. If

Mark succeeded, Feldman's career could rise to even greater heights.

They were big *if*s to overcome, *if*s surrounded by moats of molten lava and rigged with explosive booby traps.

But Feldman was indebted to Mark and greedy and therefore willing to take the risk.

And Mark was a desperate man with absolutely nothing left to lose.

It was a perfect match.

Mark showered, changed, and checked out of the motel. He put the gym bag full of electronic goodies on the passenger seat and headed east on Interstate 10 towards Phoenix.

On the way, he called Dr. Jack Stewart, his former protégé, who'd left Community General to join a high-powered medical practice in Denver.

Mark got Jack's answering service. He left a message, said it was an emergency, and then left the same message with the nurses and services who answered for Jack's partners. He also called Jack's home and cell phone and, when he stopped for gas, sent him a text message as well.

He checked in with Tyrell, who informed him that, as expected, Steve had been denied bail and would be held in custody pending trial. Mark filled Tyrell in on what he'd learned about Olivia Morales.

"It's good to know," Tyrell said. "It gives us something to use to undermine her credibility."

"That gives her a motive to want Burnside dead and frame Steve," Mark said. "The same circumstantial evidence they're using to incriminate Steve can incriminate her as well."

"Her fingerprints aren't on the murder weapon," Tyrell said. "And there aren't any photos of her planting bugs for Burnside's opponent."

"She had the same access to Yokley's weapons that Steve did and she was in Konrath's apartment building at the time of the assassination."

"But she isn't the one in jail charged with the murder," Tyrell said.

"She should be," Mark said. "She can be if you make the case against her in the courtroom."

"You've watched too many episodes of *Matlock*," Tyrell said. "It's not our job to pin the murder on someone else but rather to raise reasonable doubt regarding your son's guilt. I can use the information you've given me to attack her credibility. I'll leave it to the police to go after her for Burnside's murder once the charges against Steve are dropped."

"Is that confidence I hear in your voice?" Mark asked.

"I wish it was," Tyrell said. "Where are you?"

"Out and about," Mark said.

"Good idea," Tyrell said. "Stay that way until things quiet down. Leave everything else to me."

"You bet," Mark said and hung up.

Jack called just as Mark was entering the Phoenix suburbs.

"I got all your messages," Jack said. "The whole world knows you were trying to get in touch with me. But I'm glad you called."

"You won't be when you hear what I want from you," Mark said.

"I've been following the news. That's why you couldn't reach me," Jack said. "I took all my phones off the hook. I can't believe what I'm seeing. Whatever you need, consider it done."

"Once we get started, there's no going back," Mark said. "You could lose everything."

"So be it," Jack said. "I couldn't live with myself if I didn't help you fight this."

Mark detailed what he had in mind and the risks involved and then waited for Jack to change his mind.

"When will you be here?" Jack asked.

"Tomorrow," Mark said. "I have to pay a visit to an old friend in Phoenix first and then I'll drive up. We don't have much time."

"I'll be ready," Jack said.

CHAPTER FIFTY-SIX

Mark stopped at a mall, bought some clothes, a couple pairs of shoes, and a small suitcase to carry them in. He found a restroom, changed out of his T-shirt and shorts into casual business attire, and went back to his car, where he discovered he had no room left in the two-seater for his suitcase.

So he drove behind the mall, found a Dumpster, and threw out everything but his diplomas, his toiletries, and the bag of electronics from Tanis.

There was no room for sentimentality in his life right now. Only one thing mattered.

He put his suitcase in the trunk, closed it, and headed for his unscheduled meeting with Noah Dent.

The headquarters of MediSolutions was a three-story multi-colored cube that aggressively clashed with the rocky desert backdrop and the adobe-influenced styling of the surrounding buildings.

The lobby was decorated in stainless steel, giving it all the charm of a meat locker, which, given the company's trade in body parts, was strangely appropriate.

Mark approached the security desk and told the stocky, fish-eyed guard that he was there to see Noah Dent. The guard asked Mark for his driver's license and, glancing dismissively at it, called Dent's office. The conversation lasted less than five seconds.

The guard handed Mark back his driver's license, gave him a clip-on security pass, and walked him to the elevator. Mark stepped inside. The guard leaned in, used a key to unlock the control panel, and pressed the button for the third floor.

As soon as the guard left, and the doors slid shut, Mark hit the button for the second floor just to see what would happen. The button didn't work.

There was a woman waiting for him outside the elevator on the third floor. She was in her twenties and had both the look and the artificially cheery attitude of a stewardess. Mark was tempted to ask her for a Diet Coke and a bag of peanuts as she led him down a long row of cubicles to Noah Dent's corner office.

Dent didn't bother to rise from behind his massive desk. Instead, he leaned back in his chair and smiled at Mark. He was leaner and more physically fit than Mark remembered him. Desert living and revenge obviously agreed with him.

"I was wondering when you'd show up," Dent said. "To be honest, I've been counting the minutes."

"Do you have a speech prepared?"

"I knew you'd come looking for someone to blame for your misery," Dent said. "Here's an idea. Try a mirror."

"I feel terrible about what happened to Tanya," Mark said. "It was a tragedy. But she committed murder."

"She killed the man who brutally raped her and left her for dead," Dent said.

"If that was all she did, I would have understood. I might have let her get away with it. But she also killed an innocent bystander to cover up her crime."

"A homeless man who was dying anyway," Dent said. "She ended his suffering. It was hardly murder."

"Is that how you rationalize the actions of the people you've helped to commit murder?"

"I have no idea what you're talking about."

"Mercy Reynolds injected two brain-dead organ donors with West Nile virus so that whoever received their body parts would die," Mark said. "If you helped her do it, you're an accessory to murder."

"I *am* an accessory to murder, Doctor. The murder of Mercy Reynolds."

"You set her up to die," Mark said.

"Damn right I did," Dent said. "When I wrote her that letter of recommendation, I might as well have been signing her death certificate. I had no idea she was going to use it to apply for a job at Community General. I tried to talk her out of it, but she wouldn't listen to me. She had a bright future until she walked in there. You took that future away from her."

"She was killed for the good of the conspiracy," Mark said. "If you didn't do it, you know who did."

"Steve Sloan," Dent said. "Your son killed Mercy in a lame attempt to make her appear responsible for the crimes committed by your sycophants. I knew as soon as you discovered that Mercy once worked for me that you'd show up here, trying to blame me for everything."

"You're obviously involved," Mark said.

"I'm involved because I cared about Mercy Reynolds, yet another young woman that you've destroyed. I'm involved because my company is a victim of a body-parts scam perpetrated by your doctors. The FDA has announced a health alert and issued a nationwide organ recall that's going to cost us tens of millions of dollars."

"Revenge isn't cheap, Noah. Send the bill to Carter Sweeney."

"Who?" Dent asked.

Mark leaned on the desk and looked Dent in the eye. "I'm giving you fair warning. I won't let this stand. I'm going to devote my life to bringing you down."

"You do that, Mark. Come back often. I want to see how you rot from the inside out."

Mark turned and walked away.

The black Bentley Continental GT in the driveway of Jack Stewart's Washington Park bungalow was worth more than Liandra Haven's condo across the street. But it wasn't the six-figure price tag of the car that impressed the twenty-six-year-old real estate agent. And it wasn't that he was attractive, wealthy, and a doctor, though that would have been enough to make most single women she knew weak-kneed.

What made her swoon over Jack Stewart was the fact that he didn't behave like an attractive, wealthy doctor. He was a genuinely nice guy, which, for Liandra, was the sexiest thing a person could be.

She'd been living on his quiet, tree-lined street near Washington Park for only a month or so, but in that time she'd seen him play catch with some kids, help his next-door neighbor clean out his garage, and rescue a dog that had been hit by a UPS truck.

He always chatted with his neighbors and actually listened to what they had to say instead of talking about himself, which was very unusual for someone who was attractive, wealthy, and a doctor. Most people with his attributes believed that they were the most interesting topic of conversation imaginable, given that they also happened to be the center of the universe.

She'd spoken with him a few times, and never once did he try to impress her with anything but his natural, amiable charm.

And it was working.

She hoped he wasn't moving, but there was a big Dumpster in front of his place, and it looked like he was doing a lot of remodeling, usually the first sign in this older neighborhood that a house might be going on the market soon.

Liandra didn't want to see him go. But then again, if he was leaving, she wanted to get the listing. Whether he was or not, it gave her an excuse to say hello.

Jack was getting a late start that morning and so was she. They came out of their homes at just about the same moment. He smiled at her and she waved him over. They met in the middle of the street.

"Good morning, Liandra," Jack said, flashing a smile that seemed to make his eyes sparkle. She felt herself blushing, and that embarrassed her, which only made her blush more.

"Tell me you aren't moving, Jack. And if you are, tell me why I don't have the listing."

She wondered if she was being too aggressive, too real estate–focused, and if that would turn him away.

"I'm here to stay," Jack said. "I'm finally getting around to doing everything on my fix-it-up list. Before I knew it, I was gutting the whole place."

"I know how that is," she said, just to be saying something. "I'm glad you're not going anywhere. I still have the bottle of wine you gave me as a housewarming gift. I was hoping you'd share it with me one night."

She'd surprised herself with her admission. She was never this forward, at least not when it came to anything that didn't involve an escrow.

"Anytime," Jack said. "Come to think of, I'm free tonight. How about you? You bring the wine, I'll put two steaks on the grill, and we can eat outside under the stars."

Her face felt so warm, she was afraid her hair might spontaneously combust. "That sounds nice."

"Good, because to be honest, my backyard has become my kitchen and dining room until the remodel is done," Jack said. "How does seven sound to you?"

"Perfect," she said.

"See you then," he said, and went back across the street to his Bentley.

Liandra turned her back to him and got into her Camry, a smile on her face that she suspected would stay there all day. She hoped he didn't remember the bottle of wine that he'd given her because it was long gone, wasted on a take-out Chinese dinner she'd eaten alone, surrounded by moving boxes.

Her first stop of the day was going to be the liquor store to find a nice replacement bottle. Even if he did catch her in the lie, she knew he'd be too much of a gentleman to call her on it. Her next stop would be the department store to buy something slinky that would make her irresistible and test the limits of his gentlemanly behavior.

She was looking over her shoulder and backing out of her driveway, when his Bentley exploded, bursting apart in a fireball.

Liandra instinctively slammed on her brakes and ducked below her seat, her ears ringing from the blast. After a moment, her whole body shaking, she raised her head and peered out the car window.

The Bentley was completely consumed by fire, her view obscured by the thick black smoke rising from the car and the Dumpster, where the flames had already ignited the trash and were licking at the house.

Liandra got out of her car and ran across the street, but was immediately repelled by the heat and smoke. She stumbled back, nearly tripping over something at her feet. She looked down.

It was a severed hand, charred black.

Her horrified scream was lost in a choking cough that brought her to her knees.

CHAPTER FIFTY-SEVEN

Detective Mickey Katz had seen his fair share of shootings, stabbings, stranglings, and even a beheading, but this was his first car bombing.

The whole area outside of Jack Stewart's house was a soggy, sooty mess. Stewart's property was cordoned off with yellow tape. The neighbors, lookee-loos, and media were kept at the far end of the block by three uniformed officers.

It had taken the fire department about forty-five minutes to completely extinguish the fire, which had spread to the house, engulfing the garage. Just by doing their jobs, the firefighters had probably washed a good deal of the best evidence into the Denver sewer system.

Once the fire department released the scene, the bomb squad, the medical examiner, and the CSI guys came to collect whatever evidence was left. Everybody wore white jumpsuits, galoshes, gloves, and oxygen masks, except for Mickey Katz. He didn't bother with the mask. He'd been smoking cigarettes since he was fourteen, so he doubted that whatever carcinogens, pathogens, or other gens were in the air were any worse than what was already in his body.

Half of Jack's blackened remains were still belted into the passenger seat of his Bentley when Mickey arrived; the rest were spread out around the front yard. Mickey had spoken to the only witness, a lady realtor who lived across the street. She didn't have much to say, and he didn't have the heart to tell her that real estate values in the neighborhood were about to plummet. Murders will do that.

Jane Becher, the ME, had recovered most of Jack Stewart and was bagging up the last of him when Mickey walked over to get her preliminary assessment.

"What a waste," Jane said, bumming a Marlboro off of him.

"It usually is," Mickey said, lighting the cigarette for her.

"I'm talking about the car," Jane said. "You'd think they would have had the decency to shoot him instead of trashing such a fine piece of automotive engineering."

"You're such a softy," he said. "How soon can you confirm the ID?"

"Most of his jaw is intact and the dental records are waiting for me at the office," she said. "I can have a report for you in the morning. Unless you want to drop by and pick it up tonight."

"At the office or your place?"

"Depends if you're back with your wife again," she said.

"I'm not," he said.

"That's what you told me last time."

He shrugged. "Does it really make a difference?"

She thought about it.

"Don't come too late," she said and walked off.

He watched her go, openly admiring the way her hips moved under her jumpsuit, and that's when he saw the distraught white-haired old man arguing with an officer at the barricade. The old man appeared to be insisting on being let through. Mickey walked over to see what was up.

"I'm Dr. Mark Sloan," the man said to the officer. "I'm a close personal friend of Jack Stewart's. I need to know if he's okay."

The officer glanced at Mickey as he approached and tipped his head towards the old man. "This guy says he knows the deceased."

"Deceased?" the old man said. The word came out as barely a whisper, almost like he'd spent his last breath to say it.

Mickey could have punched the officer for his stupidity. Apparently, Mickey's feelings showed on his face. The officer thought he could improve Mickey's impression of him by talking some more.

"I'm sorry, Lieutenant. I thought it was obvious he was dead vis-à-vis the bombed-out car and all."

Mickey ignored the officer and lifted the crime scene tape. "Please come with me, Dr. Sloan."

Mark ducked under the tape and walked unsteadily over to Mickey.

"I'm Lieutenant Mickey Katz, Denver PD Homicide," he said, dropping his cigarette and grinding it out under his heel. "What was your relationship to Dr. Stewart?"

"Friends," Mark mumbled, staring past Mickey to the burned-out Bentley. "Old friends."

Mickey picked up the cigarette stub and bagged it so it wouldn't be mistakenly taken as evidence. "Do you have any idea why someone would put a bomb in his car?"

Mark nodded, his eyes welling with tears.

"Are you going to tell me?" Mickey asked.

Mark nodded again. "But you aren't going to believe me."

The doctor was right. Mickey didn't believe him. Mark's explanation was the long, paranoid rant of a crazy person. By the time Mark finished his convoluted tale, they were sitting in an interrogation room at the station, each of them on his second cup of lousy coffee.

"So you're saying Carter Sweeney and all the murderers you've put away arranged to have Dr. Stewart killed to get back at you," Mickey said.

"There was no one else left I could turn to," Mark said. "I thought Sweeney didn't know about Jack, but I was wrong. Sweeney got them all. There's no one left."

Mickey finished his coffee and examined the paper cup like he was interested in the craftsmanship. He just needed a minute to think.

He'd had Mark checked out on their ride to the station. It had taken maybe two minutes before someone called back to tell Mickey that Dr. Sloan's son was the cop who'd murdered the LA district attorney.

So Mickey knew some of the story already. What he didn't know was that Dr. Stewart had once been part of Mark Sloan's team of amateur sleuths.

"You came to Denver to enlist Dr. Stewart in your effort to clear your son and your coworkers," Mickey said. "Is that correct?"

Mark nodded. "I called him yesterday from the road. We talked and he agreed to help. We were going to work out a plan. Instead, I got him killed."

"If they wanted to kill him," Mickey said, "why wait until now to do it?"

"They knew I was in Phoenix yesterday. Noah Dent probably called them, and they guessed where I'd be going next. Or they found out somehow that I'd been trying to reach Jack. It doesn't matter. They wanted to have a big surprise waiting for me when I got here. They timed it for maximum shock value, which is why they couldn't resist blowing him up in his Bentley."

"I don't understand."

"Because it's a Bentley," Mark said. "As in Dr. Amanda Bentley."

"You don't think that's just a coincidence?"

"There is no such thing as a coincidence where Carter Sweeney is concerned. Jack and Amanda used to work together. They were very close. I think he might even have been in love with her. Don't you see how it all fits? Killing Jack in his Bentley was Sweeney's idea of a sick joke. They want to break me, but they never will. They will only strengthen my resolve."

"I see," Mickey said.

What Mickey saw was that the hour and a half he'd spent with Mark had been a complete waste of time. He put his pen back in his pocket and stopped taking notes. They were worthless anyway.

"You say that like you think I'm crazy," Mark said.

"To be honest, I have a hard time believing that Jack Stewart was murdered to prevent him from helping you."

"Do you have a better explanation?"

"I understand Dr. Stewart came from a Mob family back east."

Mark shook his head. "Jack cut himself off from that a long time ago."

"Recent events suggest otherwise," Mickey said. "Or maybe he was killed to send a message to one of his relatives. I don't know. I've only been on this case a couple of hours."

"Doesn't it strike you as odd that Jack Stewart, my former protégé, was murdered only days after Sweeney was set free, I was fired, and my son, Amanda, Jesse, and Susan were jailed?"

"I don't see the connection."

"*I'm* the connection!" Mark yelled.

"You haven't worked with Dr. Stewart in years and he had nothing to do with Sweeney's arrest."

"All that matters is that Jack worked with me once, that I cared about him, and that he was the only one left who could help me," Mark said. "*That's* why he had to die."

"It's an interesting theory, one that I'll definitely keep in mind," Mickey said, rising from his seat. He would call Detective Morales in LA and get the real story on Mark Sloan once the doctor had left. "Thanks for taking the time to talk with me. I'll have an officer drive you back to your car."

"I knew you wouldn't believe me," Mark said sadly.

"I believe you've lost someone you care about and that it happened during a very stressful time in your life," Mickey said. "You have my sympathies."

"I don't want your sympathies," Mark said. "I want Carter Sweeney back on death row."

CHAPTER FIFTY-EIGHT

The venerable 112-year-old Brown Palace in downtown Denver was a big step up from the Super 8 in Quartzsite and the Ramada Inn that Mark had stayed at on the road somewhere on his way up from Phoenix. For one thing, neither of those hotels employed a full-time historian, though the wino who was urinating into a potted plant in the lobby of the Ramada when Mark arrived might have qualified.

There were seven hundred pieces of ornate wrought-iron grill-work that ringed the grand lobby of the Brown Palace from the first floor up to the seventh. Two of the wrought-iron panels were upside down. One of those panels was installed incorrectly by design, to symbolize the imperfection of man. The other was put in wrong out of spite by an angry worker, thus proving the meaning of the first improperly installed panel.

Mark felt like one of those panels—old, flawed, and spiteful. He was sitting in his dark room, looking out the window at the volcanic granite walls and Gothic spire of the Trinity Methodist Church across the street, when there was a knock at his door.

He looked through the peephole and saw three men standing in the corridor. The one standing closest to the door looked like a male model, the kind who posed as businessmen in magazine ads for European cars, fine suits, and first-class air travel. There were just enough dashes of gray in his hair to make him seem established, respected, and educated but not so many that he seemed old.

The two men standing deferentially behind him at the door were muscular and had faces that had been reshaped over the years by fists. They were clearly his bodyguards.

Mark opened the door. "Yes?"

"Dr. Sloan," the man said, "I am Elias Stewart, Jack's uncle. May I come in?"

Mark stepped aside. Elias turned to his men.

"Wait for me in the suite," Elias said and then came into Mark's room.

Mark closed the door and faced his guest. "I'm sorry about Jack."

Elias nodded. "He admired you, Dr. Sloan. You were a major influence on his life."

"And his death," Mark said.

"That's why I am here," Elias said. "I was in Seattle on business and came here as soon as I got word. They had to use dental records to positively ID him. You understand what that means? He was practically cremated by that bomb. We can't even give him a decent burial. That isn't right."

"No, it isn't."

"How much do you know about our family, Doctor?"

"You're very close," Mark said.

"I meant about how we earn our living."

"Your primary interest is in the scrap metal business," Mark said. "Your other business ventures are varied."

"That's a polite way of putting it," Elias said. "But there is no need for such niceties between us. You know who and what I am. Jack loved his family but wanted no part in scrap metal or our other less legitimate enterprises. We understood that."

"Even when he was helping me and my son solve homicides?"

Mark sat on the edge of the bed facing Elias, who took a seat in one of the two easy chairs.

"We don't do a lot of business in California, and we did even less while Jack lived out there, to minimize the potential for conflicts," Elias said. "I believe Jack felt that by helping you in your investigative pursuits he was doing some kind of penance for the sins of his father. And his uncle. But if he had any resentment towards us, he never expressed it. We respected him for that. We knew where he drew the line and he knew where we did."

"It's good that your differences didn't drive you apart."

"It wasn't easy, for him or for us. We were relieved when he left Los Angeles and gave up his detective work for you," Elias said. "But it was one of those old murder investigations that got him killed, wasn't it?"

Mark shook his head. "It wasn't anything he did for me that

got him killed. It was what he might do. But most of all, they killed him because they knew it would hurt me."

"Who are they?"

"If I tell you," Mark asked, "will you kill them?"

"Eventually," Elias said. "After they've begged me to do it."

"Then I can't tell you," Mark said.

"Don't you want to see these people punished for what they did to Jack?"

"Punished, yes. Tortured and killed? No. I don't think Jack would have wanted that either."

"I could make you tell me," Elias said.

"You probably could," Mark said.

"But you were family to him," Elias said. "I don't hurt my family. So I will have to do this without your help."

Elias got up.

"Wait," Mark said. "Please."

Elias sat down.

"We both want the same thing, to see that the people who killed Jack are punished," Mark said. "I'll help you if you agree to do things my way."

"Your way got Jack killed," Elias said.

"I know," Mark said. "But I need them alive. It's the only way I can save my son."

"And live with yourself."

"I don't much care about that anymore," Mark said.

"Then we are more alike than I thought. If that's how you feel, why reject my methods?" Elias said. "They are very effective in matters of this sort."

"I'm all for employing your methods," Mark said. "Within limits."

"I'm not a man who has ever lived within limits," Elias said.

"And I'm a man who has lived within them all his life. Maybe we could meet each other halfway and accomplish our goal."

"I presume you would be the one setting these limits?" Elias said. Mark nodded. "Give me an example of one of your limits."

"No bloodshed," Mark said.

"That's like me asking you to perform surgery without a scalpel."

Mark shrugged. "Sometimes it's necessary for me to explore alternative forms of medicine."

Elias considered Mark's proposal for a long moment. "If I

agree to this arrangement, how do you know that you can trust me not to slit the killer's throat?"

"Because if you're anything like Jack," he said, "you're an honorable man who stands by his word."

"Don't be so sure," Elias said.

"I'll take my chances," Mark said, and then he told Elias everything that had happened, who he believed was involved, and why they had killed Jack.

"It seems to me that there may be more to this than you think," Elias said.

"What do you mean?"

"Sweeney is out and, presumably, in some debt to the murderers who are still in prison," Elias said. "Like Malcolm Trainor and the Ganza family."

"I don't see what you're getting at," Mark said.

"Killing Jack may have served two purposes. It may also have been a message to me not to see your downfall as an opportunity to increase our business interests in the Southern California market."

"This isn't about you."

"It is now," Elias said. "He killed my nephew."

"That wasn't what I meant."

"It doesn't matter why Sweeney did it," Elias said. "The end result is going to be the same. I can see an easy way to resolve this."

"But it won't get my son and Amanda, Jesse, and Susan out of jail."

"Why should I care?"

"Because Jack did," Mark said.

Elias grimaced, and Mark saw a flash of anger in his eyes. Mark could see that using the memory of Jack against Elias would have diminishing returns and that he should use such leverage only sparingly.

"Okay, we'll do it your way." Elias stood up, took off his jacket, and draped it over the back of his chair. "But it's only going to work if there's some blood spilled."

"I won't allow you to hurt anyone."

Elias grinned, like Mark was a child who'd amused him. "It's not going to be anyone, Doctor. It has to be you."

It took Mark a moment of thought, but then he saw Elias's point. Regardless, Mark knew that according to the rules that Elias lived by, at the minimum he deserved to be beaten for the misery he had caused.

In a way, it would almost be cathartic for them both. Mark's only fear was that once Elias tapped into his rage, he wouldn't be able to stop. And Mark couldn't clear Steve, Amanda, Jesse, and Susan from the grave.

Elias studied Mark's expression and seemed to read Mark's mind.

"Don't worry, Dr. Sloan," Elias said, rolling up his sleeves. "I'm like a surgeon. This is an operation I've performed many times and I haven't lost a patient yet."

"You might as well call me Mark."

Elias walked into the bathroom, got a towel, and wrapped it around the knuckles of his right hand.

"You can call me Elias," he said. "When you're conscious again."

Chapter Fifty-nine

Noah Dent's home was tucked up against a barren hillside and surrounded by tall palm trees. It was his oasis in the desert. His yard was landscaped with cactus and rock around a waterfall that spilled into a black-bottom pool.

He was reclining on a chaise longue in his swimsuit under the shade of an umbrella, sipping a Bloody Mary and browsing the *Wall Street Journal*. It occurred to him, as it often did at times like this, that he'd come a long way from Toronto.

It hadn't been easy to get where he was, but he never once regretted his decision not to go into his father's lucrative bathroom fixture business. The ubiquity of Dent toilets and urinals had made Dent the brunt of jokes throughout his childhood ("I piss all over you every day," "Dent was born pissed off," "Hey, Noah, you look a little flushed," etc.).

The idea of hearing those comments for the rest of his life was his vision of hell. But the same comments that embarrassed and stung Noah Dent actually amused and flattered his father, who took tremendous pride in the fact that, in Canada, Dent was a household name. When Noah bought the Scottsdale house, his father shipped him a toilet as a housewarming present. Dent would have smashed it with a sledgehammer but for the fact that his dad came to visit once a year. The last thing Dent wanted was any of his friends making the same tired jokes he'd spent his life running from.

Dent was so preoccupied with basking in his own success that he wasn't aware of the two men until they showed up on either side of his chaise longue.

At first he thought they were the pool guys. But they weren't Julio and Eduardo. They were muscled, grim-faced men who wore polo shirts that clung too tightly to their bodybuilder frames and sunglasses that balanced unevenly on their misshapen noses.

They grabbed Dent by the arms and lifted him off the chaise. He opened his mouth to protest, but one of the men slammed a fist into his gut, knocking the wind out of him. He almost passed out. The other man slapped a strip of duct tape over his mouth. They dragged him around the side yard to a black Lincoln Navigator that was idling in his driveway.

They lifted the cargo hatch, flung Dent inside like a piece of luggage, and then rolled him over, binding his wrists behind his back with duct tape. They slammed the hatch closed, and he felt the car start to drive away from his house.

Who were these men? What did they want with him? Was he going to die?

It took a few minutes for the pain to fade and for him to get his breath back. He was on top of plastic sheeting and his head was up against the handle of a shovel.

Plastic sheeting and a shovel. Not very good signs as far as his life expectancy was concerned.

He wanted to cry.

That's when he became aware of someone else lying in the trunk beside him.

Dent rolled on his side and found himself looking into the bruised and bloody face of another man.

There was duct tape over the man's mouth and his arms were pinned behind his back. Blood was spattered on his shirt and caked in his hair. The man looked at him with one eye, the other swollen shut. His gaze was unfocused, showing no recognition, no emotion, and barely any spark of awareness.

It was Dr. Mark Sloan.

Dent looked into Mark's eye and screamed, the sound muffled by the tape over his mouth.

The two musclemen dragged Dent out of the Navigator and let him fall onto the hard, hot asphalt before lifting him to his feet. He could see now that they were at a public storage facility in a desolate area somewhere outside of Phoenix. There was an open unit in front of them, the floor lined with plastic sheeting. There was nothing else in it except for a stool and a single lightbulb dangling from the ceiling.

They led Dent inside the storage unit, sat him down on the

stool, and then walked out, pulling the rolling corrugated-metal door down behind them.

Dent was left in total darkness. He heard the car drive off. He got up off the stool.

"Sit down," a voice said evenly.

Dent did as he was told.

The lightbulb came on, revealing a man who must have been standing in the dark recesses of the storage unit all along.

The man was casually dressed and leaned on a baseball bat.

"My name is Elias Stewart. I'm a very bad man. I make my living off drugs, gambling, and extortion. And when I get mad, I hurt people. My nephew Jack was a doctor. He chose a different life for himself. I respected him. And I was proud of him. But most of all, I loved him. Jack's mentor was Dr. Mark Sloan. Because Jack was a stand-up guy, he'd do anything for his friends, especially someone who meant as much to him as Dr. Sloan did. You know what happened to my nephew? He was killed by a car bomb shortly after agreeing to help Dr. Sloan free his friends from prison."

Elias paced in front of Dent, who was shivering, and not because he was cold.

"When I heard the news, I was so hurt and so angry that I beat my dog to death with my bare hands. Besides crapping all over my yard, my dog never did anything wrong to me. I liked my dog. But I was angry, Noah, and I lashed out. I am still angry. So I found Dr. Sloan and asked him some questions. Dr. Sloan was reluctant to answer them, so I had to use some persuasion."

Elias swung the bat at Dent's head, barely missing him. Dent whimpered.

"Dr. Sloan has principles, even when it comes to the people he hates. He knew what I'd do to whoever was responsible for killing my nephew, and he couldn't live with that. I told him he wouldn't have to. He wouldn't have to live with anything anymore. See, I blamed him for what happened to Jack. It's not very rational, I know. But that's me."

Dent shivered again as he considered the meaning of that last statement and realized that the plastic sheeting and shovel probably meant there was a shallow grave in Mark Sloan's immediate future.

And his own.

"After some persuading, Dr. Sloan told me who he thought killed Jack and why," Elias said. "I hope you don't need persuading too. Since I killed my dog and beat Dr. Sloan, my arms are sore."

Elias ripped the duct tape off of Dent's mouth. Dent whimpered.

"This is a terrible mistake," Dent said.

"I have to agree with you there. Whoever thought that killing Jack was a good idea is going to discover just how wrong he was. So tell me, who was that person?"

"I don't know."

Elias swung the bat close enough to Dent's face that he could smell the wood.

"Wrong answer," Elias said. "Let me try a different approach. How did you meet Mercy Reynolds?"

"If I tell you," Dent said, "will you promise not to hurt me?"

"I promise that if you don't tell me I will hurt you. Very badly. I doubt your mother will be able to identify what's left of you. How's that?"

Dent couldn't stop shivering.

"Mercy came to see me and asked for a job. She said that she and I shared something in common, a hatred for Mark Sloan and Community General Hospital," Dent said. "She told me that Mark was responsible for her boyfriend's death."

"What did she want from you?"

"She wanted to work for me long enough to learn our procedures and so that I could recommend her for a nursing position at Community General."

"Did she tell you that she intended to work with funeral homes to steal body parts and frame Dr. Bentley for it?"

Dent didn't answer. He just shivered. Elias sighed, stood as if preparing for a pitch, and raised his bat.

"Yes!" Dent shrieked.

Elias lowered his bat. "You went along with the scheme even though it would cost your company millions?"

"It's not my money," Dent said. "I'm just a hired hand. Besides, they can afford it."

"What about infecting organ donors with West Nile virus? Was that your bright idea, too?"

"I didn't know anything about that," Dent said. "I would never harm another person."

"You don't think sending Dr. Bentley to prison for a crime she didn't commit is doing her harm?"

"It's not physical harm," Dent said. "There's a difference."

"Of course there is. Completely destroying someone is much more noble and pure than beating a man to death with a baseball bat. You aren't a man—you're a worm. You took the coward's way. A man faces his enemies."

Dent cowered, still shivering with fear. He was afraid he might soil himself.

"You said you wouldn't hurt me."

"No, I said that I *would*—unless you gave me a good reason not to. So you knew about Mercy's body-parts scheme but not that she was going to inject organ donors with West Nile virus. But you figured that as long as Dr. Sloan's friends were suffering, it didn't matter who died, right?"

"I felt terrible about the murders. But what could I do? If I reported what I knew, I would have gone to prison myself as an accessory. I had to keep my mouth shut. They knew that."

"They?"

"Whoever Mercy was working for," Dent said.

"Who were they, worm?"

"I don't know," Dent said with a whine.

"You better think of someone, because if there's no one else I can punish for Jack's death, it's going to be you."

"But I was here when he was killed," Dent said. "I can prove it."

"I'm not interested in proof. Does this look like a courtroom to you?" Elias said. "Who did you call after Dr. Sloan visited you?"

"Nobody," Dent said.

"Wrong answer." Elias hefted the bat. "Let me persuade you to answer correctly."

"Wait!" Dent screamed. "They'll kill me if I talk."

"I'll kill you if you don't. Die now or die later. Your choice."

"Olivia Morales," Dent said. "She's an LAPD detective. She hates Sloan, too."

"I wasn't too fond of him myself." Elias turned his back to Dent and lifted the roll-up door, filling the unit with harsh sunlight as he walked out.

Dent squinted against the blinding glare, but once his eyes adjusted to the light, he discovered he was all alone. His tormentor was gone.

He hunched forward and began to sob.

CHAPTER SIXTY

In the hours that Noah Dent spent alone, sitting shirtless and barefoot, his back against the rough cinder-block wall of the storage unit, he reached some important conclusions.

His first inclination was to run barefoot across the hot desert to the first phone he could find, call Olivia Morales, and tear her head off for killing a mobster's nephew and bringing hell down on them all.

But what would that accomplish besides searing the flesh off his feet?

If Noah warned Olivia about Elias Stewart, she'd undoubtedly realize that he'd had ratted her out. She'd probably kill him for it and spend the rest of her life running from the Mob.

No, the best thing Noah Dent could do was keep this nightmare to himself. As soon as somebody finally showed up at this godforsaken place, and he got a ride back home, he'd pack up everything, withdraw all his cash from the bank, and disappear to an island somewhere. He'd leave it to his attorney to sell his house and get the cash to him wherever he was and under whatever new name he invented for himself.

Mark Sloan was dead and Tanya was avenged. And Noah Dent had paid dearly for it.

His task was done. It was time to start anew.

He didn't give a damn about Olivia Morales, Carter Sweeney, and whoever else was involved in the plot against Sloan.

They were on their own. If Dent was lucky, Elias Stewart would kill them all.

Ever since DA Burnside was assassinated and Chief Masters was fired, the new police chief had kept the LAPD on emergency status, putting as many uniformed officers on the streets as she could, hoping the show of force would maintain control.

So far it had.

Olivia Morales hated being back in uniform and Kevlar, driving a squad car on patrol, and dealing with radio calls.

She was stuck that night in a black-and-white that smelled like puke, cruising the long Valley boulevards, the idea being that just seeing cop cars all over the place would dissuade the angry populace from taking their aggression out on local businesses.

The only time she got out of the car was to arrest an unruly drunk or break up some petty domestic squabble.

God, how she hated it.

But it would be over soon, and it was a small price to pay for the sweet retribution she'd enjoyed. Steve Sloan was in prison and Mark Sloan was ruined. The Sloans would suffer their entire lives for depriving her of the only man she'd ever loved.

Olivia felt no remorse over killing Mercy Reynolds or Neal Burnside. Mercy was a sociopath and a liability and had to go. Burnside was executed for the misery he'd inflicted on Olivia.

Fair is fair.

But Rusty Konrath was different. He was an innocent victim, a decent kid whose only mistake in life was renting the wrong apartment at the wrong time. She knew that she would always be haunted by the look of horror and bewilderment in his eyes when she shot him.

In a way, though, that guilt was a good thing. It made her feel better about herself, assuring her that she still had a conscience and wasn't an entirely bad person.

She wanted to kill Dent, but Sweeney argued that anything Dent could say would only incriminate himself. Dent couldn't harm them. She didn't agree, but Sweeney had been right about everything so far, so she was willing to go along with him.

That was before she got the call yesterday from Mickey Katz, a cop with the Denver PD, giving her a heads-up on Dr. Jack Stewart's murder and Dr. Sloan's accusations. The Denver PD wasn't taking Sloan's rantings seriously, especially after she filled Katz in on the details of the scandal.

She was certain that Sweeney was responsible for killing Dr. Stewart. The timing of the bombing and Stewart's association with Dr. Sloan were all the evidence she needed.

But since she didn't kill Jack, that meant Sweeney had farmed out the job to someone else, even though they had agreed that she would do all the killings that were necessary. It wasn't that she enjoyed the task. It was simply a matter of efficiency, practicality, and safety. She was an experienced homicide investigator. She could manage the crime scenes before and after her bloody work.

This wasn't just a betrayal of trust. It was an act that put her at risk.

Olivia hadn't talked to Sweeney about it yet because she wasn't quite sure how she wanted to handle the situation. More than once she'd picked up the cell phone to call him and then tossed it back onto the passenger seat in anger. She had to strategize this the same way he would, to see every possible outcome of her actions.

She was still mulling her options when she got a call from the dispatcher to investigate a report of a prowler behind the Goodwill store on Owensmouth.

Probably another drunk. And she'd just finished cleaning up the puke from the last one.

Olivia arrived in the alley within a minute of getting the call. The alley was dark and lined with trash bins, the mobile homes of the homeless. One of the bins was in the middle of the alley, blocking her path.

She got out of the car and pushed the bin out of the way. That was when she saw the man standing in the middle of the alley. He wasn't any drunk. His stance and the expression on his face instinctively told her that he might as well have been death himself.

Olivia reached for her gun.

He was faster. He shot her twice in the chest with his silencer-equipped gun, the muffled pops in sharp contrast to the impact of the bullets, which knocked her flat on her back. Her head banged against the pavement.

The Kevlar vest she wore under her uniform stopped the bullets from her flesh but not the force they carried. She felt like she'd been struck twice with a sledgehammer, the air completely knocked out of her.

She couldn't get her arms to move, but even if she could have, it wouldn't have mattered. The man kicked her gun out of her reach.

She fought to stay conscious, gasping for air, each breath like a dagger jammed into her lungs.

The man stood over her, placed his foot on her throat, and aimed his gun at her forehead.

"My name is Elias Stewart," he said. "Jack Stewart was my nephew."

Olivia looked straight into his eyes. She could see that this was someone who had killed before, and would kill again, and gave no more thought to it than brushing his teeth.

This wasn't just an aggrieved relative. This was a professional.

And then it hit her.

Jack was one of *those* Stewarts. It was a miracle she was still alive, though that was bound to change in the next few seconds.

It never occurred to her that Jack was one of *them* because Stewart was such a common name and Mark Sloan was someone she thought would never let a mobster's nephew into his inner circle.

That was a fatally incorrect assumption.

How could Sweeney have been so stupid?

Or did Sweeney know all along about Jack's "family" connections? And was this just Sweeney's way of getting the Mob to kill her for him?

She wouldn't put it past the clever bastard—not that there was anything she could do about it now. Her brains were about to be splattered all over the alley.

"I don't give a damn about Mark Sloan, his family, or his friends," Elias said. "You could have done whatever you wanted with them. But you shouldn't have touched my nephew."

She would have agreed, but she couldn't speak. It was hard enough just managing to breathe, a luxury she was fairly certain she wouldn't be enjoying much longer.

"I'm postponing your execution for twenty-four hours. That's how long you have to give me the person who killed my nephew. If you don't, I will finish what I started here tonight."

He leaned down and shoved a card into her breast pocket.

"Call me," he said before lifting his foot from her throat and walking away. "Tick, tock."

CHAPTER SIXTY-ONE

The beach house that Carter Sweeney was renting was two doors down from Mark Sloan's home. Sweeney got the place on the cheap because it was the house where Cleve Kershaw and his lover had been murdered not so long ago. The house was supposedly haunted, but Sweeney didn't see how the ghost of a movie producer and a bad actress could terrify anyone, least of all him.

Sweeney wanted to be here when Mark Sloan eventually returned from his wanderings, broken and defeated. It would only add to Mark's misery to know that the man who'd destroyed him, and everything that mattered to him, was not only free but living close enough to borrow a cup of sugar.

He stood outside on his beach deck, leaned over the edge of the wooden railing, and craned his neck to take in the view of Mark's house in the moonlight.

If things worked out as Sweeney planned, Mark's complete financial ruination wasn't far off. Soon, Sweeney would be able to add the extra humiliation of taking Mark's house from him and moving in himself.

Oh, how sweet that would be.

Once Mark was destitute, forgotten, and scavenging in garbage cans for food, perhaps Sweeney would take pity on the doctor and hire him for odd jobs. Like washing his car. Trimming his shrubs. And cleaning his toilets.

As Mark's reputation crumbled, Sweeney's image was buffed, shined, and reimagined. In the space of just a few days, Sweeney had gone from convicted killer to a victim of corruption and injustice. Now Sweeney was being hailed as a courageous fighter for truth, justice, and the American way. All he was missing was blue tights, a red cape, and a big *S* on his chest.

He was even seriously considering entering the mayoral race.

Community leaders and potential backers in both parties told him that if the election were held today, he'd probably win.

His father would have been so proud of him.

Sweeney's only regret was that his sister, Caitlin, wasn't at his side to share in his glory.

He would find a way to set her free. Or, at the very least, get her out of prison and into one of those country club mental institutions that make most five-star resorts look like dive motels.

There was plenty of time for that. And so much more. The Carter Sweeney era in Los Angeles was only just beginning.

The doorbell rang. Sweeney answered it and found himself looking down the barrel of a gun.

Olivia Morales pressed the gun to his forehead, backed him into the entry hall, and kicked the door shut behind her. She was wearing a T-shirt, jeans, and a very angry expression.

Nevertheless, Sweeney remained calm. Very little unsettled him anymore.

"Give me one good reason why I shouldn't kill you right now," she said.

"I can't think of any," he said. "Pull the trigger. You can blame my murder on the ghosts."

"I met Elias Stewart tonight," she said. "He shot me twice to introduce himself. If I wasn't wearing Kevlar, and if he wasn't in such a jolly mood, I'd be dead now."

"What's that have to do with me?"

"He's peeved that you killed his nephew Jack."

"Who is Jack?" Sweeney asked.

Olivia cocked the trigger of her gun. "Do you really think this is the best time to play dumb?"

"Humor me," Sweeney said. "Consider it my last request, if that helps your motivation."

"Elias Stewart is one of the biggest Mob bosses on the East Coast and a major player on this one, too. Dr. Jack Stewart was Dr. Mark Sloan's apprentice once. Jack moved to Denver and Jesse Travis took his place. Sloan called Jack for help. The next day, Jack gets into his two-hundred-thousand-dollar Bentley and is blown to bits."

"I see," Sweeney said, processing the information, extrapolating all the possible scenarios, implications, and explanations.

He didn't know about Jack, and he didn't know about any Mob connections. But given what he did know now, Olivia was right to assume that Sweeney would have neutralized him in some fashion. The timing certainly suggested that was exactly what Sweeney did, even though he hadn't. It was all very interesting to Sweeney.

And a little disturbing.

"Elias wants the person responsible for killing Jack in twenty-four hours or I'm dead," Olivia said.

"Then you wouldn't dare deprive him of the pleasure of killing me." Sweeney turned his back on her and walked out to the deck to enjoy the view again. After years in Sunrise Valley, he couldn't get enough of the fresh air and the endless horizon.

Olivia simmered for a minute, then jammed the gun into the holster on her belt and followed him outside.

"So you admit you're responsible," she said.

"You think I broke our agreement and killed Jack Stewart without consulting you first," Sweeney said. "Thus betraying you and jeopardizing everything."

"Pretty much, yeah."

"But what you really think is that I did it so the Mob would kill you for me, thus removing the one person outside of prison who can tie me to the frame against Steve Sloan and the others."

"Yes," Olivia said. "I do."

"I hate to disappoint you, but I had nothing to do with it." But the truth was, it was such a great idea that he wished he *had* thought of it.

"Convince me," she said.

"Does it matter? If I was in your position, I'd sacrifice me to Elias Stewart regardless of the truth to save myself."

"I'm not you," she said.

"Right. You're a much better person," Sweeney said. "I'm sure that just before Mercy Reynolds, Rusty Konrath, and Neal Burnside got a bullet between the eyes, they were thinking what a wonderful human being you are."

"I killed them for you, remember? And although I may be a killer, I don't betray my friends."

"Are we friends?" Carter Sweeney asked, cocking an eyebrow. "Really? I thought we were simply two resourceful people who shared a mutual interest."

"So if you didn't kill Jack Stewart, who did?"

"What you should be asking is how did Elias Stewart get to you?"

Olivia scowled at him. "That's easy. Noah Dent, our friend in Phoenix. I tried to reach him, but he's disappeared."

Right after his anticipated visit from Mark Sloan, Sweeney thought. It was a troubling development.

"Where's Mark Sloan?" Sweeney asked.

"He's also gone," she said. "He was staying at a hotel in Denver. His car and his stuff are still there. The hotel management called the police this morning. Housekeeping found blood all over his room."

It was obvious to Sweeney what had happened. Elias got to Mark and made him talk. For all of Mark Sloan's many faults, the one thing he wouldn't have done was help a mobster intent on bloody revenge. Mark was far too principled for that. The old fool. So if Mark gave up Dent, then it meant Elias had broken the good doctor. Probably permanently. After that, breaking Dent would have been easy for Elias.

Sweeney hated Mark, but the likelihood that the doctor was dead was a big disappointment. He didn't want to be denied the joy of Mark's long-term suffering.

This changed everything. Elias wouldn't be satisfied until he'd killed anyone even remotely connected with his nephew's death. Since Sweeney didn't know who was responsible, the only way to save himself would be to offer up a suitable fall guy.

Or woman.

Olivia Morales was the natural choice. The question now was how to make that happen and how to convince Elias that she'd acted on her own.

Actually, it would be easy.

"It's clear to me what's happened," he said. "One of Elias Stewart's rivals saw an opportunity to take out Jack and make it look like someone else was responsible. It's what I would do if I was one of them, if only to distract him and destabilize his operations."

"Perhaps you did," Olivia said. "Perhaps that's the deal you had to strike to get Malcolm Trainor and his buddies to sacrifice their funeral home operations for your frame against Amanda Bentley to work."

"I didn't, but you may still be on to something," Sweeney said. "Trainor may be the one responsible for this. Do you know how to reach Elias Stewart?"

"He gave me a number," she said. "It's probably for one of those disposable cell phones."

"Next time you meet, he'll kill you, even if you deliver me or someone else to him."

"I know," she said.

"Give me the number and run," Sweeney said. "I'll call him and try to convince him that Trainor is the one he wants."

In fact, Sweeney had no intention of calling Elias. He would contact Trainor and, through the Mob accountant's sources, get word to Elias that Morales had killed Jack on her own and was now on the run. Sweeney hoped that after killing Mark, Dent, and Morales, Elias's bloodlust would be sated.

"And if you fail?" Olivia asked.

"We're no worse off than we are right now."

"How do I know you won't pin everything on me?"

"You don't," Sweeney said. "But again, you will be no worse off. You'll be gone and I'll still be here. I'm the one who is the most vulnerable."

"You're damn right you are," she said. "Just remember, I can prove that you arranged the entire frame against Steve Sloan and his friends. I'm the one person who can take you down."

"Believe me, I know," Sweeney said, and found himself glad that things were working out this way.

Olivia's cell phone rang. She yanked it off her belt and answered it. The caller's voice on the other end was loud enough for Sweeney to hear.

"We are so glad to hear that," a man's voice said.

"Hear what?" Olivia said.

"That you can prove what I've been saying about Carter Sweeney all along."

It was Mark Sloan.

When Elias Stewart shot Olivia Morales and kept her busy, one of his goons must have placed a listening device in her phone.

"I didn't know," she mumbled to Sweeney.

He held his hand out for the phone. Olivia, stunned, handed it to him. He leaned over the railing and peered past her to Mark's house.

Mark stood on his deck, a phone to his ear, another man standing beside him. The doctor waved at him.

"Good news, Sweeney," Mark said. "They've kept your cell for you."

"The man beside you," Sweeney said. "Dr. Jack Stewart, I presume."

"Alive and well," Mark said.

And in that moment, Sweeney saw the entire scheme that had

ensnared him, one that hinged on the same assumptions about Mark Sloan's character that had enabled his own plan to work.

He didn't feel anger. He didn't feel disappointment. He didn't feel anything at all.

The front door burst open and a team of men in FBI Windbreakers rushed into the house, guns drawn. The one in the lead, a middle-aged man with gray hair, flashed his ID.

"Barton Feldman, FBI," he said. "You're under arrest."

CHAPTER SIXTY-TWO

The sky was a clear and cloudless blue, the smog blown out to sea or into the Valley by a cool wind that made the heat not only bearable but pleasant. The waves were frothy and dappled with light and, in the distance sailboats jumped over the swells.

The long picnic table on the beach behind Mark Sloan's house was covered with the leftovers of lunch: BBQ tri-tip, potato salad, fruit, and seashell casserole. Steve, Amanda, Jesse, Susan, Tanis, and Jack were enjoying their generous portions of homemade Chocolate Decadence à la Sloan as Mark, who sat at the head of the table, finished filling them in on everything that had happened.

They all knew, of course, that Sweeney was back in Sunrise Valley and that Olivia Morales and Noah Dent had agreed to testify against him in return for whatever leniency was possible for themselves—which, in Olivia's case, meant sparing her from death.

What they weren't so clear on was how Mark had managed to pull off the con that allowed Tanis to stop running and freed the rest of them from jail.

First, Mark told them, he carefully set the stage by calling just about everyone in the Denver phone book and leaving messages for Jack, so word would get around that he was desperate and overwrought, which wasn't all that far from the truth.

He called in the debt that Barton Feldman owed him and convinced the former Denver-based FBI agent to arrange for an unidentified cadaver to be put in Jack's car during the night. Jack himself rigged the bomb and purposely engaged his pretty neighbor in conversation so there would be a witness to his death.

In reality, Jack was safely hidden behind the Dumpster in his driveway when he activated the bomb, and then he easily slipped away in the flames and confusion.

Feldman visited Jack's dentist, swapped the cadaver's X-rays with Jack's to assure a positive ID, and the con was set in motion.

Mark put the surveillance devices that Tanis had given him to good use, leaving a bug behind in Dent's office, which captured Dent's call to Olivia. He also gave a bug to Elias, who had one of his men plant it in her cell phone while she was pinned to the ground under his foot.

"Was Elias in on the con?" Steve asked.

Mark shook his head. "It was crucial that Elias believe that Jack was really dead, to ensure that his rage was genuine. I wanted Dent and Morales to see the pain and fury in his eyes. I knew that would sell the con better than any tricks I could come up with."

Steve glanced at Jack. "Is Dad going to have to look over his shoulder the rest of his life?"

"I ironed things out with Uncle Elias," Jack said. "He understands why doing this was important to me and that I paid a big price for it. That said, he's doubly glad he gave Mark that beating now."

Mark still looked like a prizefighter who'd lost in the sixth round.

"How did you fake blowing up your Bentley?" Jesse asked.

"I didn't," Jack said. "That was the big price I was talking about. I'm expecting to get reimbursed, which is why I'm so glad to hear that you all got offered your old jobs back."

"I didn't," Mark said. "As long as Janet Dorcott is there, I'm not welcome in the building."

"We are, but we're not so sure we're going to accept their offer," Susan said.

"They don't really want us," Jesse said. "It was more of a publicity gesture."

"I don't know if I'd ever feel comfortable working there again," Susan said.

"The same goes for me," Amanda said. "They've shown just how little faith they have in me and my integrity."

"I'm not exactly rushing to return to the LAPD either," Tanis said. "I'll face disciplinary action for the covert ops we did for Masters. And I have a bad feeling that they'll find a basement below the basement to stick me in."

Jack looked at Steve. "What about you?"

Steve shrugged. "Maybe I'll become a private eye. I hear they get all the girls."

Jack sighed. "Looks like I'll be driving a Festiva for a little longer than I had planned."

"This is a good thing," Mark said.

"You've obviously never driven a Festiva," Jack said.

"What I mean is, we're about to enter a new chapter in our lives," Mark said. "We have a world of possibility in front of us."

"We do?" Jesse asked.

"You have possibility," Jack said. "I have a Festiva."

For the first time in ages, Mark didn't know what tomorrow held for him. It was exciting and scary, but in a good way. He felt revitalized, as if he'd been given a second chance at life.

Perhaps he had.

Perhaps all of them had.

The question now was what they would all do with the opportunity they'd been given.

Whatever path they chose, he knew one thing would never change.

They would always be a family.

Don't miss the rest of
the series based on the hit TV show

Diagnosis Murder

by **LEE GOLDBERG**

Available wherever books are sold or at penguin.com